The Knitting Fairy

A Crabapple Yarns Mystery

Jaime Marsman

"What do you get when you combine a novice to the world of fiber working in a yarn shop with the owner, a mysterious, fairytale inspired character? You get Jaime Marsman's magical, whimsical story of *The Knitting Fairy* which is sure to be enjoyed by knitters everywhere."

—Penny Sitler
Executive Director of The Knitting Guild Association
www.TKGA.com

"Amidst the characters, humor, and mystery is the fun of witnessing a non-knitter's assumptions and observations turn to affection and obsession. It made me wish to be a new knitter again!"

—Sally Melville
www.sallymelvilleknits.com
www.sallymelvilleknits.blogspot.com

"A heartwarming and witty novel, guaranteed to make you smile. Molly Stevenson's newfound love of yarn brings her comfort and friendship but leaves her with many unanswered questions. Appealing to the non-knitter as much as the knit-a-holic, this wonderful and enthralling mystery detailing the weird and wonderful goings on in Crabapple Yarns knitting store, will have you totally hooked."

—Geraldine Curtis, UK Hand Knitting Association
www.ukhandknitting.com

"A page-turning mystery with yarn shops and knitting – what else could you ask for!"

"Whenever an author combines stories and stitches, I smile. Jaime Marsman has done just that in her new book, *The Knitting Fairy*. With a nod to Agatha Christie as well as fairytales about Brownies who appear when no one is looking to complete domestic tasks for those in need, Marsman has crafted a tale that combines mystery, fun, and knitting. Filled with phrases like, 'she kitchenered Old Mrs. Harrison's toes together,' 'Oh, honey, let's go home and cable,' and 'as Louise reached into her small knitting bag, I had a distinct feeling of foreboding,' knitters will find themselves laughing through each chapter, wondering who the knitting fairy could be!"

"What I loved best about *The Knitting Fairy* is how perfectly Jaime captured that as knitters we actually fall in love with knitting. She reminded me of the butterflies, excitement, and joy of falling in love with my first skein of luxury yarn, falling in love with perfectly tensioned stitches and the euphoria of completing my first project. Not only did *The Knitting Fairy* remind me of why I fell in love with knitting in the first place, it made me pause (as a deadline-driven professional) to think that I still need to stop and smell the roses from time to time."

"It is obvious that Ms. Marsman is writing about what she knows: books, libraries, and yarns. I really enjoyed following Molly's adventures in learning to knit and solving mysteries. *The Knitting Fairy* always keeps you guessing!"

The Knitting Fairy

A Crabapple Yarns Mystery

Jaime Marsman

Print ISBN: 978-1-937331-27-6
E-Book ISBN: 978-1-937331-28-3

Cover art by Josh Hickey
Copyright @ 2012 ShadeTree Publishing, LLC
1038 N. Eisenhower Dr. #274
Beckley, West Virginia 25801

Visit our Web site at www.ShadeTreePublishing.com

DEDICATION

This book is dedicated to the best little dog that ever was. Nipper. He was the greatest little friend in the whole world, and I miss him. It's possible that you did not know Nipper, and this is sad. I know you would have loved his little furry self too. He lives in Heaven now, but he will always live forever in my heart... and now it makes me happy that he will live forever in this book... because each time you, dear reader, read this dedication, you will think of Nipper - the best little dog that ever was.

KNITTING

The Merriam-Webster definition:**
- To form by interlacing yarn or thread in a series of connected loops with needles
- To tie together

The definition that <u>should be</u> in the dictionary:
- The mystifying and magical process whereby linear fiber is twisted and reshaped by needles of varying sizes not only knitting fabric together, but hearts and minds as well, resulting in lifetime friendships, a sense of self-satisfaction, and personal identity.

**knit. 2012. In *Merriam-Webster.com.* Retrieved June 22, 2012, from http://www.merriam-webster.com/dictionary/knit

Prologue

My life is hanging on the door of my refrigerator, and it has been for years. It lives under a little magnet shaped like a worm that says, "Let the Book Bug Bite." The magnet shouldn't surprise you. After all, I am a librarian.

Did you know that some people go their whole lives without a plan? They never know when they're happy because they don't know what makes them happy. They never know if they're successful because they have no idea what success looks like. So pathetic. People with no sense of purpose. So often, they are drifters blowing in the wind - and, like the song says – hoping that the answer is blowing in the wind with them. Personally, I think the only thing that is blowing in the wind is dust, and the only thing it inspires me to do is sneeze.

To my eternal relief, I <u>do</u> know where I am going. And if I ever start to wonder, all I have to do is look on my refrigerator at "The Plan" (a.k.a., my blueprint for life success). Of course, getting the rest of the world to conform to The Plan can sometimes be a challenge. For instance, I am 27-years-old, and between you and me, I'm a little behind on several key elements of The Plan. It's not worrying me too much, though. Not yet, anyway. It's just a little odd that something so well thought out and well-written would have trouble translating to real life. Of course, when I wrote The Plan, there were several variables I did not (and frankly could not) figure into the equation. One of them being Mrs. Goldmyer. But, we'll get to her in a minute.

So, here I am. The Plan has moved me along nicely for years, and now I'm just waiting for Phase II to get off the ground. Don't tell anyone, but I've been going to the refrigerator a little more than usual lately. There is, in my brain, a very tiny, little, horrible and sneaking suspicion that it may be possible that I may have missed something important along the way. Possibly. It's only a wisp of a fear that perhaps I wasn't as thorough as I had thought I was. Perhaps The Plan has a fatal flaw that I won't see until it's too late. And, sometimes, just

1

sometimes - I catch myself studying The Plan and wondering... *is it for me or against me?* But then The Plan winks at me from its perch on my refrigerator, and I relax. It's all good. The Plan has everything under control. I just need to stick to it.

***

My name is Molly Stevenson, and I live in Springgate. I wasn't born here. I was actually born in a small town about 20 minutes north, but I love it here. It's a fairly good-sized town. You can (and believe me, I have) get lost in Springgate, so clearly it is not too small. Actually, I would call it a "baby bear" town – you know, not too big...not too small...just right. If you don't know what I'm talking about, there's a certain children's book you should dig out and read again.

All in all, I guess, it doesn't really matter where I live because I'm the sort of person that nothing much ever really happens to. Ha! I know exactly what you're thinking right now... "Yeah, yeah, I've heard that a million times before." And you probably have. But that doesn't mean it isn't true for me (and really you shouldn't be so quick to jump to generalizations either). In all honesty, though, it's not like I spend a lot of time looking for things to happen either. I like my life the way it is. It's all in The Plan.

You could say that I live a quiet life. I say quiet life mainly because I am a librarian, so naturally, my days are spent in a library, a place of infamous quietude. Where one does try to be quiet. I'm not completely sure why that is, though. Books are worlds within worlds. Don't you think that's something to get excited about? I do. And take it from me (and everyone that has ever gotten shushed by a librarian), it's a little hard to get excited and stay quiet at the same time.

I can't help the thrill that runs from my head down to my toes when I enter the library every morning and I see all the rows and rows and rows of books, waiting like silent friends for me. Isn't it a wonderful thought that no matter what you do or who you are, you can for about 300 pages be someone else, see life through someone else's eyes, and even experience the nearly impossible?

Every morning before Mrs. Goldmyer comes in, when I am supposed to be preparing the library for the day – which means that I am supposed to make the coffee (which I don't drink), turn on all the computers, open the doors, check the drop off box and dust the front desk – I walk down one or two rows, running my fingers along the cracked and worn spines, trying to imagine what wonderful story awaits in each one...never dreaming that my story would ever be as interesting as the ones I could find here in a book. But...all that changed on one soft, almost-spring day in April when I met Mother Goose, and my life changed forever. And now we're getting ahead of ourselves again. Let's start at the beginning.

Chapter 1

Overdue. Way Overdue.

It was just one of those days. Have you ever had a day where you wake up and everything that you think should happen during the day doesn't? And everything that shouldn't happen, happens? A day where you find yourself doing something so completely out of character that you're sure you must be still in bed dreaming? A day where you can no longer see your carefully constructed life charted out in front of you? A day that changes *everything*? This was one of those days although I didn't know it yet. It was very sneaky as it began like any other day, and so I suppose that I was a bit smugly confident that it would end like the others as well. But, as most people know (and I was about to find out) you can plan and plan or you can let it go and live the life you're supposed to live...

It truly was a wonderful day – the kind that you wished would go on forever. A day where you felt like hugging every person in sight just because the smell of spring was in the air and you were filled with so much love you felt that you might just possibly burst if you didn't share it with someone else. Of course, people don't do crazy things like that, but that didn't stop me from thinking about it. It was a day where you could even ignore the little piles of dirty snow melting in the corner of the parking lot because you knew they would soon be gone. One of those kinds of day.

You know what? I'm not usually this verbosely dramatic. Sorry about that. It happens when I get excited. I'll try to control myself and stick to the facts...

The air was cool against my cheeks as I made my daily hike from my little apartment across town to the Springgate Library where I am Assistant Librarian. Quite an impressive title, is it not? The truth is, I am little more than gopher-girl to the tyrannical Head Librarian, Mrs. Goldmyer. Her first name, you ask? I don't think that she has one. Oh, and if you're thinking that it's a little rude to label someone tyrannical, it's okay...you just don't know Mrs. Goldmyer.

I do love this library, though. And no matter how cruel and demanding Mrs. Goldmyer could (and would) be, the library itself more than made up for it. It was actually a former church and still retained the peace that many old churches have. The rows and rows of books standing squarely on their shelves lined the former sanctuary in a great square with consecutively smaller squares of shelves within the square. The circulation desk was the former narthex. It was quaint and charming. And absolutely stuffed with books. It was my favorite place in the whole world – even with Mrs. Goldmyer there. And that's saying something.

Thankfully, the ancient oak doors that opened onto the street, although beautiful and hand-carved, now had another row of more practical doors behind them. I said thankfully because it tended to be quite chilly in the cooler months as patrons entering and exiting the library let in the most delightful drafts that you can imagine. I had once foolishly suggested to Mrs. Goldmyer that we move the circulation desk farther away from the front doors so that we could stay a bit warmer. When I say, "we", I actually mean "me" because she, as Head Librarian, very rarely has time to do the more mundane tasks of the library. She has a nice cozy office just off of the narthex that used to be the pastor's office, with a little space heater under her desk. Did I have a space heater? Uh, no. And yes, in case you were wondering, that was also considered a foolish question. When I presented this particular silly question to Mrs. Goldmyer, I was informed (in her usual nasty and brisk manner) that such idle questions only proved how wasteful I was as a person and such things would not be tolerated, and that, should I persist in making imprudent statements and asking senseless questions, she was sure there were a great deal many more people "out there" who were more qualified and experienced for the job than I was, and she was sure that they would be easier to work with as well.

Whew. (Did I mention that she was also the Queen of Run-On Sentences? It was actually quite a problem, because sometimes, by the end of the sentence, I had forgotten how it all began. This made responding a little difficult. I would take notes, except she might get the wrong idea.)

She was probably right – but only about the experienced part. I had a college degree in Librarianship, which was why I was even considered for the position, but other than working at the circulation desk for my college, I had no other experience to speak of. That's why I had practically jumped at the chance for this job.

When I think back now, remembering my excitement when only two days after my interview I was offered the job, I cannot help but feel a little foolish for being so naive. At the time, I couldn't believe my good fortune. Now looking back, I realize that I was probably the only person who, after having met Mrs. Goldmyer, would even consider the job. And, she, on the other hand, was getting pretty sick of not having a gopher girl. I guess we were just destined for each other.

"Excuse me?" the soft comment startled me from my daydreams. I quickly straightened away from the desk where I had been slouching in order to greet...well...Mother Goose.

Of course it wasn't Mother Goose. It couldn't possibly be Mother Goose. Everyone knows that Mother Goose is a literary character from a children's book.

I firmly repeated this (in my head, of course). Twice.

But, if Mother Goose was real – which we all know she is not – she would look just like the figure currently staring down her unfortunately long, crooked nose at me. Her (suspiciously) white hair shone in the fluorescent lights like a halo, and it was neatly coifed under a large straw hat decorated with tiny little fruits and flowers that jingled and bounced with every movement. The hat tied under her chin with a large pink ribbon. Her little periwinkle blue eyes twinkled behind dainty wire-rimmed glasses that were perched somewhat precariously on the aforementioned elongated, crooked nose. She wore a flowing, pretty dress the color of irises in the springtime. A wispy white shawl was tucked around her shoulders.

My jaw must have dropped at some point, because her expression turned a little wary. She took a small step back and looked up and down the desk. "I beg your pardon," Mother Goose said, "I thought that this was the circulation desk."

Giving myself a mental shake, I forced a smile, "Of course it is," I said, slipping easily into my 'Librarian mode'. "How can I help you?"

Her confidence restored, she stepped to the edge of the desk. "I would like to return this book," she said. And with that, she produced a fairly large, hard-covered book from the basket slung over her arm. It landed with a slight thump on the desk, emitting a small cloud of dust from between its pages. I wiggled my nose and willed myself not to sneeze.

"I see," I said, logging into the computer, "and did you enjoy it?"

"Oh yes," she said happily, "I most certainly did. I read it over and over. It's really just like an old friend to me." She smiled at me, and her face erupted in little wrinkles.

Ah...a kindred spirit. I smiled back at her, "I know what you mean."

She leaned conspiratorially over the desk. "Actually," she whispered, "I almost forgot that it belonged to the library and wasn't my own."

"That happens," I reassured her. Picking up the barcode scanner, I flipped the book open, my fingers automatically searching for the back page. "That's strange," I muttered, "the barcode must have fallen off."

I looked up at Mother Goose who looked back at me innocently – perhaps a little too innocently?

I set the barcode scanner down and flipped the book back over to its front side. Instead of the usual card holder pasted on the front title page there was an old, antiquated version of the same. Frowning slightly, I pulled the worn card from its slot with some care, as the paper looked like it might crumble. Squinting, I tried to read the return date. I blinked and read it again. The card fell to the spotless counter as I gaped at the old lady in astonishment.

Did I imagine it or was Mother Goose now looking the tiniest bit guilty? She wrinkled her nose and shook her head slightly, giving me the benefit of watching all the fruit jump alarmingly. "I'm afraid it is a trifle overdue—" she began.

"A trifle?—" my voice cracked. I cleared my throat and tried again. "I'm afraid it's 45 years overdue."

She put a hand to her mouth, "Oh dear, how time does fly."

THE KNITTING FAIRY

Chapter 2

Mother Goose – Springgate Library's Most Wanted

Mother Goose wrinkled her nose again. Was it my imagination or was there now a mischievous twinkle in her eyes? "Forty-five years must seem like a lot of time to a youngster like yourself," she said. "But let me assure you, it goes quicker than you think. I really am sorry about not returning the book sooner. I hope no one was waiting for it."

I blinked. "Uhhh...no, I don't think anyone is waiting for it," I said slowly.

She gave a great sigh of relief. "Well, that is certainly a blessing," she said, "I would just have felt terrible for keeping it for so long if someone had been waiting more than five years or so to read it. It seems hard to believe that it's been 45 years. Are you sure about that, my dear?"

I blinked again. At what point had I lost complete control over this situation? Had she actually called me a "youngster"? It had been a long, long time since anyone, had referred to me that way. I nodded my head slowly, "Yes, it's definitely 45 years overdue." Her face fell. For some reason I had the urge to try to smooth things over. "I can see how 45 years can slip by," I admitted. "Please don't feel too terribly bad about this. No harm has been done. As a matter of fact, we're partly to blame if you never received an overdue notice. And, it's funny that you should mention it because I was actually just thinking today about age and Life Plans and the whole process of—" I stopped myself before I could finish. What was the matter with me? I risked a quick glance around the desk. Mrs. Goldmyer would not approve of this sort of conversation at the circulation desk or anywhere else in her library.

11

"Yes—" Mother Goose prompted me gently. The fruits and flowers swayed hypnotically on her straw hat. "Do go on, dear."

Something in her eyes drew me toward her. Or maybe it was the swaying fruit. She really looked interested in what I was going to say. Almost unwillingly, I leaned farther over the desk and lowered my voice. "I was wondering when—" I stopped again, flushing slightly and feeling inexplicably flustered. "Oh, never mind," I laughed self-consciously. "I don't know why I'm telling you this, and I certainly don't know why you would be interested."

"Oh, but I am interested," she protested. It was her turn to lower her voice. "Actually—" she said.

"Aunt Carolyn!" Mother Goose turned as a tall, thin, impeccably dressed woman rushed across the room, coming towards the circulation desk. I could tell Mother Goose was not entirely thrilled to see her, but she forced a smile anyway. The woman bent over (way over) Mother Goose...I mean Carolyn, and planted a kiss somewhere in the air next to a bobbling cherry. "I'm so glad I saw you," she gushed. "I was just looking for a new book to read and I saw your hat over the stacks of books. It is quite a hat you know, Aunt Carolyn. I'm really not sure that I would ever have the nerve to wear something quite that...that—" her words seemed to fail her, but she went on determinedly. "Anyways, since we're both here and it's almost lunch time, why don't you let me buy you lunch."

I never really saw Mother Goose agree, but that didn't stop her niece. With a regretful look, Mother Goose waved goodbye as her niece took a firm hold of her arm and led her away.

I watched, shaking my head. Whatever had gotten into me today? Acting in such a way with a patron? It must be the spring air. I bit my lip, wondering what to do. What could possibly be the proper protocol for checking in a book that was over 45 years overdue? The book didn't even have a bar code. I knew one thing for certain. This story wasn't going to have a happy ending. Mrs. Goldmyer was going to freak.

The library was starting to wake up. The little bell attached to the door tinkled happily as another patron came in. What they didn't know was that besides the cute little bell, a more practical, but infinitely more dull, electronic bell sounded by the circulation desk and also in the back office. I knew that I would have to make up my mind fast when I saw Mrs. Heath come in with her darling son, Lucas, in tow. I could only hope that Mrs. Goldmyer hadn't seen them yet. I figured that I should have about four minutes (if I was lucky) before the commotion (and Mrs. Goldmyer) forced me to leave my post at the circulation desk and save the library from certain doom – I mean, Lucas Heath. I shuddered. We were still reeling from the darling boy's last visit.

But, the question still remained. What should I do with this book? I seriously doubted that it was even in the computer. If I had more time, I would check, but any move toward the keyboard with no library patrons standing near the desk would immediately draw the suspicion of Mrs. Goldmyer. It amused me to no end that she kept trying to catch me doing something horrible and life-shattering to the circulation desk computer. It wasn't even networked or hooked up to the internet or anything. Did she think that I would single-handedly take down the entire library system? Perhaps delete all the patrons? Even if I knew how (which I didn't), I know exactly who would have to fix any mistakes like that. Me.

So, what to do? I picked up the book again, turning it over and over in my hands. The leather was old and worn and cracked in several placed. I ran a hand down the spine over the worn lettering and smiled. It was so easy to picture Carolyn, her feet tucked up under her, reading and re-reading the same book year after year. Its yellowing pages and worn-out print must have truly been like an old, comforting friend. Why bring it back now? A dormant sense of guilt?

I shrugged my shoulders; the reason was not important. The essential question was - what was I going to do with it? Mrs. Goldmyer was going to have a fit. That was a given. She might even charge Carolyn the full price of the book. There would be absolutely no sympathy for an elderly woman who had selfishly hoarded a library book for so many years.

Frowning, I contemplated the silent book. Mrs. Goldmyer was not a pleasant person on her best days. Somehow I doubted that even charging Carolyn the full price of the book would satisfy her certain ire. But, what else could she do? I pondered the question, still frowning. What would a vengeful Mrs. Goldmyer do with a book that had been returned 45 years late? What horrible fate would await Carolyn? Her library card cut in half? A viciously worded letter? Ostracized at the local supermarket as the gossip began? We had several grocery stores, but I had full faith in Mrs. Goldmyer's ability to cover them all.

Then, it hit me.

I was paralyzed as the full weight of what Mrs. Goldmyer would do washed over me in a sickening wave of horror. I knew what she would do just as surely as I knew that I was standing here. She would charge Mother Goose <u>all</u> of the late fees.

I frantically tried to remember the exact wording of the penalties in the library codes. Alright, smarty-pants, if you're thinking that, as Assistant Head Librarian, I should know all the codes by heart, let me assure you that since the code book is about a hundred pages thick and presumably written by Mrs. Goldmyer when she was feeling especially contrary, it's really not too hard to imagine that the details were a little fuzzy. As best I could recall, it was solely up to the Head Librarian's discretion whether the late fees or the full price of the book would be charged.

I tried to follow the twisted workings of Mrs. Goldmyer's mind, but found that I simply did not have the deviousness for it. Surely, I thought desperately, surely even Mrs. Goldmyer would demand payment on whichever total was the smallest. Surely there would be some sort of safeguard against a situation like this.

An image of Mrs. Goldmyer's beady little eyes floated to mind. Maybe not.

The leather under my hand was screaming for attention, and as I looked down, I realized that Mrs. Goldmyer would never let Carolyn simply pay for the book – she would have to pay the late fees. Head aching from the strain, I forced myself to reason as if I were Mrs. Goldmyer... The book was 45 years overdue, not lost. The book was now in our possession, and we wouldn't have to replace it; so therefore, the price of the book was not an issue. The patron should be punished for the blatant and total disregard he/she has shown not only to the library but also to the other patrons as well. The late fees would be assessed and demanded.

Carolyn is a grown woman, a little voice in my head argued. She should have known better than to keep a library book for over 45 years. She will have to face her mistakes like everyone else.

I thought of the sweet little wrinkled face and was besieged with indecision. I mentally calculated the cost of the late fees. The amount was staggering. There had to be a way around this situation that wasn't going to bankrupt Mother Goose.

I was half tempted to stash the book in my purse and "accidentally" forget to bring it back. The idea had merit. I could probably even get away with it. Probably. Apparently, we didn't even know that the book was missing. Biting my lip anxiously, I could feel time ticking by. A decision had to be made quickly. With an almost audible sigh (Mrs. Goldmyer has ears like a hawk), I regretfully decided to abandon my purse plan, which was really too bad. It was such a beautiful plan, and I was really sorry to see it go. But alas, my beautiful purse plan had one fatal flaw. And for that reason alone, I could not follow through with it. That reason, unfortunately, does me no moral credit. My purse was way too small to fit a book that size.

A small rumbling could be heard from the general direction of the Children's Section. I didn't have much time left. I knew what I should do. There was only one sensible option. Leave the book on Mrs. Goldmyer's desk with a note explaining the situation. Then, the problem would be out of my hands and into the appropriate hands of the Head Librarian. She would deal with the matter as she saw fit. It was not my job or responsibility. Leave the book on her desk, and I would be done with it. It really was the only course of action.

So, naturally, that's not what I did at all. Just because you're a shy librarian doesn't mean you're always sensible. Keep this in mind - never judge a book by its cover. Ha! (Just a bit of librarian humor. Sorry!)

Like a bolt of lightning from the sky, inspiration struck. The simplicity of my new plan was absolutely blinding in its brilliance. As nonchalantly as possible, I took the book over to the Damaged Book Bin. Every Thursday, we took the books that had been returned damaged and sent them out for repairs. Today was Tuesday. I had two more days to figure something out. Brilliant, more time. And what would I do with all this wonderful extra time? Perhaps I could simply hunt down Mother Goose and tell her to just take the book back. My conscience let out a shriek of indignation. No, I guess not. Besides, I didn't even know her last name. It was almost a bit appalling to me how quickly my sense of library morality deserted me in favor of a nice, old, library-book stealing lady.

Whoever said lightning never strikes the same place twice was wrong because, not two seconds later, inspiration struck again. I could simply replace the book on the shelf. It was as easy as that.

Clearly if Mother Goose had not been receiving overdue notices, we didn't even know that it was missing. I only had to wait for the perfect opportunity when Mrs. Goldmyer wasn't watching to retrieve the book from the Damaged Books Bin and put it back on the shelf. It couldn't be any simpler.

Could my conscience live with that? I mentally probed it; yes, I think it could. Brilliant, absolutely brilliant. I actually felt a bit smug about the cleverness of my plan as I placed the book conveniently under a few other books in the bin. Thanks to my care and devotion to library maintenance, the wheels on the Damaged Books Bin did not squeak or groan as I pushed the bin back into place.

So, was the problem solved, you ask? Of course not. Thanks to my combination of cowardice and procrastination (in other words, my Brilliant Plan), I had only bought myself some time. But hey, when one is dealing with Lucas and Mrs. Goldmyer at once, time is a wonderful gift.

Looking up, I saw the latter barreling toward me, her thick practical shoes clomping with purpose toward the circulation desk. I decided to beat her to the punch and slipped around the counter gracefully. With a quick wave of my hand, I said in my friendliest voice, "I'll be right with you, Mrs. Goldmyer, but I'm afraid I had better go check out what's happening in the Children's Section."

Her mouth opened and closed. She looked very annoyed about missing the opportunity to instruct me to do that very thing.

Grinning to myself, I headed towards the Children's Section. I had won the small battle with Mrs. Goldmyer, and now I was ready to face the larger one against a smaller, but equally formidable foe – Lucas the darling boy. As I mentioned before, the library was set up like squares within squares. The Children's Section was in the center (theoretically so that parents could keep an eye on their dear children while looking for books themselves). Lucas' mother, however, believed in letting Lucas "become his own person". In reality, this meant that she spent hours going through the shelves of books while I scrambled to keep Lucas from completely destroying the library in his quest find himself.

Fun times.

I was quickly advancing on the Children's Section and ready to peel Lucas off of the bookshelves, which he was undoubtedly trying to climb again. This time, he had made it half way up. "No Lucas," I said, raising my voice, "You are not Jack and that is most definitely not a beanstalk!"

I had only myself to blame. In a foolish effort to hold his attention, I had taken to reading Lucas stories while his mother browsed. He loved them. Probably a bit too much. I really had to find this kid a story that didn't involve swords, climbing tall

17

objects and – as a book of children's poems whizzed past my head – and oh yes, throwing. Lunch time couldn't come too soon.

***

Waving goodbye to Lucas, I couldn't help the little grin. We had ended up with Pooh Bear. There wasn't too much in Pooh that a darling little boy who is "becoming his own person" could do much damage with. Other than Tigger, of course. And that was the reason for my little grin. I had very wisely omitted any mention of the bouncing Tigger when I read it. I doubted his mother would be smart enough to do the same.

My friends, I don't think you can imagine my horror and dismay as I turned around to see Mrs. Goldmyer pushing the Damaged Books Bin back into place. Her thin lips were pinched together and she surveyed the rest of the library grimly from behind her thick, black-rimmed glasses. Her hair was pulled back so tightly that I was sure her eyes must hurt. She stalked back to her office.

My throat was suddenly very dry, and I had almost an uncontrollable desire to hide under the circulation desk. My fingers clenched the edge of the counter so hard that they turned white. Had she seen the book? What was she doing in the bin? Would she say anything? Did she find it? Should I go confess? Attempt to explain?

I consoled myself with the thought that perhaps she was only putting a book in there herself. I tried to think, but it was hard to concentrate over the noise in the library. What on earth could that dreadful banging noise be? Had Lucas returned? Were the books jumping from the shelves? It was when I realized that the banging coincided quite well with the thumping in my chest that I realized I was hearing my own heartbeat.

"Pull yourself together," I said sternly. "You're falling apart."

I glanced again nervously towards her office, but the door was pulled firmly shut. Feeling nauseated and nervous, I was overcome with guilt. Had I done the right thing? What on earth had possessed me to hide that book? Was I crazy? Perhaps I should go and confess. Or try to laugh it off as a silly mistake. I briefly considered outright lying, but I knew I couldn't live with myself if I did that. And, to be completely honest, I'm a terrible liar. I'd never get away with it.

Self-doubt and remorse aren't good companions, so I went back to work and tried to ignore them. I could feel them hovering over my shoulder, and so I concentrated on working even harder. Without realizing what I was doing, I found myself checking books in with a gusto I seldom felt. The distraction worked all too well. I didn't notice Mrs. Goldmyer behind me until it was too late. I jumped in spite of myself.

She raised one pointy eyebrow, "It really is a shame that this is not the caliber of work that we usually see from you Ms. Stevenson."

Somehow she always made "Ms." sound like an insult.

I gritted my teeth. "I always strive to do my best, Mrs. Goldmyer," I replied honestly.

The eyebrow went up again. She really had a knack for it. "I wonder if I might have a word with you in my office." It wasn't a request, and as I trudged obediently behind her to her office, one single thought stood alone in stark contrast to the swirling guilt and panic flooding my mind. You may be wondering what that thought was. Was I kicking myself for feeling sorry for Mother Goose? Well, yes, but that wasn't it. Guilt? Yes, guilt was in there too. But still...there was another emotion that kept rising to the top. Remorse? Yes.

Yes, indeed, I was definitely feeling remorseful. And if you guessed remorse, you would be right. You might be surprised that I was not, however, feeling remorseful about hiding the book. Nor was I feeling remorseful for taking pity on Mother Goose. No. I am a bit embarrassed to admit that I was mostly sorry that I didn't have a bigger purse.

Chapter 3

A Healthy Shove Down My Career Path

Lunch time found me sitting in the park. It was a beautiful park nestled in the heart of downtown Springgate. I often found myself taking lunch hours there. The library was a magical and mystical place, but a breath of fresh air at midday always helped clear the head (and the lungs from magical book dust).

Today, I sat with my back against an old, oak tree. Its rough bark was against my back. I felt a special friendship with this tree that let me sit beneath its branches. Years ago, the tree's long roots had begun creeping towards the surface, and now they made the perfect place to sit amid the soggy ground. The roots weren't exactly dry, but what's a little dampness when one is communing with nature? I tilted my head back so that I could see straight up the tree. I could see the sky quite clearly between the crazy maze of branches that shifted and swayed in the spring breeze, but it wouldn't be long before those branches were covered in green and soon I would be sitting in shade.

Spring is the most exciting time of the year. Trees, tired of shivering in the bitter winds of winter, now quivered with expectancy. They were hoping and dreaming of the day when their long branches would once again be covered in warm green leaves. The plants in the garden to my left looked so little and forlorn with their pitiful branches sticking out of the half-thawed mud. But there was promise in the air. The plants could feel it; I could feel it too. Already, you could imagine that those bare little branches were straightening just a little, reaching hopefully out to the sun.

It was a good life lesson, and I pondered it carefully. A lesson from nature. Even when everything looks bleak and bare from a long, hard winter, the hope of spring pulls you along. I

21

took a deep breath of the promise-filled air and closed my eyes tightly - trying to ignore the stinging.

"Well, hello again," a pleasant voice rang out. I took another deep breath and, blinking rapidly to dispel the tears, forced myself to open my eyes to greet the intruder. It's a good thing I was sitting down because otherwise I would have fallen over. It was Mother Goose.

Do you believe in fate? I don't. I do, however, firmly believe that God has a plan for each of our lives (not to be confused with The Plan, of course). I had always imagined His plan to be a wispy, floaty thing that gently guided you through life. A little voice deep inside that whispered advice when you were in doubt. A quiet certainty that The Plan was pulling you in the right direction. Never, ever did I think that He would use Mother Goose to almost literally drag me down my own path.

"H-hello," I stammered, "How are you?"

She was untying the ribbons of her straw hat, as she smiled serenely at me. "Quite well, thank you dear," she said. "And you?"

I took another deep breath and said very convincingly, "I'm fine."

Her eyes narrowed at me, "Are you sure?"

Hmmmm...I told you that I was not a very good liar. At this point, I didn't know whether that was a comforting thing or not. She sat down next to me, pulling her dress up so that she could sit Indian-style on the tree roots. I couldn't help but grin.

She grinned back at me. "Now that's more like it," she said approvingly. "It's such a nice spring day. Much too nice to not be happy." She looked thoughtfully up at the sky, "I'm not so sure that winter won't rear its head again, though. You can almost feel it in the air." She peered at me intently, "Now, why don't you tell me what's bothering you?" She laid her straw hat on the ground, arranging the fruit and flowers so that they wouldn't tangle.

I shook my head, "It's really nothing." Another lie. I hoped it was more convincing this time. How could I possibly tell her that I was fired because I tried to hide the fact that she

22

brought back an overdue book? I was ashamed. And embarrassed.

Not surprisingly, my lie was again caught and exposed. She gave a very unladylike snort. "I think I know trouble when I see it, young lady," she said. "If you don't want to share it with me, that's fine. But don't lie to yourself. Trust me, it won't make you feel any better."

Whoa. Mother Goose with an attitude.

There was, however, no answer that I could give her. The world was getting watery again, and I blinked my eyes very hard and stared determinedly at the grass. In the distance, the sound of church bells rang through the air on clear, sharp notes, striking the hour. Mother Goose twitched slightly and looked at the watch hanging around her neck. "How long is your lunch hour?" she asked. "You wouldn't want to get into trouble by being late from lunch. I've lived here a very long time, you know, and one thing I am certain of is that Mrs. Goldmyer is not too forgiving of that type of thing."

I sniffed and started at the ground again. "I don't have to get back to the library," I said in a very small voice, my fingers plucking at the grass. I didn't dare raise my eyes.

Confusion was evident in her voice, "You have the rest of the day off?" she asked.

Clearly lying was out of the question, so I decided to bite the bullet and just tell her the truth. I raised my eyes to meet hers. "I was let go this afternoon."

Her mouth formed a perfect "O". I broke eye contact first and looked off into the direction of the playground where small children, invigorated by the smell of spring, were running and playing. How could they be so completely oblivious to the fact that 100 yards away a girl who had just been fired for doing something she ordinarily never would have done was sitting under a tree having a conversation with Mother Goose? How did this day get so crazy? Perhaps I was still asleep and dreaming. Somehow, though, I doubted that even my imagination was clever enough to come up with this scenario. And besides, I

23

don't remember my rear end hurting from sitting too long on a tree trunk in any of my dreams. Ever.

"May I ask for what reason you were fired?" Mother Goose asked gently.

"Conduct unbecoming a librarian," I said with some chagrin.

"Conduct unbecoming a librarian," she repeated slowly, her eyes never leaving my face. "Now, why do I have a hard time believing that?"

I didn't answer her. She was a very sharp lady. It took her all of five seconds to jump to the correct conclusion. "Does this have anything to do with my library book?" she asked just as gently as before.

I broke eye contact again and stared over her shoulder. The situation was just too bizarre for words.

"I am sorry," she said sincerely. "I had no idea I would be the cause of so much trouble." She made a small fist and smacked herself in the forehead. "I should have brought that book back years ago. The truth is," and here she paused to look around, "the truth is Mrs. Goldmyer and I have what you might call an ongoing disagreement about something, and I never felt the urge to go back to the library." Tears shone in her eyes. "I never thought that it would cause trouble for someone else."

Now I felt like a worm – a double worm. She felt bad for making me feel bad. And I felt bad for her feeling bad for me. And, to make it even worse – I didn't know what the right words were for a situation like this. "Please don't cry," I said desperately, "I loved working at the library, but it was probably only a matter of time before I got fired anyway. It's really for the best. We really weren't kindred spirits. And to be quite honest, I'm glad I don't have to think about seeing her everyday anymore." I stuttered my way through the speech a bit, and as I did so... I realized that I was telling the truth. I had loved the library. I still did. But I would not miss being ridiculed and mistreated every day. I would not miss the feeling that no matter what I did I would never meet the standards that Mrs. Goldmyer set forth.

Mother Goose sat back and contemplated me with surprisingly shrewd eyes. Silence hung in the air between us. The only sound was the laughter from the children and the occasional chirp of a feathered friend sitting on a branch above me.

"Well, you could come and work for me." She broke the silence so abruptly that the bird flew off with an indignant flap of its wings.

I gaped at her, "Excuse me?"

Looking back, I can see that this is the exact moment – the precise point in time –when everything changed. Had I wanted my life to continue on according to The Plan, I should have started running. Really fast.

She picked up her straw hat again and began the process of putting it back on. "Yup," she said, "That's the thing to do. I just know it. You'll come to work for me, and everything will work out fine, you'll see." her eyes twinkled at me. "Trust me, I have a great feeling about this."

"But, but, but—" I stammered, while she tied the ribbons under her chin again, "You don't even know me...and come to think of it, I don't know you either."

She made a vague gesture with her hand. "We'll get to know each other," she assured me.

This was all going way too fast. One simply didn't get fired and hired within the same two hours. It just wasn't done that way. "What kind of business are you in?" A little fact that might be nice to know.

"I own a yarn store," she said.

I waited politely for her to explain herself. Evidently she thought she had, and as I stared at her, she stared back at me without blinking.

She got to her feet, and I did the same. I tried to discreetly brush the dirt off the back of my khakis. She obviously wasn't going to say anything else. So, I cleared my throat and ventured forth with "yarn store?"

Her eyes wide, she nodded slowly, "Yes, dear, you know... a store where you can buy yarn."

"Right," I said slowly, "a yarn store to buy yarn. Of course." Oh boy.

Evidently she felt that I had finally caught on. "Yes," she continued enthusiastically, "We're right downtown - well, almost right downtown. It's off of Main Street on Roberts Alley. Perhaps you've seen us? Crabapple Yarns?" I must have shook my head at the appropriate moment, because she went on, "Well, we've been open for over 20 years now—" she trailed off. "Whatever is the matter, dear?"

I felt like I was in a daze. "You mean that you actually own a store that only sells...yarn?" Unfortunately, I felt my voice go up and end on a note of disbelief. I hoped I hadn't offended her. Was the park spinning?

She shook her head, and the fruit went flying, "Oh no," she said with a smile, "of course not."

I let out a sigh of relief. The park came back into focus. Good. Maybe she wasn't so crazy after all. "We also sell needles and books and all of the things that go with yarn."

To my dismay, the park began its slow orbit around me again. I took a step back so that I could feel the comfortable solidity of the tree behind me. Coherency usually wasn't this much of a problem. "And you find that you have, err, umm, well—" how could I say this without hurting her feelings? Perhaps it would be best just to get to the point. "I mean you do have customers, right?" I rubbed at a particularly troublesome spot of dirt on the seat of my pants so that I wouldn't have to look at her.

Instead of being offended, she let out a merry peal of laughter. "I can tell you're not a knitter, are you?"

I shook my head, "No, I'm afraid not." Crazy, definitely crazy.

She took my arm as if we were old friends and started walking me out of the park. She certainly had a very determined nature. "My name's Carolyn, by the way," she said. "What's yours?"

"Molly Stevenson."

"Nice name," she said approvingly. "I can tell we're going to be great friends. Now, you just come along with me, young lady. I'm going to take you to my store and then we'll talk some more about your future career path."

I felt what was left of my control over the situation slipping away like water down a drain, but I felt that I should at least try to protest a little. "I really should—" I began.

She took a firmer grasp of my arm, "Nonsense, Molly." She sent me a sympathetic look. "It's not like you have anywhere else to be, is there? You lost your job because you didn't want me to get into trouble. Now, let me repay the favor by offering you something in return."

I shrugged mentally. What did I really have to lose, after all? It was a beautiful day for a stroll downtown, and it might be interesting to see what a yarn store looked like. It's not like I was really going to work for her or anything.

THE KNITTING FAIRY

Chapter 4
Denying My Inner Knitter

The downtown area of Springgate was a wonderful place to be. Unlike other towns where restaurants, bakeries, clothing stores, toy stores, and gift shops were relegated to dreary little strip malls scattered along busy streets, Springgate kept a beautifully maintained downtown area. It was like stepping back into the past. Churches and businesses coexisted peacefully in one of the most tranquil settings that you could imagine. On the corner was a candy store that made its own fudge. The smell wafted for blocks. Pigeons played at your feet as you walked along, hoping that you hadn't been able to resist the popcorn in the park and were going to share.

Of course I had walked downtown many times, but I had never come across Carolyn's yarn store. You may think that this is strange but you have to remember that I just moved here a little over a year and a half ago. On the weekends, I still went home quite a bit to see my family. So when I did get downtown, I mainly went to the stores that I always went to. Alright, I admit it – the candy store was my favorite stop. I never ever thought to look for a yarn store. But, seriously... who would?

I confess that I'm making it sound a little more idyllic than it really was. Like every city, it had its quirks and faults, but all in all, it truly was a beautiful place. My mind was spinning again and Carolyn, thankfully, let us walk along in companionable silence.

Smaller streets split off of Main Street at regular intervals, and it was at one of these streets where Carolyn eventually turned. I suppose it was more of an alley than a street. It was just a little street that connected Main Street to Church Street, which ran parallel to Main Street. Towards the left, the only thing you could see was the wall of the department store across the street. Painted in fading letters across this part

29

of the building were the words, "If Colson's doesn't have it - you don't need it!" But, on the right side of the street, three stores were snuggled into a relatively small space. About 20 parking spaces lined the front of the stores.

The first store we passed was a small bakery. The smells coming out were mouth-watering and my stomach growled loudly, protesting the absence of lunch. I made a mental note to stop there on my way back. The second store on the street was a hardware store. I tried to look in as we went by. It was somewhat dirty-looking and had very poor lighting. I wondered how it stayed in business when the big hardware chain store at the end of Main Street held everything that you could possibly want – and it was clean. Both the bakery and the hardware store were fairly common-looking places, big plate glass windows in front proudly displaying their wares.

Carolyn's store, on the other hand, was anything but common. As we paused in front of it, I had to stand completely still in order to take it in. It was not a large place. It wasn't small, either. It was absolutely...perfect. Made completely from fieldstone and brick, it was a two-story, English cottage looking place. A large window occupied much of the front. The roof rose to a sharp point in the front with the chimney, also made from stone, coming straight out of the point of the roof. I tilted my head and squinted, was it...

"Yes," Carolyn said with a sigh, "the chimney has a bit of a lean."

"It's perfect." I must have said it out loud, because Carolyn let out a sigh of agreement. A wooden sign stuck out over the entrance with "Crabapple Yarns" engraved in red and gold lettering. Under that, a ball of yarn with knitting needles tucked through it proudly proclaimed it to be a knitting store.

There was a large straw mat in front of the antique wooden door. To my delight, the door had large, old-fashioned iron handles. Carolyn stepped back to allow me to enter first. I felt almost reluctant to enter so sure that anything would be a disappointment after the enchanting exterior. I grasped the cool metal handle and gave a slight tug. The tinkle of a bell alerted the store to our presence. I took my first step in and stopped in my tracks.

I had entered a land of enchantment. We had obviously ventured through a portal into another world, for places like this didn't exist on earth. Wood floors gleamed in the sunlight, warm and welcoming. Ancient, but colorful, rugs were sprawled across the gleaming surface at irregular intervals, creating an immediate sense of warmth and home. Wooden cubbies lined the walls and strange and wonderful "things" poured forth from them, dizzying and intoxicating in their color and texture. Everywhere I looked, items (I assumed that they were knitted) hung on various surfaces...a little fuzzy purse, a shawl that looked like it belonged to a fairy queen for surely it had been knitted from a cobweb, a warm-looking sweater, scarves draped everywhere...How long I walked around the store, I have no idea. I do, however, have a vague recollection of a counter across the room where a lady sat knitting. When I finally came back to my senses, I was sitting on a cushioned chair in the front of the store. Carolyn was across from me on a rich tapestry loveseat, her feet tucked up under her. I met her twinkling gaze with a look of wonderment.

"I had no idea—" I began and then stopped. How could I tell her that I had thought she was a bit loopy...alright, I had thought she was downright delusional, when she told me what line of business she was in. She still could be... but this store... this store was...

Her grin was from ear to ear. "Everybody reacts the same way, dear," she said, her grin both triumphant and sympathetic. "Everyone who is denying their inner knitter thinks that knitters are crazy."

"Denying their inner knitter?" I asked, curious despite myself.

She lowered her voice, and looked around like she didn't want anyone to hear her, "You know, non-knitters."

"Right," I said, "non-knitters." I looked around the store again. It was a magical place. Carolyn had done well to create the perfect atmosphere for her customers. If she did, indeed, have customers. I tried to think if I knew anyone who knitted. I wracked my brain for several seconds. My grandma, of course, had knitted. She probably would have loved this place. But, the yarn she used didn't look like what Carolyn had here...I don't know what the words I was looking for were, but grandma's yarn looked...different.

I folded my hands on my lap, tightening my fingers around themselves. I suddenly felt very out of place and self-conscious in this little haven. Surely I did not belong here. I belonged between stacks of books and computers and little cards with due dates stamped on them. The Plan would not approve of this at all. I belonged with things that were logical...dependable. I wouldn't know the first thing about yarn or even about selling...anything. Librarians weren't salespeople. Librarians were helpers. Carolyn's store was a little self-contained world - a lot like a book in the library. One world among millions. Librarians didn't belong in one book. Librarians belonged in a library and helped other people pick out books. Working here could be scary. It would be all too easy to become...involved.

Too bad though, I thought, looking wistfully around the store. It could have been interesting.

I suddenly had an overwhelming need to escape this small store.

"Thank you, Carolyn," I said abruptly, "for helping me forget about my problems for a little while. This truly is one of the most beautiful shops I have ever seen. I really have no idea what one does with all the things in here, but I feel more peaceful for just coming in. I promise I'll stop by quite often and see how you're getting along." A little line was forming between her eyebrows, and so I plunged on. "I know you feel sorry for me, but don't worry, I'll get another job. I wouldn't know the first thing about selling or yarn or customers or anything like that. Please don't feel like you have to—"

"How much did you make at the library?" she asked, as if I had never spoken.

My grand speech halted in midair and plunged to the floor. "Excuse me?" I asked weakly.

She repeated the question, and for some strange reason, I answered her. The frown deepened, as did the wrinkles across her forehead. "Oh dear," she said, "I could never afford to pay that much. And you live in an apartment?" I nodded obediently. "That can't be cheap either."

She put a hand to her cheek and tapped a finger absently, lost deep in thought.

The need to leave intensified. I considered making a run for the door.

Carolyn looked up with an expression that I was learning to recognize. I should have run for it when I had the chance. "I have it," she said triumphantly, "why don't I pay you (and here she named a figure) and then you can live upstairs for free."

My mind reeled again. "I think I need to sit down," I said.

"You are sitting down," she said.

"Oh." It was all I could manage. The idea was tempting and completely ludicrous at the same time. I briefly wondered if perhaps she really wasn't completely sane. She hardly knew me. Yet, here I was. Not six hours ago, I had been contemplating my life and its lack of adventure, and now, I was sitting in a yarn store because I had been fired, and a nice old lady was offering to let me live in her enchanted cottage and a job all at the same time. Perhaps some of you still don't think that's much of an adventure, but for me, this was huge.

I was still debating what to do when I heard someone say, "Alright, I'll take it."

Uh-oh. I think it was me.

A delighted grin spread across her face, which was once again covered in equally delightful little wrinkles. "I knew it," she said, "I just knew from the first time that I saw you this morning that we were bound to do great things together."

I would have replied, but at the moment my mouth was too dry and my heart was thumping like a marching band to the tune of "What have I done? What have I done?" I wanted to stand up and pace to relieve some tension, but I had a sickening feeling that my legs would not support me. What have I done? What have I done? It was a catchy rhythm and my head began pounding along in time with my heart. I put a hand to my stomach, feeling slightly queasy.

It was like someone had taken a hammer and shattered my nice comfortable world. I felt the pieces lying in shards around my feet. Panic was like a butterfly in my stomach. The events of the day had suddenly become too much.

I had been fired. Me. Fired. I had never been in trouble before. Reality slammed down hard. I had been fired. How would I ever tell my parents? I was ashamed of myself. Mrs. Goldmyer had been absolutely correct in firing me. What in the world had I been thinking? Hiding a book? It was practically fraud. My conscience shrieked in indignation at the exaggeration. Well, maybe not fraud. But still, Carolyn had been wrong. I had been wrong. She hadn't returned the book for 45 years. I should have followed protocol. If only I could turn back time. I would...and here my brain was stopped in its tracks by my heart, as I acknowledged the truth to myself. I would not have done anything differently. No one deserved to have to pay a library fine in the thousands of dollars. After all, if the library hadn't sent her overdue notices, it was partly the library's fault, anyway. But still, fired. For the second time today, I felt like a worm. A worm trapped above ground with a new job that it was absolutely unqualified for. The butterfly was beating its wings frantically.

"You've had a hard day, dear." It was Mother Goose's voice that brought me back to the present. "I know you must be feeling very low right now. You've had a terrible blow. I know what it feels like to be fired." My eyes shot up to meet hers. Who could ever fire Mother Goose? "Try not to dwell on it too much. You'll have to forgive me for saying so, but Mrs. Goldmyer is not a nice person. As a matter of fact, she has either fired every person that has ever worked for her or they have quit out of sheer frustration. So, keep that in mind. You might have been a little misguided in your actions, but you are a wonderful person, and you're going to come through this just fine."

At some point during her little speech, my eyes had filled with tears, and I looked up at her, not quite knowing what to say. She came to sit on the arm of the chair next to me and gave me a one-sided hug. I froze. She was totally invading my personal space, and she didn't even seem to notice. "Why don't you go home now, have a nice hot bath and some lunch." Her eyes twinkled at me. "I heard your stomach growl. And then tomorrow, come to the store around 8:00 in the morning. I'll give you a crash course in yarn and get you started knitting."

Panic again. It was becoming a very familiar emotion. I stuttered, "Ummm...me...knit?" My voice rose to an almost hysterical pitch.

She patted my arm again, "Of course, you'll have to learn how to knit so that you can help the customers."

Of course, I thought desperately. Why hadn't I thought of that?

And with that, she bundled me out of the door, calmly hushing my protests and sent me home. Not for the first time I really, really regretted having a mouth that spoke for itself.

Chapter 5
Making Friends With The Yarn

The next day dawned dull, cold, and rainy, matching my mood. With a sinking feeling of dread, I realized that I would not be spending my day among my friends (the books in the library). I would be spending my day in a yarn store, of all places. I would learn how to knit today. I groaned and pulled the pillow over my head.

As I was eating breakfast at my tiny kitchen table, The Plan mocked me from its perch on the refrigerator. "Shut up," I said. But it didn't. The silent mocking hurt my ears, so I flipped the paper over. "That will teach you," I said unhappily, sticking the book bug over it. "You need to learn that you're not always right." But, like me, it wasn't a lesson that it wanted to learn.

I arrived at Crabapple Yarns right on time. Even in the drippy rain, it was still a magical place. I knocked timidly on the door. Carolyn's smile was the only sunshine in the day. "Good morning Molly," she all but sang. "Are you ready to begin your adventure in knitting?"

My eyes must have been wide and apprehensive because she laughed good-naturedly, "Come on, it's not scary."

I walked into the store, and she carefully locked the door behind us. Oh great, now I was trapped.

On the large wooden table near the center of the store, Carolyn had spread out an assortment of yarn and needles. She rubbed her hands together gleefully. Today she was dressed in a yellow gingham jumper with a snowy-white lace blouse underneath. A scarf in a coordinating shade of yellow went around and around her neck and still managed to almost scrape the ground as she walked.

I approached the table somewhat reluctantly and picked up a pair of needles. They were smooth and unexpectedly warm in my hand. I waited politely for Carolyn to jump right in with a knitting lesson.

She grinned and pulled the needles from my fingers. "Oh no, dear," she said, "first you have to become friends with the yarn."

I could hardly wait.

An hour later, I was still trying to grapple with the concepts of the different weights of yarn. Fingering, lace, worsted, bulky...all strange words that now had new (but precious little) meaning to me. I also had a vague idea of the different fibers that yarn could be made out of. Good grief. Who knew that there were so many? And better yet – why were there so many?

Why couldn't people just pick one and go with it, for pity's sake? Did one really need to blend five different animal fibers into one yarn? Was there really a point? Did it really make a difference if it was 45% wool and 50% llama and 5% acrylic? Why couldn't they just live without the acrylic and throw in a little more wool? For that matter, what do you think the llama really added? I bet the llama didn't even want to be part of the yarn. I bet the llama would have been just as happy to keep his own wool on his little backside.

When I worked up the nerve to (very politely, mind you) inquire the reason for this absurdity, Carolyn only surprised me by throwing her head back and laughing in a very unladylike manner.

I was not so amused. Surely it would be easier if there were only a few choices. If it boggled my mind it must also boggle the minds of whatever customers she might possibly have. Wouldn't they be happier without quite so many choices? I decided, however, to keep my opinions to myself. I don't like people laughing at me. But I do have to say one thing – some people sure know how to make life complicated.

By 9:30, I was sitting by the table with two needles and a ball of yarn and was diligently trying to knit. "Just the garter stitch, dear," Carolyn had said, "We'll tackle purling tomorrow." I really didn't know what she was talking about, but it sounded like things were going to get harder. Gritting my teeth, I inserted one of the sharp pointy sticks into the loops of yarn on the other needle. I felt like I had about fifteen thumbs. My hands fumbled terribly as I tried to balance needle, yarn, and the other needle.

This was ridiculous.

This was insane.

This was really, really boring.

I probably didn't have to worry too much. There couldn't possibly be that many people in the world who considered this fun. For the hundredth time, I wondered exactly how Carolyn stayed in business. Perhaps she was independently wealthy. Perhaps she was really an undercover spy who used yarn to smuggle secret, coded messages. Or perhaps a mastermind criminal and the store was a front for something sinister. As long as she could afford my paycheck and didn't try to involve me in larceny or mayhem, I supposed it didn't matter all too much.

"Great," she praised me, her eyes glowing with an excitement that I did not feel, "You've got it."

After knitting every stitch on the left needle onto the right needle, I looked up at Carolyn with a questioning gaze, "Now what?"

"Now you switch hands and do the same thing all over again."

"Excuse me?" I asked as politely as I could, "That's it? That's all there is to it? I just repeat the same step over and over and over?" I'm afraid that disbelief practically dripped from my tone, but I quite simply could not help it.

I've always had a somewhat abstract respect for knitters. I've seen people knitting before, of course, and it's very impressive the way that their needles flash in the light and their skilled fingers twist and bend the yarn in mysterious, lightning fast motions. This is all that they do? Push a needle through a loop, wrap the yarn around, and pull it off to the other needle? It was hardly worth talking about. I sighed. Surely Carolyn did not expect me to actually knit a whole scarf? I would die of boredom.

For some reason, my tone did not throw her off; her grin simply grew wider, like she knew something I did not. It was more than a little annoying. "Yep, that's it. Well," she amended, "that's the knit stitch. Tomorrow we'll learn the purl stitch. And once you know the purl stitch, you can do anything."

I don't think my face conveyed the appropriate joy, but she still grinned anyway. She glanced at the clock and her expression took on a look of alarm. She grabbed a bag that had been sitting on the table, and pulling the needles and yarn from my hand, shoved them unceremoniously in.

"Hey," I protested feebly, "What's going on?"

Her smile was a bit forced, "Why don't you take this home and work on it today. Come back tomorrow morning at the same time and we'll continue our lesson."

I was confused. "Don't you want me to stay?" I asked. "I thought I was working for you—"

"You started working for me this morning," she assured me. "Don't fret about that. But it would really be better if we had our lessons together before you worked here when the store was open. I'll explain later, I promise." Her expression was panicky as she glanced at the clock again. Clearly she did not want me to be here when the store opened. That was strange, but I nevertheless obligingly stood up and within seconds found myself standing outside of Crabapple Yarns with a bag of knitting in hand and a befuddled expression on my face. Shrugging, I turned to go home. In the future, I would have to remember to keep a firmer grip on my mouth.

Chapter 6

Humble Pie Can Be Tasty... But So Are Cinnamon Rolls

I didn't make it past the bakery. The aromas drifting out were too tempting to pass by, so I settled the bag of knitting farther back on my arm and pushed open the door of the bakery. As bakeries go, it was a nice little place. Small, clean, mouth-watering. It could use a little bit in the area of decorating, but I suppose that the owner felt his wares more than made up for whatever was lacking in ambience. Still, some comfortable seating would have been nice.

I walked up and down in front of the glass display cases trying to decide which pastry I was most hungry for. If I had to walk past this store every day, I was sure to gain five pounds a week. The person sitting behind the counter and frosting sweet rolls looked up at me with a practiced smile. "Can I help you?" he asked. I guessed his age to be somewhere in his early 30's. He was tall and way too skinny to be a baker, with a great shock of red hair and freckles.

I smiled at him. "I can't quite make up my mind," I admitted, "everything looks so good."

He recommended the cinnamon roll, and I found myself back out on the street with my knitting in one hand and a cinnamon roll in the other. This was kind of fun – meeting the new neighbors. I decided that I just might like working in a community setting like this. I debated whether or not to go into the hardware store, but in my current state of mind, I figured that I just might come out with a hammer or something crazy like a coping saw – and frankly, I did not have any more hands to carry anything.

The sun had decided to come out. It was going to be a warm day again. I had my spring coat with me, and so I decided that it was too nice of a day to go home and knit. I might just fall asleep. What if I went into the park and knitted? I could always sit on my coat. At least if I got bored, I would be bored in a pleasant atmosphere. And, hopefully, there wouldn't be too many people there at this hour to see me. That could be embarrassing.

Three hours later found me sitting under my favorite tree.

My back muscles were screaming in protest, but I paid them no attention. My cinnamon roll sat half-eaten. I sat hunched over my needles, my hands becoming a little more confident with each stitch I created.

It didn't even occur to me to be bored. I was hypnotized as the little loops came off the needle and grew with each row of knitting into something that I was creating.

Me, Molly Stevenson creating.

I had singlehandedly taken a long piece of yarn and knitted it into a scarf that now lay before me curling into the grass by my toes.

It was amazing. It was...strangely satisfying. It was comforting. And, I had to admit, it wasn't boring at all.

With dismay I realized that I had knitted all of the yarn that Carolyn had given me. I felt an irrational surge of annoyance. Why hadn't she given me more yarn than this? How was I supposed to spend the rest of the afternoon with no yarn?

I dropped the unused needle into the grass and wound the scarf around my neck. One end was still on the needles (I had no idea what sort of process was involved to get them all off so that they would stay together), and so I let that end hang down my side as I admired my handiwork.

I think I really did a good job, considering that this was the first thing I had ever knit. It was actually quite beautiful. Carolyn had given me a lovely yarn that was all the shades of spring, and as I had knitted with it, it had formed stripes all by itself. I gave the scarf an affectionate pat.

What a clever yarn. And wasn't I clever for knitting it?

I settled back against the tree and my muscles breathed a sigh of relief. That was the one thing that was a bit strange. Carolyn had lectured me that knitting was a great stress reliever. She had cited it as helping lower blood pressure and releasing tension. What a salesman. What a crock. If that really was true, why was I was so sore?

My fingers twitched restlessly towards the needle in the grass. My next lesson wasn't until tomorrow morning. What was I supposed to do with the rest of my day? I thought of all the books waiting for me at home. I could read. Reading was my favorite thing to do. So why did the idea seem so undesirable to me right now?

The only thing I wanted to do was knit some more. But I was out of yarn.

I could go back to Crabapple and get more. But, I had the distinct impression that Carolyn would rather that I were not there. I paused. That was certainly odd, wasn't it? Was she trying to hide something from me? Was there some reason she didn't want anyone to know I was going to be working at her store? That was crazy. Why would she hire me if she didn't want anyone to know I was there?

I shrugged mentally. It didn't really matter right now. My thoughts went back to knitting. Who knew something so simple could be so addicting? Yesterday, I would have laughed in your face if you told me that I would ever crave something as silly as yarn. Perhaps they put some kind of drug in the yarn to make it addicting. It's possible, I guess. I examined my hands carefully for any sign of change. It could be some kind of drug that comes in through your fingertips or something like that. At least that would explain my sudden and complete need to have more.

I could go to another store and buy yarn, I reflected. Where I would go, I had no idea. I suppose I could look in the phone book. Maybe they had a "Yarn" entry in the business section. My phone book was currently holding up one end of my lopsided desk, so that could be a problem. Besides, somehow it didn't seem right to buy yarn at another store. It would be like betraying Carolyn. I snorted to myself. I wasn't even officially working there and I was already quite the loyal little employee, wasn't I?

So I did the only thing that was a real option to me at the moment. With a sigh, I picked up my beautiful hand knit scarf and began the tedious process of unraveling.

Chapter 7

A Creature From Outer Space – Or Something Like That

My lessons with Carolyn were going very well. Today was Friday. It was our third lesson. Yesterday I had learned to purl. The endless combination of knits and purls was a bit overwhelming. Words like ribbing, seed stitch, garter stitch, and stockinette stitch swam through my head as Carolyn drilled me in the world of knitting. I doubted that I would retain even half, but it was still exciting to learn – and it was a start. Unlike our lesson on Wednesday, I was now excited to learn all that I could, and I felt like a sponge absorbing Carolyn's wisdom.

She had been quite amused when I had returned on Thursday with my much-knitted scarf. Of course, she had been thrilled with my progress and had praised me for being so diligent and finishing up all of the yarn. She was also impressed with how even my stitches were. With my eyes on the ground, I confessed, somewhat reluctantly, that I had indeed knitted the scarf several times over. I'll never forget the look on her face. She had known all along that I would love knitting. If I wasn't enjoying myself so much, I would have been really annoyed by her smugness.

"I think," Carolyn said thoughtfully, "That tomorrow would be the perfect day for you to start your new career."

I was in the middle of a row of ribbing, and my heart jumped in my chest. It seemed to be doing that a lot lately. Now that I knew how much more there was to knitting than a couple of sticks and string, I was insanely nervous about how much I did not know.

She smiled warmly at me, "Well, as you know, I also have one other employee, Louise. She won't be working tomorrow, so it will be just you and me." She patted me on the arm, "Don't worry, dear, you'll do fine."

I set my knitting down carefully on the oak table so that the stitches wouldn't fall off the ends. "So," I asked just as carefully, "you wanted me to learn about knitting before I started working, right?"

Even though the store was not yet opened, and we both knew the door was locked, she looked around the store anyway. Was it my imagination or were her cheeks a little pinker than usual? "Oh Molly, I—" She then hesitated and looked at me rather strangely. It was a decidedly odd look. She had her head tilted to one side and was peering at me intently over the rim of her glasses. Almost as if she were making a decision. Almost as if she were going to confide something terrible... I held my breath. "My dear," she said, "there are a few things I should—"

As you can probably tell, I've read a few mystery books in my time, and I have to tell you that as soon as she started speaking, a finger of delicious apprehension went up my spine. And, it was not totally unexpected. I knew there was something wrong here at Crabapple Yarns. I mean, who hires someone and then doesn't want them on site during store hours? That, in itself, is just plain weird, and if it had happened in any other setting with any other person, I would probably be running down the road for my life. But something held me here. Carolyn's secretive ways did not alarm me – much that is. What her secret could be, I had absolutely no idea. I didn't, however, for one minute believe that it was anything that would cause me personal harm. She didn't strike me as the type of person who would knowingly put me in danger.

One of these days, I hope my dormant sense of reality kicks in.

And on top of that, this place was just a little too perfect. Do you know what I mean? If I weren't having so much fun, I would be kicking myself for getting involved here. Just you wait, I told myself gloomily, Carolyn will turn out to be a blood thirsty cannibal or a psychotic murderer who skewers her victims with knitting needles or... I know, I know. You're probably thinking

46

that I should stop reading so many books. But, as you may (or may not) know, the truth is always stranger than fiction. What did scare me a little was that I could dream up some pretty strange fiction.

In spite of the crazy thoughts flying through my head, I waited for her to continue with an expression that I hoped was pleasantly expectant and confidence-inspiring. In classic gothic style, whatever she was about to say died on her lips as her eyes became saucers. I followed the direction of her gaze to the door, which as I said before, we knew was locked, just in time to see it burst open. Sunshine flooded the doorway, and I had to shield my eyes from the sudden glare. On the threshold stood a creature the likes of which I had never seen before.

A scream died in my throat, and I clutched at the edge of the table wildly. Something long, thick and matted stuck out in quivering tentacles from the general direction of the head. Each tentacle was a different color that ended in fur, and they whipped wildly about the room. Light flashed from its eyes, and its entire body was brown and furry. Brown-colored liquid sloshed to the floor at my feet, and I jumped to avoid being hit by its drippings.

It was hard to tell – everything happened in such a rush. But the creature also appeared to have more than two legs. It dragged its third leg along the ground behind it; its gait rocky and uneven.

My eyes were burning and my head was swimming. It took several long seconds for me to realize that I was holding my breath. Carefully, very carefully, I sucked in a breath of air and froze again as the creature reached out a fur-covered arm towards me. I shrank back, letting out – I'm afraid – a very undignified squeak. It did not, however, shoot lasers or ooze more brown goo. The arm continued its orbit to the tentacles that still flung madly about its head and gave a solid tug. The creature stepped away from the glare of the sun in the doorway and vanished.

With another gasping breath, my vision cleared.

Oh...

Feeling extremely foolish and more than a little flustered, I bent over my knitting needles again, as if I were in the middle of something extremely complicated and couldn't stop. I tried to look as normal as I could. Which...probably wasn't too normal.

"Whew," the lady wearing a long fur coat, glasses and carrying a cup of (now spilled) coffee said. "It's a little chilly outside today." The crazy apparatus that she apparently wore as a hat was calmly tucked into the bag she carried over her shoulder, and she finished pulling a floor lamp through the door.

Maybe it really was time for me to stop reading so many books.

"Louise," Carolyn said, her hands planted firmly on the counter, "what on earth has gotten into you? What are you doing here?"

Louise? Wasn't that the name of the other lady who worked here? And was it just my imagination or did Carolyn sound upset? Is it possible that she had been startled by the sudden apparition in the doorway as much as I? Or was it possible that this person was the reason for me not being able to be at the store all week? Setting my needles aside once again, I examined the strange person with renewed interest.

She had enormously large glasses that completely overshadowed her thin, narrow face. Her eyes were small and hawk-like. As she peeled off her coat, I could see a beautiful sweater, which for some reason, I automatically assumed that she had knitted. See how much I was already changing? For the first time in my life I contemplated the idea of knitting something to wear. In public. The sweater looked like little crooked squares that had been woven together in all the shades of blue. Unfortunately, it did nothing for her plaid pants. Or the combat boots. Her hair was about four inches long. It fell about an inch above her ears and she wore it straight and plain. Her bangs ended just before her glasses began. While Carolyn was comfortably plump, this lady looked like a twig wearing clothes. She had a thin and pointy nose. She looked like someone who knew a lot about a lot of things and wouldn't mind pointing out your own lack of knowledge.

She was currently staring at me. I stared back.

Chapter 8

In Which We Learn That Louise Is No Fun At All

"Louise," Carolyn repeated, "What on earth are you doing here? You scared us about half to death."

Louise raised a bony thin arm to point at me and demanded, "Who is that?" She looked like a shriveled forest sprite or an Omen of Impending Doom standing there with her arm outstretched and her face grim. Her voice was as dry and raspy as I expected it to be.

I found that I had to close my mouth and swallow before I could speak. "I'm Molly," I said. I gave myself a mental smack in the head. Brilliant. As if that explained it all.

What can I say? I've never been good around intimidating people. Without thinking, I straightened my blouse and sat up a little taller. The way that she was staring at me made me wonder if my hair was sticking up. I bravely resisted the urge to check.

Carolyn came from around the counter to take the lamp from Louise. "Oh for goodness sakes, Louise," she snapped irritably, "this is Molly, our new employee." I was a little bit surprised. I had never heard Carolyn speak like that. Of course, I had never seen a creature from outer space turn into a little twig woman either.

She was still staring at me. I felt like squirming some more. "Our new employee." she repeated slowly in her dry, raspy voice. She stood still – as if she were waiting for the punch line.

The lamp must have been heavy, because Carolyn was having trouble dragging it across the floor, too. "Here Carolyn," I said, "let me do it. Where do you want it?"

She gave me a small smile of gratitude and gestured to the sofa. "Over there," she said to me, and turning back to Louise, she said, "Yes, Louise, our new employee. Her name is Molly Stevenson. She's a fairly new knitter, but an excellent

51

learner, and I know she's going to be a valuable asset to our store. She's also going to be living upstairs."

I could feel her eyes boring holes into the back of my head as I dragged the cast iron lamp over to its spot next to the sofa. Getting down on my hands and knees, and trying to keep my skirt decent, I looked under the sofa and found a plug. I stood up and wiped my hands with satisfaction. The lamp looked very pretty there. It had a beautiful lampshade, the perfect color of golden apples. I dusted the lampshade with the corner of my sleeve. Still not ready to return, I proceeded to straighten the lampshade. The sofa pillows needed a little fluffing, too. So, I fluffed those and then wiped my hands together. *Chicken.* Gathering my courage, I turned to meet Louise's stare.

But she was no longer staring at me. She was staring at Carolyn. Like Carolyn had lost her marbles. Like someone had invited the bull into the china shop for tea. Like she was letting Attila the Hun play with small children. I felt a brief sting of resentment. I wasn't that bad.

They continued their stare-down. Louise broke down first. "You're hiring someone now?" she asked in a tight voice. "Are you sure she—" her voice trailed off. For about the hundredth time I wondered what I had gotten myself into here. I mean, come on, this was a yarn store, not the CIA. Did people commit international espionage with yarn? Who knows? Perhaps they did. Perhaps I should check into it.

Carolyn was already bustling back towards the counter. "I think I know what I'm doing Louise," she said in a voice that I would never argue with. Evidently Louise wouldn't either. She shot me another glare before she decided to completely ignore me. I would soon learn that ignoring someone was her chosen method of self-defense.

In a gesture that must be a habit, she smoothed the hair over her left ear and her demeanor changed instantly. It was like I wasn't even in the room and she had forgotten that I existed. "Mr. Morrie called yesterday right before we closed and said that the lamp was fixed," she said. "I thought I'd stop by this morning and see if you needed any help, and on my way past the hardware store, Mr. Morrie handed me the lamp. He said the cord was so frayed, that it was a miracle that only the lamp caught fire and not the whole store and that he thought it looked—"

Whoa.

Carolyn eyed Louise, who promptly stopped talking. "I guess we can be thankful that it was only the lamp," she said, "and that Mr. Morrie was able to fix it so nicely."

Louise and Carolyn exchanged silent significant looks that went on for almost a minute. Who knows – maybe they were communicating by telepathy.

Carolyn broke the silence first. "Thanks for coming by Louise," she said firmly, "but I think that Molly and I can handle everything here today. You're gone for the weekend, right? Well, we'll see you on Wednesday—" She kept up a steady chatter and before I think even Louise knew what was happening, Louise had her coat on, her "hat" on and she soon found herself gently but firmly back out on the street.

I don't think I was imagining things when I heard Carolyn sigh as she re-locked the front door. I was still rooted in place and did the only thing I was capable of. I closed my mouth.

After Louise had left, Carolyn walked slowly back to the counter, refusing to meet my eye. Feeling awkward and quite unsure why, I sat back down by the table and resumed my knitting. She said nothing and busied herself with work behind the counter. She clearly did not want to talk about Louise. Or the lamp.

Trying to look normal, I shot small looks at Carolyn from time to time over my knitting. It looked like she was cleaning. Weird. Very weird. For some reason, it also made me a little angry. An explanation of some kind would be nice. And, yet, I said nothing. Agatha Christie would be so disappointed in me right now. My needles clicking were the only sound I dared to make. Time passed slowly, and as the hands approached my normal leaving time, I rose to my feet and began gathering my supplies in silence.

As I crammed my needles into their bag, I kept my head down, "So—" I had to clear my throat because it was so dry, "tomorrow then?"

Carolyn had to clear her throat as well as she came around the counter to meet me, "Molly," she began. Something in her expression forced me to meet her eyes. They were as kind as ever, but there was something else in her expression – something I couldn't quite define. "Molly," she said again, "I apologize for this morning. I hadn't expected Louise to stop by."

She unexpectedly ran a hand through her hair, and looked away. The small action moved me to compassion. In all the time that I had known Carolyn (which, of course, was a really, really long time), I had never seen her unsure of herself. She was upset... and a little... scared? There had to be more to Carolyn's current emotional state than Louise's surprise visit. Other than ignore me and imply that I was a disaster waiting to happen, Louise really hadn't done anything to make Carolyn so upset. But, she was clearly agitated, and I felt foolish for taking something personally, which I now realized had actually nothing to do with me. Perhaps it had to do with the lamp? Was Louise really going to imply that the cord had been frayed on purpose? Did someone want Crababble Yarns to burn to the ground? That was not an entirely pleasant thought. I decided not to think about it.

Impulsively, I squeezed her arm. "You don't have to explain, Carolyn," I said, "It's alright."

I finally allowed myself the laugh that had been building since I saw Louise take off her "hat." "Do you know that I thought Louise was an alien creature or something when the door burst open like that."

Carolyn, seemed relieved to drop the subject. "It really is quite a hat," she said, and she was smiling now, too. The warmth was back in her eyes, and I was glad.

My knees felt weak as I left Crabapple Yarns. I wasn't used to living on such an emotional roller coaster. Deciding that a cinnamon roll could have amazing therapeutic value, I decided to stop by the bakery. My feet must have felt the craving before my head because I realized with a start that I was standing right in front of the door. I hoped that I hadn't been standing there for a long time. My mouth was already watering. There was something quite beautiful about these cinnamon rolls. Oozing succulent frosting, they were the most amazing combination of sweet, crunchy, chewy and just the littlest bit of salty. I attempted to walk nonchalantly to the counter, while the man behind it grinned at me. He wasn't fooled.

"Cinnamon roll?" he asked.

I tried to pretend that I was contemplating the other delectable options, but I wasn't fooling anyone. He was already reaching for a bag to put the roll in, and as he reached his hand in to grab the closest on the tray, he happened to glance up at me. Something in my face stopped his hand. Rolling his eyes, he said, "Alright, which one?"

I bit back a smile. It was only our third day, but already we were developing our own little routine. Trying to look casual, I pointed to the juiciest cinnamon roll in the middle of the tray, "That one please."

With a heavy sigh, he rested his arms on top of the counter and looked at me seriously. "The one in the middle?" he asked with a long-suffering look.

"If it's too much trouble—" I risked a small smile.

He rolled his eyes again and dug out the cinnamon roll. I paid him, and as I was leaving, I turned back to wave goodbye. He was looking down at the cinnamon roll tray, and he said (to himself, of course), "Now I'm going to have to re-arrange the whole tray."

I grinned to myself. There was nothing worse than an unbalanced tray.

THE KNITTING FAIRY

Chapter 9
So Far, So Good

Saturday.

So far, so good.

I was actually fairly pleased with myself. I had been working for almost an hour now, and no one had asked me anything too hard or intimidating. I had mastered the art of the cash register program and was actually quite good at stacking purchases into the cute little plastic bags. I sent the last customer out the door happily clutching her yarn to her chest.

I'm a little embarrassed to tell you this, but when Carolyn turned the open sign on the door, I was waiting for the parade of grannies. Didn't grannies knit? Wouldn't you say that grannies had the market on the knitting world? Cute little old ladies like Carolyn with sweaters that smelled faintly of mothballs and sturdy support shoes that clomped across the floor? Well, my friends, you are wrong, because, to my astonishment, we had not had a single granny as of yet. We had a couple of older ladies, but they would hardly qualify for "granny" status yet. We had a young woman and a 12-year-old girl, if you can believe that! Where were all the grannies? And, how did all of these other people know about knitting? Clearly I had led a sheltered life at the library.

My stomach growled, and Carolyn patted my arm as she went past. "Time for a cinnamon roll?" she asked.

She straightened the novelty yarn display with the confidence of one who has done this many, many times before.

"How did you know about that?" I demanded.

Her Mother Goose face grinned impishly at me. "Once you've worked here awhile, you'll know," she said. "Why don't you run out and get me one too." She slipped some money into my hand, and I pushed it back at her with a smile.

"My treat," I said, practically running towards the door.

I once again left the bakery with a smile in my heart and with the baker once again bemoaning his maladjusted tray. All in a day's work. You would think that he would, by now, know which cinnamon roll I would want and put it on the outside. I shrugged, maybe he liked re-arranging his trays.

I walked quickly back to the yarn store. It was quite nippy today; the balmy spring weather was momentarily in hiding. The forecast was even calling for snow – if you could believe anything the weatherman said. I certainly didn't.

As I approached Crabapple Yarns, my feet didn't make it to the door. Clutching my bakery bag tightly, I decided to just take a quick peek through the window. It was one of my secret pleasures. I loved looking in through the front window. It was so comforting. So homey. If you stood in just the right spot, you had the most tantalizing and scrumptious view of the shelves and the seating area. It was like looking at a picture postcard. I wished that Carolyn's store was out on Main Street so that more people would pass it. Surely, surely, everyone would want to come into a store as lovely and warm as this one.

You may find it hard to believe, but words failed me as I gazed through the window. Something tugged at my heart. It happens every time. It's a hard feeling to describe. Actually, in some ways it is a little bit bittersweet. The coziness was enchanting, but I also felt a pang of something I couldn't quite identify. Something told me it might be a little bit of something suspiciously like longing. What I could be longing for, I had no idea. I was very happy.

I shivered and realized that I had been standing in front of the window for quite some time. I hoped Carolyn hadn't seen me. I hoped the rolls weren't cold. I peeked closer through the window trying to see where she was. She was standing by the counter with the phone held to her ear. Her normally sweet face was scrunched into a terrible scowl, and though I could not hear what she was saying, I felt a shiver of something go down my spine. Swallowing hard, I backed away from the window, took a deep breath, and went back through the front door.

She was just walking toward the counter as I entered. The phone was not in her hand now. I cleared my throat and she turned to greet me with her usual warm smile. "Did you bring me one too?" she asked pleasantly.

I stared at her blankly. She tilted her head quizzically, "A cinnamon roll," she said patiently. "Didn't you go to the bakery to get us one?"

"Oh, oh, yes, a cinnamon roll," I stammered, "I went...I have, yes, that's right, I did go to the bakery—" I held the white paper bag out in front of me, as if it were proof. She took it, giving me a strange look. I cleared my throat and tried for some coherency. "I thought you were on the phone." Well, that was subtle.

Her pleasant smile didn't falter, but she creased her brow with a small frown. "The phone?" she said, "No, I wasn't on the phone."

I couldn't believe my ears. She was actually lying to me. I didn't think she was capable of something like that. I gave her a chance to come clean. "You weren't on the phone just now?" I asked again. What was I doing? Interrogating Mother Goose? Didn't she have a right to her own private personal phone calls? Who made me the phone police?

Still, her smile remained intact and the furrow left her brow, "Oh yes," she resolved, "just now I did answer the phone, but it was only an advertisement." She disappeared through the back into the small kitchen and returned with two plates and two forks. She was soon sitting on the front sofa, her feet tucked up under her and a serene smile on her face. "I wonder what their secret ingredient is. There's just something about their cinnamon rolls, isn't there?"

Alright, fine. If she was going to be that way, there wasn't much I could do about it, was there? I mean, you tell me – what was I supposed to do? What would you do if you were me? I was almost ninety percent certain she wasn't telling me the truth. But, then again, I couldn't just call her a liar now, could I? Well, I could. But, then I just might get my little rear end fired again. I could just see it now... "conduct unbecoming a knitter—"

Perhaps I was completely wrong. Perhaps it was an advertisement. Perhaps Carolyn has a strong aversion to salesman. While it was true that I didn't know Carolyn very well - or for very long, I did know one thing: Carolyn was essentially a kind person. And kind people don't lie without a reason. What did you just say? Kind people shouldn't lie at all? Well, you're right – they shouldn't. But, if they do, then they probably have a good reason. I felt the faint stirrings of a new challenge. I would just have to pay closer attention and figure out this little mystery for myself. Without getting fired. Or skewered by knitting needles. And without a criminal record.

Chapter 10
Knitters Are Crazy

My bones felt like they were sticking out of the bottom of my feet. Carolyn locked the front door and I collapsed onto the tapestry sofa with a great sigh. "How many hours were in this day?" I asked with a groan. She grinned. Although she did not throw herself on the chair, she settled in with a great deal of satisfaction. To my great amusement, she slipped off her shoes and put her feet up on the coffee table. She wiggled her toes at me.

"I love this store," she said with a happy sigh, "but I love the end of the day, too."

A reply at this point would have been impossible, so I settled for a grunt of agreement. We passed several minutes in comfortable silence before I had the energy to stir. "You do this every day?" How was it possible that all of this had been going on almost literally underneath my nose and I knew absolutely nothing about it?

"Well, Saturdays are one of our busiest days," she said. "And today was unusually busy."

"I never would have believed that there were so many people who actually buy yarn." I could have slapped myself, but Carolyn was not offended. She let out a merry peal of laughter, and her delightful face once again was covered in little wrinkles. I couldn't help but smile back at her.

I rolled over to my side and looked up at Carolyn. "Are there any books that you would suggest I read to understand knitters?" I asked.

"What on earth do you mean?"

"Well," I was picking my words as carefully as I could, "it seems to me that knitters are very particular about what types of yarn they use, what colors they use, and what the colors mean and what the patterns mean and why they knit certain things and why—"

"Okay, okay," she held up one hand. She looked like she was trying not to laugh. She sat up so that her hands were resting on her knees and then put both hands in front of her mouth. Did she really think that I couldn't see her smile? "You certainly learned a lot today, didn't you?" She waited for me to nod. Her expression softened, and the amusement slowly died away, "Molly," she said, "this is a whole new world for you. I completely understand. I still don't know everything there is to know about knitting and I've been knitting for longer than you've been alive. I certainly don't expect you to learn everything in a couple of days." She reached across the coffee table to pat my hand, "Don't worry about it so much. The best way to learn is through experience. You'll catch on. I believe in you. And I'm here to help."

She had a way of making me feel like crying when she said things like that. She would have made a great politician.

"I'm glad you were here for that lady this afternoon in the pink sweater." Carolyn let out a very unladylike snort and put her feet back up on the coffee table. "I seriously considered calling the mental institution to see if they were missing someone."

Seriously. You should have been here because, this afternoon, a lady wearing a bright pink sweater had floated in. She had a flower stuck behind her ear. Her perfume wafted in tangible waves around her. I coughed discreetly. It was burning my eyes. "Did you see the color of the sky this morning?" she asked in a perfect sing-song voice. After we discussed the fact that yes, indeed, I had seen the sky this morning, she had stated in her beautifully modulated voice, that she was so inspired by the sky that she would like to knit a scarf in that exact shade of blue.

Yeah. It was right about then that I knew I was in big trouble. Carolyn was absolutely no help. She was slacking off, helping three other customers at the same time. I knew it wasn't fair, but I sent her a plea for help through face language across the store. I contorted my face as much as I could, but she did not respond.

And so I was forced to cross the floor and help the pink sweater lady pick out yarn the color of the morning sky. When I pulled out the first skein of yarn, she dropped her flighty attitude for two whole seconds. She screwed her face up in disgust, "I said the sky this morning, not that ugly shade." She all but snarled it at me. Yikes. Another lesson learned. Knitters were dangerous. Thankfully, Carolyn had ditched her other three customers to come and bail me out. The blond in the pink sweater finally left Crabapple Yarns happily clutching her skein of beautiful sky-blue yarn. Yes, my friends, it was then and there that I knew knitters were a strange bunch.

Carolyn yawned and stretched. "Oh my goodness," she said suddenly, "I forgot to get the mail." She pulled herself to her feet and headed towards the front door. The phone rang as she had her hand on the handle.

"I'll get it," I said, swinging myself to my feet reluctantly. My foot had fallen asleep, and as I made a grab for the phone, I managed to bump the small table it was perched on. The phone tumbled to the floor, ringing incessantly. Wretched thing. I made another grab for it only to slip on the floor rug. Tingles were going up and down my leg. Choking back a laugh, I answered the phone with a somewhat breathless, "Hello?"

"Took you long enough to answer the phone," a harsh voice said. Caught unawares, I could not find a reply quick enough. "I suppose you think you're pretty smart. Do you think you're safe now?" There was a breathless sound that could have been laughter. "Who's the new girl?"

"Who is this?" I demanded.

There was a sudden intake of breath and the phone went dead in my hand.

I stared at the phone in bewilderment before pushing the disconnect button. I set it carefully down on the table, staring at it. Carolyn came back through the door, her eyes on the mail in her hand. "Who was it?" she asked, flipping through envelopes.

I cleared my throat, "I don't know."

Something in my voice must have alerted her that all was not well, and her eyes flew to my face. "Why Molly," she said, "what on earth happened?"

I looked down at the phone on the table. It looked so innocent. "Do you have prank calls here very often?" I asked.

An expression flickered so fast over her features that I was not sure if I had even imagined it before she smiled carelessly, "Oh, is that all." she said. "Don't let it upset you. Probably just kids having fun."

"That wasn't fun for me."

She patted me on the arm. "I'm sorry, honey," she said, "but I wouldn't let it worry you. Why don't you go on home, and I'll see you on Monday." She smiled warmly at me. "I was really proud of you today. You're a natural."

I went home, wondering, not for the first time, what on earth I had gotten myself into.

Chapter 11
This Store Would Be More Fun Without Customers

I was at the store quite early on Monday. Carolyn always arrived early. She said she liked to commune with her yarns. Yep. That's what she said. Commune with her yarns. For me, it wasn't communing with the yarns that drew me there so many hours before the store opened. It wasn't the atmosphere either – although, I have to admit, I loved the soft feeling of warmth that surrounded my heart as I sat by the large oak table, happily working on my stitch techniques. It wasn't the glow that surrounded Carolyn as she leaned over the table to check my work either nor was it the quiet feeling of community as we worked together to straighten the shelves. It wasn't even laughing so hard we almost fell off our chairs after I had knitted two whole rows with my tail. (If you're not a knitter, you won't know what that means. Yes, I now speak "knitter" too.).

No, my friends, I felt the need to be there early so that I could absorb as much of knitting as I possibly could before the store opened. I almost felt feverish with the desire to improve my knitting skills. I was petrified of being found out as a brand new knitter. Carolyn had never mentioned that she didn't want everyone to know that I was a new knitter, and for some strange reason, I never asked for an explanation either, but something told me that I should know as much as I could and quickly.

Carolyn surprised me on Monday. Before we opened the store, she did something that I totally did not expect. "Molly," she said, "I realize that I have never asked you what your beliefs are concerning religion, but I always like to start my days here with prayer. Do you mind?"

"Uhhh...no," I had replied uncertainly, "I believe in prayer—"

She had graced me with a beautiful smile and grabbed my hand. "Good," she said. "Let's pray."

Whoa. Whoa. Whoa. Help. Heart palpitations. Pounding. Wait a minute. Hold everything. Did she expect me to pray out loud with her? Right here? Right now? I wasn't sure I was comfortable with that. I had no idea what I should say. Or maybe I shouldn't say anything. She didn't give me time to worry about it.

"Dear Lord," she said, "Thank You so much for another beautiful day. We love the sunshine, and we love You. Please bless us as we go about our day and keep us all safe in Your Hands. Amen." She gave my hand a brief squeeze before she went to go turn on the cash register.

I just stared at her waiting for my reeling mind and galloping heart to catch up. Whoa.

The store was much quieter today, and I had time to fully appreciate the beauty of the yarns that filled the store. Carolyn and I circled the store together, as she explained, once again, the different types of fiber. She was such a patient woman. I was still feeling very unsure of myself. I was literally petrified of the day when someone would ask me a question on what type of yarn they should buy. What if the lady in the pink sweater came back and wanted to knit the sunset? I decided to add on to Carolyn's prayer. *Please God*, I prayed, *Don't let it be today.*

So far, I had not seen any evidence of more prank phone calls, and for that I was glad. I was beginning to seriously wonder, however, what exactly Carolyn was hiding. There were times when I could plainly see that something was troubling her. I had nothing concrete to go by, but there were times when the spark would dim in her eyes and she would bite her lip anxiously. My only problem was that I had absolutely no idea how to go about discovering what the trouble was. If I happened to ask about the reason for her sudden quietness, she would only smile brightly and proceed to chatter about something else. My veiled inquires fell on deaf ears, and I was left wondering how (or even if) I should proceed.

Of course, I consoled myself; it was only my second official day working at Crabapple Yarns. I really couldn't expect to know the deep dark secrets of the store until I had been working there for at least a week.

There was one thing that I was beginning to get excited about. I had spoken to my landlord, and in two months, I would be moving out of my small apartment to the top floor of Carolyn's store. We had agreed that beginning next week, we would start cleaning up there.

So far, I had not seen Louise again, but I knew that she would be back on Wednesday. Carolyn informed me that she worked only part-time and during the busiest hours. We would be working together several days a week. I could hardly wait. I'm sure that Louise was counting the days as well.

Late Monday afternoon, the doorbell chimed merrily and two women came through the door, chatting happily. Or, should I say that one woman was chatting happily, the other woman was looking like she felt a little intimidated and in way over her head. I knew the feeling. My heart lurched in instant empathy with her.

"And see, Lacey," the chatty one said, "this is the wool that I was telling you about. It stripes all by itself."

Lacey was clearly not a knitter. After only two days (alright one and a half) of working at the store, I was very good at knowing what knitters did. They grabbed all the yarn in sight – cuddling the yarn, smelling the yarn, holding the yarn up to their faces, rubbing the yarn, talking to the yarn. Basically, they couldn't keep their hands off of it. They did not stand back from the shelves like it might jump out to bite them. They did not stare at their knitting friends like they had just sprouted antennae.

"Come on Lacey," the lady urged, "you have to at least feel it."

Lacey obediently stuck one finger out to poke the skein of yarn. She looked like she was testing fruit at the supermarket. And, judging by the look on her face, she'd probably have more fun with the fruit. I bit back a smile. From across the store, I could see Carolyn, who was working with a customer to pick out yarn for a baby blanket, was also amused.

Amusement aside, my heart began pounding. This could be it. This could be the big one. What if these ladies had a question before Carolyn was done with the other customer? I might have to handle these ladies all by myself. What if the chatty one turned nasty like the lady with the pink sweater? Gulp.

Besides that, I hadn't had time to go to the bakery this morning, and my stomach was loudly protesting the absence of its favorite breakfast food. People shouldn't have to go through stressful situations on an empty stomach. It should be against the law.

Oh dear, as soon as I helped this customer by the counter check out, I would have to make a move. Soon. Very soon. What in the world was taking Carolyn so long with that baby blanket lady? I'm sure the baby didn't care what yarn its blanket was made out of. For goodness sakes, I thought desperately, just grab the yellow stuff on the first shelf and be done with it.

Lacey looked like she was ready to flee. And believe me, I know that look when I see it. "Helen," she said dubiously, "I'm not sure if—"

But she did not get a chance to finish. Helen obviously sensed her poor friend's distress. She was a good friend. So what did she do for her scared little friend? Sit down on the sofa and calm her down? Uh, no. Suggest they have a cup of coffee until Lacey's heart stopped beating erratically? Nope. Helen was already dragging Lacey across the floor, giving her a crash course on knitting and fibers and needles and just about everything else. Every time Lacey started edging towards the door, Helen would grab another skein and thrust it at her, describing its fiber content, its pros and cons and its various uses. I have to give Lacey credit. She obediently poked her finger into each skein and tried her best to look impressed. After a while, I felt sorry for the skeins.

After the customer by the counter had paid for her purchase and was safely out the door, I knew that I could put it off no longer. Rats. I left behind the relative safety of the counter to go and greet Helen and Lacey.

"What do you think of this one?" Helen was asking Lacey. "Wouldn't this make a fabulous scarf?"

"I don't know," Lacey replied skeptically, "It looks like a wild animal."

She was right, it did. It was orange and red and black and white with pieces of checked ribbon and bits of fluff sticking out of it at random intervals. "Good afternoon ladies," I said smoothly. "Please let me know if there's anything I can help you with." I smiled politely at both of them, congratulated myself on my professionalism and began the wonderful process of retreating.

"Uhhh...well, actually," Lacey said.

Uh-oh.

I couldn't believe my ears. They were actually going to take me up on my offer. The nerve. What did they think this was? A knitting store or something? Taking a deep breath, I turned back around to face them and gave them my most expectant smile.

"Helen is going to teach me to knit. I'm afraid I'm a bit overwhelmed. Do you have any suggestions for a beginning project?"

I wondered what would happen if I just walked out of the door. Right now. Just walked out of the door.

To my complete and utter surprise, I heard someone answering her in a fairly confident voice. "Well, when I first learned how to knit, I started with a scarf." Wow. I think it was me. It was a good answer too. A very good answer. Do you see any reason that she had to know that it was just last week that I knitted my first scarf? Nope, me neither.

Helen nodded emphatically and shook the skein of wild animal in the air, "That's just what I was telling her," she said, "and don't you just love this yarn?"

Lacey and I both stared at it skeptically. Once again, I found myself answering them. And once again, to my surprise, I sounded like I knew what I was talking about. "It is a lovely yarn," I agreed, "but perhaps for a beginner, something a little less...errr...fuzzy would be easier." Where in the world were these wise words coming from?

Before I knew it, we were back at the self-striping wool yarn, and Lacey was picking out a color that would go with her favorite coat. I was feeling rather proud of myself, and as I met Carolyn's eyes across the room, I could tell that she was also proud of me. I was glad that I hadn't tried the escape through the door routine – although I mentally filed it away. You never know when something like that could come in handy.

The door tinkled again, and (gasp!) a man entered. He peered through the store, and when he spied us standing by the shelf along the back wall, his face split into a wide grin, as he crossed the room in a few long strides. I soon discovered that he was Helen's husband and a charming man. After greeting his wife with a hearty kiss, he patiently took a seat by the fireplace and paged through a hunting magazine. Carolyn very cleverly, subscribed to several men's magazines to appease waiting husbands, sons, brothers, etc. – the ones that were brave enough to come in, that is. It only confirmed my opinion that she was one of the smartest women I had ever met. Mother Goose was definitely a student of human nature.

The wool that Lacey choose came wound in hanks, and I soon had a crash course in how to use the skein winder – excuse me, the swift. Yes, it was very easy to use. Yes, it made skeins a lot easier to use. However, I made the mistake of admitting it was my first time to use this particular device and soon I had quite the audience. Lacey was excited to watch the colors of her beautiful yarn swirl round and round, Helen was very excited to offer her expert advice, and Carolyn was very excited to see two of her customers so excited. Even Helen's husband eventually wandered over to see what all the fuss was about before retiring back to his hunting magazine. It is just amazing how stressful something as simple as winding yarn can be when one has an audience. Another lesson learned in the yarn store.

After about fifteen hundred hours, Lacey and Helen and Helen's husband were on their way out the door, but not before both Lacey and Helen thanked me for all of my help. I smiled to myself. Boy, did I have those two fooled. Ha! Maybe I could make it in this business after all.

Just before we were going to close, the door opened again to admit a tall, thin woman. I recognized her as Carolyn's niece from the library. She did not see me, as I was sitting on the floor by the sock yarn. Some of the customers had gotten a little crazy sorting through it, and I was trying to restore a little bit of order. I was having a rather difficult time of it as there were hardly two skeins the same color. This made things a bit challenging. It seemed that knitters were just crazy about knitting socks. I know... I think it's weird too. And, not only that, but they are very picky about what color sock yarn they buy. Apparently, there *is* a difference between a little red, a little blue, and some yellow versus a little red, some blue, and a little yellow. Good grief.

"Aunt Carolyn," she called, her voice calm and well-modulated, "I was just in the neighborhood, and I thought I would stop by and see if you wanted to go out for dinner."

Carolyn was behind the counter, trying to restore order to the mounds of shopping bags. I was soon learning that this is what one did after a long day in the yarn store – restore order. "Oh, I don't know, dear," she answered, "I thought I would maybe stay a little later tonight and start moving things out of the apartment upstairs."

"Why on earth would you want to do that?" I think she was a little bit upset that her dinner invitation wasn't being snapped up. Her calm demeanor slipped a notch, and she paced the floor. Despite her agitation, she was immaculately dressed, not a hair out of place, and even from my position on the floor, I could see that there wasn't a wrinkle in her business-like suit. She abruptly ceased pacing, but one well-manicured hand rested on her hips and she drummed her fingers against her skirt.

Carolyn paused in her efforts to push the hair back from her face. "Why because Molly is moving in upstairs," she said calmly.

Her jaw dropped in a most unbecoming manner as she gaped at Carolyn. "Who's Molly?"

I decided that it might just be a good time to make my presence known. I stood up somewhat reluctantly to meet this paragon of walking perfection. As I stood, I knocked against the shelf of sock yarn that I had been trying to straighten. As luck would have it, a rebellious skein of sock yarn jumped back off the shelf. I wanted to look graceful as I picked it up – I can't tell you how much I really wanted to. But, I tried too hard and ended up stumbling, knocking the shelf a bit harder. I was wearing blue pants with a long pleated white shirt. This morning, both the pants and the shirt had been nice and crisp. Now, they were a wrinkled mess. My hair had fallen out of its barrettes, and I felt like a total slob. From the curl of her lip, I could tell that Carolyn's niece thought that I looked like one too. I shrugged my shoulders mentally and held out my hand to her.

"I'm Molly," I said, smiling my friendliest smile at her. "Your aunt hired me last week."

I don't think my friendly smile had any effect on her at all. She closed her mouth with a little snap and took my hand. Her handshake was limp and cold. It was like holding a dead fish. I wondered if the rest of Carolyn's family was more like Carolyn or her niece. It was hard to imagine a whole family of dead fish.

"So nice to meet you," she murmured. She dropped my hand as soon as it was polite to do so. She didn't exactly wipe her palm against her skirt, but I had the feeling that she would as soon as she was out of sight. No, on second thought, she would probably pull a cute little bottle of antibacterial soap out of her perfect little pocketbook to disinfect her perfectly manicured hands. Oops. That sounded a bit snide, didn't it? Sorry.

"Since when are you hiring?" she demanded. "You never mentioned to me that you were going to hire someone new. Did you advertise?"

"I didn't think I needed to let you know, dear," Carolyn said in a very, very polite voice. "You've never shown much interest in the inner workings of my store before."

That shut her up. I grinned at Carolyn from behind her niece's back. I could have sworn that one eyelid dropped just ever so slightly in a wink back at me.

Her niece turned so that she could see the both of us at once. She looked me up and down appraisingly before plastering a smile across her face, and for a moment she reminded me of a store mannequin. "Well, I'll stop by and see you again sometime," she said. "We'll do dinner then."

And with that, she was gone. I let out the breath I hadn't realized that I was holding. Silence filled the room. The only thing that remained of our late visitor was the lingering smell of her perfume. I wiggled my nose trying to escape from it. "She certainly is...elegant," I offered tentatively.

Carolyn grinned. "Yes, she is quite elegant, isn't she? She works very hard at being elegant." Carolyn was wearing a wonderfully cabled Aran vest, and she tugged unnecessarily with the hem. "Somehow I always feel a bit of a mess when she's around," she admitted.

I felt it might be in bad form to agree with her, but I smiled anyway. "What's her name?"

"Irene Donley," she said, "my sister's daughter." And that was all she said.

I decided to change the subject. "Did you really want to get started on the apartment tonight?" I asked. She looked really tired, and if Mother Goose didn't want to take care of herself, I would have to do it for her. "We could just take the night off and you could show me how to do a cable."

I dangled the bait temptingly and without compunction. I knew that she was too tired to move anything, and I also knew that she couldn't resist sharing her knitting knowledge either. Later, I would have to take some time to consider this seemingly inherent character flaw of knitters – the compulsive need to turn everyone else into knitters too. I was glad that I didn't seem to possess such a flaw. Perhaps it was something that one acquired. If so, I would be certain to take preventative measures to guard against it.

She cocked her head to one side and regarded me down her long nose with narrowed eyes. I stared back at her with my most innocent expression until she finally cracked a smile. "Why, Molly," she said, her periwinkle eyes twinkling, "I do believe that you're trying to tempt me into a night off."

"Would I do that?" I quizzed.

"Well," she paused to consider, "I do believe you would. And you just did." And with that, she began going around the room turning off lights. The store was exceptionally well-lit, because, as Carolyn explained, you must have good lighting in order to tell the difference between mustard yellow and golden yellow. Any knitter would tell you that. As a result, there were lamps, twinkle lights and little tea lights scattered throughout the store, all in addition to the overhead lights, of course. Also as a result, you can imagine that it took quite a while to turn them all off.

"Molly," she said, turning off a light over the sock yarn, "you know, you haven't even seen the apartment upstairs. Wouldn't you like to at least take a look at it tonight?" The idea was tempting. "And just wait until you see the window seat." That finished it. I wasn't the only person who was good at talking people into things.

As I helped her turn off lights, I couldn't help but think about how well laid out the store was. Wooden cubbies brimming with yarn lined the walls. To the untrained eye, it may look as though the yarn was arranged to make the store look as charming as possible, but to an experienced knitter, such as myself, you could see that actually a lot of thought had gone into making it look thoughtless. All of the wool was towards the back of the store in the cubbies, the baby yarn had its own section, the washable wools their own section, the sock yarn their own section and so on. In the back wall there was a door that led to the back room which was actually quite a large room in itself. It contained a storage room and the very important bathroom. There was also a little kitchenette where Carolyn made coffee each day and the occasional sandwich. This was where you could find the door that led to the staircase to the upstairs apartment.

Back in the main store, continuing across the back wall, the needles, circulars, straight needles, double-pointed needles were arranged neatly across the wall space between the door that led to the storage room and the corner. Shelving of various sizes and configurations filled a great portion of the store. As I said before, lamps and lights were everywhere. On the counter, there was a beautiful Tiffany lamp that literally glowed with beauty. I was terrified of the day that I would knock it off the counter. I held my breath each time I went past. The hardwood floors gleamed in the light, and the rugs added a touch of color and practicality.

Across the room, running perpendicular to the front windows was the counter. And in front of the windows, behind the window display was a comfortable seating area with an overstuffed sofa and chairs, a little wood burning fireplace right between the two windows and a little oak table between two of the chairs. None of the materials on the chairs or the sofa matched. There was a tapestry loveseat and a checkered overstuffed chair, but somehow it didn't matter. They coordinated and clashed perfectly. Nestled right smack in the heart of the store was the large round table where I had learned to knit and where Carolyn told me they had many classes.

After we had turned out all of the lights except the overhead ones, Carolyn headed towards the door in the back. Following close on her heels, we quickly passed through the kitchenette and Carolyn pulled out a key to open the door that led upstairs. "There is another door," Carolyn explained, "upstairs on the landing. It goes directly outside. But then you have to go down the stairs outside." She turned the key and flipped a switch. Instantly, the stairwell was flooded in light.

Now, you may be thinking that it's pretty strange that I would have agreed to live in a space that I had never seen, and actually, I would have to agree with you. My heart was pounding a little harder than usual as we ascended the staircase. I don't know why, but for some reason I was expecting shadows and dust and darkness and cobwebs. Maybe even the hint of a ghost. But the stairs were beautiful. They switched direction halfway up, doubling back the opposite way. I'm no expert on wood, but they appeared to be made out of the same type of beautiful, dark, shining wood like the floors in the store. The handrails were carved elegantly. I ran my hand along them lovingly as we went up.

Carolyn was right. At the top of the stairs, there was a landing and a door. I was happy to see the very practical-looking deadbolt in addition to the regular lock. Looking past the landing, the only thing you could see at the moment was another door. Carolyn pulled out another key. "Two doors keep out the drafts, you know, she said. Did I mention that she was a woman after my own heart?

She opened the door to the apartment and went through, turning on lights as she went. The apartment was lovelier than I had ever dared to hope. The ceilings soared to the roof in dramatic slopes. There was not much headroom along the outside walls. It was an open floor plan. From where I stood, I could look across the entire apartment. Across the room, with a view from the front windows was what would be the living room. There were two windows that overlooked the street. The one on the right was graced with something I had always, always wanted. A window seat. In between the windows there was a charming little fireplace. It was in the same location as the one downstairs. I guessed that they must share the same chimney. I didn't know fireplaces could do that. Let's hope they could do it without smoke billowing in through the top one when the bottom one was lit.

The kitchen was immediately to my right and the bedroom was over to my left. The bathroom was in front of the bedroom. There were boxes here and there and it definitely could use a good cleaning, but I knew without a doubt that I would love living here. It already felt like home.

THE KNITTING FAIRY

Chapter 12
In Which Something Odd Happens

On Tuesday, something very odd happened. At the time we all agreed that it was strange, but it was not until much later that any of us recognized the significance of what happened. Are you intrigued yet? Don't worry. I'll get to the point soon. I promise.

You might be interested to learn that in the course of time between Saturday and today, I had finished another scarf and was actually beginning a sweater. Impressed, aren't you? I knew you would be. Carolyn had assured me that it really was not much harder than the scarf I had just knit, and I was more than willing to trust her on it. I loved the color, too – a beautiful gray tweed. She had tried to talk me into socks as my next project, but I saw absolutely no sense in that. Sometimes she really is very strange.

I was currently wasting my time knitting a little piece of practice knitting to make sure I was using the right needle size. I didn't particularly care whether or not I used 7's or 8's, but Carolyn was emphatic. She said that if I wanted the sweater to fit, I must do the practice knitting. The term she used was "gauge." I told her that if the sweater was a little too big, I would just wash it in hot water until it shrunk a bit. This made her shudder, so I finally gave in.

Carolyn was currently knitting a scarf herself among her other projects. It was absolutely gorgeous, the color of raspberry sherbet. She was using a frothy mohair and larger needles to knit the scarf in a simple lace pattern. What's mohair, you ask? Oh, my dear friends, if you don't know what mohair is – run, don't walk, run to your nearest yarn store. You don't know what you're missing.

I discovered very early that Carolyn was one of "those" knitters. If you're not a knitter, then you probably don't know what I mean, but upon careful observation of the slightly strange habits of knitters, I have already learned that are several types of knitters. One type of knitter is the multi-project knitter. You know... a knitter who has more than one project going at a time. The reason for this is unknown.

The first time I chatted with a customer who admitted to having three projects going at once, I had been incredulous. Covering my laughter, I had politely waited for her to leave the store before sharing this piece of juicy news with Carolyn. Expecting her to be as shocked as I was, I was the one who was shocked when she burst into laughter. It was really annoying when she did that. It was even more annoying that she did it so often. I know that I am quite an entertaining person at times, but it was a little disturbing to be almost the sole source of Carolyn's amusement. After all, when one is thrust into a new world called knitting, one cannot possibly be expected to understand, comprehend, and sympathize with all of the idiosyncrasies of the new world within the first 72 hours. When she was done laughing and wiping her eyes and fixing her scarf that had come unwound due to her laughing, she merely patted me on the arm and told me that someday I would understand.

Yeah. Now, while I have never had a reason to doubt Carolyn yet, I saw no reason why I would be crazy enough to have multiple projects going at the same time. Perhaps she had been around yarn fumes a bit too long. Why on earth would you even want to have more than one project going? What would be the point? Seriously? Knitting was knitting. It seemed just a bit ridiculous and over-indulgent.

But, I rolled my eyes, wisely said nothing, and went back to work. It was obvious that Carolyn was one of "those" knitters too, and there was no sense in talking to her. The reason I am sharing this with you now is because Carolyn's scarf was the first "incident." And here comes my point – just like I promised.

Because she has so many projects going at once, Carolyn chooses to leave her projects strewn about the store so that no matter where she lands, if she has a few minutes, she can do a little knitting. I know, pretty obsessive, right? I mean, if someone is so addicted that they can't even be bothered to cross the room to get their knitting, I think you would agree with me that professional help might just be the best option. But are you going to look Mother Goose in the eye and tell her that? I didn't think so.

Anyways, we're getting off the subject here. What I was trying to say is that Carolyn has several knitting projects scattered throughout the store at all times. When she sits down to chat with a customer or have a bite of lunch (or now that I'm here – a cinnamon roll), she picks up whatever project is closest and knits. It really surprises me that she hasn't found a way to just wrap the skein of yarn around her neck, tuck the project down her shirt and stick the needles into her hair so that her knitting is always with her. I'm almost afraid to even suggest it to her in joking because she just might take me up on it.

Yes, you're right. We're getting off the subject again. On Saturday, I remember watching Carolyn hold the scarf up to another customer. They had laughed about how it just might be long enough to wrap around a flag pole. That had opened up a whole can of worms about whether or not it was appropriate to dress inanimate objects in hand-knitted garments. And if so, was a scarf the best thing that one could knit a flagpole? Perhaps a turtleneck would be a better option. Yeah. I'll say it again – knitters are a crazy bunch. After the customer had left, I saw Carolyn set the scarf back down. Since then, I saw her knitting many things, but I didn't see her knitting the raspberry scarf. Too many boring details for you? I apologize. But you have to know the details if you're going to truly understand what happened next. Patience is a virtue.

Anyways, on Tuesday, Carolyn and I were settling down to dive into our (surprise, surprise) cinnamon rolls, when a customer came in. It was Helen. She needed a little help with one of the instructions in her pattern. Carolyn graciously put her delectable roll down and reached for her closest piece of knitting to show Helen how to SSK. Don't ask me what that is – I really couldn't tell you. What I could tell you, however, was that there is no way that I would have set *my* roll down so close to Helen. She looked hungry.

Carolyn reached across the sofa to the small ottoman and picked up her raspberry scarf. It fell open in a long fold. The SSK forgotten, we gaped. Well, Carolyn and I gaped. Helen didn't, of course, realize anything was wrong. Helen let out a knitter's squeal – yes, knitters have their own language, which we can discuss later – and reached for the scarf which was, by my untrained eye, over a foot long. It was absolutely gorgeous and appeared flawless in its lace pattern. I couldn't believe my eyes.

"Carolyn," I gasped, "when did you have time to knit all of that?"

Carolyn was still staring at the scarf like it was an alien from another planet. "I just don't understand," she murmured. "Who would have done this?"

The tone in Carolyn's voice alerted Helen that something was wrong. She stopped her admiration of the scarf to look from Carolyn to me and back again. "What's wrong?" she asked.

Ignoring Helen, I kept my eyes on Carolyn. "Are you saying that you didn't knit that scarf?"

She shook her head. I narrowed my eyes at her suspiciously. I tilted my head and gave her my best you'd-better-not-be-fooling-me librarian look. Carolyn did not flinch from my gaze. She looked as baffled as I did.

"On Saturday, that thing was only three inches long," I stated.

"I know," she said.

"You didn't knit on that thing at all. I saw you knitting your sweater, your socks, and your purse, but not that thing."

"I know," she said.

"That thing is over a foot long now!"

"I know," she said, "and stop calling it 'that thing'."

Helen was still looking back and forth between me and Carolyn. "Are you saying that someone else knitted this scarf?" she asked. We both nodded. She grinned, "Must be some

82

customer couldn't keep their hands off of your beautiful mohair."

We paused to consider. You could almost hear the wheels in our brains spinning. Had I seen one of the customers knitting Carolyn's scarf? I tried to think back to Saturday and then yesterday. How many customers were in the store for any long length of time? It would have taken quite some time to knit that much, although there are some very fast knitters. Show-offs. Carolyn was already shaking her head. "No, my dears," she said slowly, "we didn't have any customers on Saturday that were here long enough to do this, and yesterday we were slow all day."

"Perhaps someone took it home with them and returned it this morning."

Again Carolyn shook her head. "No, you're our first customer. No one else has been in."

"So, if someone took your knitting home with them they would have had to return it sometime before you opened," Helen mused. "Who else has a key?"

"Just Louise and I," Carolyn said, "and Louise is still out of town. She called me at home last night to let us know that she won't be back until Friday."

I feel really badly that my heart gave a little joyful leap at this news. Really, I do.

"So what you're saying is that no one knitted on your scarf on Saturday or Monday, no one could have taken it home because no one could have returned it, and no one knitted on it this morning." Helen paused. "Is that what you're saying?"

Carolyn shrugged her shoulders helplessly. "I guess so," she said. She took the scarf back from Helen and turned it over and over in her hands as if expecting it to talk to her. "I can't believe that someone had time to knit this while I wasn't looking. I just don't know when—"

You have to believe that what popped out of my mouth next was completely un-thought-out. I had no idea what trouble it would cause. How was I to know that the six little words that came unbidden to my mind and unchecked out of my mouth would change the course of all of our lives forever? I mean, really, how was I to know?

"Maybe it was the knitting fairy," I said.

I guess you could say that what happened next was all my fault.

Chapter 13

Decisions. Decisions.

(Or... How "The Plan" Tried To Lure Me Back)

Helen's face lit up with delight. She was a very lovely woman in her mid-thirties with dark brown hair and dark brown eyes. When she smiled, she lit up with the whole room. Right now her eyes were glowing. "I love it," she breathed, "I absolutely love it. A knitting fairy."

Carolyn rolled her eyes, "Oh Helen," she said with a tolerant smile. "Don't be ridiculous. There is a logical explanation for this."

We sat there in silence for quite some time, but no logical explanation was forthcoming. Finally, it was Carolyn who stood, up, brushed the crumbs from her blouse and patted her silver hair. "Well, I don't know who knitted it," she said, "but I hope that they had fun. Perhaps someone will confess someday."

Helen and I both nodded in agreement, but I could tell by Helen's face that she was thoroughly taken with the concept of a knitting fairy.

Like I said, Carolyn's scarf was the first incident. At the time, I thought that it was probably going to be the strangest event of the day. What could be stranger than a knitting fairy? Right? Boy, was I wrong.

About 2:00 in the afternoon, one of the strangest things EVER happened. I was standing behind the counter, helping a customer check out. She had over 20 skeins of yarn and a list of colors that she needed. She was knitting a baby blanket out of a pattern in a magazine. She had the list of colors from the pattern, but she didn't necessarily want it in those shades. So, instead, we had substituted some colors for others. It had all made perfect sense when we were standing by the cubbies. Now, it was becoming a little muddled.

"So," I said with a small sigh, "you're going to use the Mandarin Orange instead of the Pink Bubblegum and the Spring Green instead of the Sky Blue, the Lime Green for the Bright Green and the—"

She was scribbling furiously on her pattern as I talked, and we bickered cheerfully back and forth about which shade of purple we had decided she would substitute for the Eggplant and the Violet when the doorbell jingled cheerfully. A man walked in. Please forgive the phrase, but really the only way to describe him was tall, dark, and handsome. Broad shouldered and wearing a beautiful navy blue suit, he had a quick, wide smile that would brighten even the darkest of days. The sound of his laughter could win over the crankiest of people, cheer the saddest of hearts, and change the most stubborn minds.

Yes, I knew him. You might be very surprised, though, to know how I knew him. You see, when I said that the sound of his laughter had been known to win over the crankiest of people, the person I really had in mind was...Mrs. Goldmyer (a.k.a, his mother). Yes, that's right. His mother. Cold, unfeeling, critical and mean-spirited Mrs. Goldmyer had somehow managed to give birth to one son, her emotional opposite. Mr. Goldmyer, you ask? I have no idea. You can ask Mrs. Goldmyer if you like, but I wouldn't suggest it. If I didn't know better, I would say that there was no Mr. Goldmyer. But that could hardly be possible, now could it?

His name was Nathaniel Goldmyer. Isn't that a nice name? I knew, however, that he preferred to be called Nathan. He was (sigh) a lawyer. A very good lawyer. Mrs. Goldmyer loved to brag about her son the lawyer, and kept anyone and everyone abreast of his current activities and cases. It was actually the only time that she looked almost happy. He used to stop by the library every once in a while, and although we never really talked, he always took a few seconds to say hi to me if I happened to be up front at the desk. Not that I paid any attention to such things, but I might have happened to notice that he only visited the library at certain times of the afternoon.

If I just happened to be at the desk at that same time each day, it could probably just be chalked up to coincidence. Probably.

So, what in the world was Nathan Goldmyer doing walking into Crabapple Yarns? Well, at the moment, he was currently making his way across the floor towards...ME? I gulped and looked at the lady across the counter. She looked up at him, but there was no recognition on her face.

I looked to see what Carolyn thought, but then I remembered she was in the kitchenette, making herself some lunch. He was still finding his way across the room toward me, a pleasant smile upon his face. "Hello Molly," he said kindly, once he had reached the counter.

"He-hello," I stammered in surprise. So, he did know my name. Amazing. Wonderful. Happiness.

He looked from between me and the customer. "I was wondering if I might have a word with you," he said.

I pulled myself together and smiled, "I'll be right with you as soon as we finish here."

He nodded in agreement, and left the counter to examine the store. We finished discussing which shade of purple she should use, the customer paid for her purchases and left the store, giving me a knowing smile as she left.

I noticed Nathan had taken a seat at the large oak table in the middle of the store. Although he was not a heavy-set person, he certainly seemed to command a lot of space around him. I was suddenly very, very nervous, but I came around from behind the counter and sat down on the opposite side of the table. There was still no sign of Carolyn. How could such a little woman take so long eating lunch?

I ran a hand nervously over the polished oak surface, wondering what on earth I should say. "It certainly is a surprise to see you here, Mr. Goldmyer," I finally said.

His mouth turned up in each corner with a little smile, and his eyes glowed with humor. "Mr. Goldmyer?" he teased. I felt myself flushing, and his playful smile abated, "Call me Nathan, or better yet, Nate."

I nodded shyly, but allowed myself a smile in return. "It certainly is a surprise to see you here, Nathan," I said. "I didn't know you were a knitter."

This time, his smile was wide. "I always thought you had a good sense of humor," he admitted. His face sobered, and he leaned slightly across the table towards me. "I know we don't know each other very well," he said, "but I felt that I just had to come over. I found out yesterday that my mother had fired you for...for—" ...and here words seemed to fail him.

"Conduct unbecoming a librarian?" I supplied helpfully.

"Err...yes," he said. "Well, I thought it was very strange that you weren't working last Wednesday, but I merely assumed that it was your day off. When I visited Mother yesterday and I still did not see you, I began to wonder and questioned Mother as to the reason for your absence. She confessed that she had let you go last Tuesday." Here he paused to regard me steadily. "She said that you had tried to unethically return a book to the library without going through the proper procedures. That you had failed to report a missing book, and as such, had showed a total and flagrant disregard for the rules upon which the library depends for its existence."

I resisted the urge to squirm, and sitting straight in my chair, didn't flinch from his intense gaze. I suddenly felt very sorry for the witness who was ever unlucky enough to be cross-examined by him. "Yes," I said slowly, "I believe that I did do that."

"Why?" he let go of his lawyerly demeanor and allowed a little bit of pure human emotion show through - confusion.

"Excuse me?"

He regained his composure immediately. "I know my mother is a hard person to work for. I know that she's very exacting and demanding and doesn't show appreciation for others very well." That was probably the understatement of the century. "But I also know that she valued you very highly as a treasured employee." Huh? Could have fooled me. "She deeply regrets her actions of last week and has sent me as her

Jaime Marsman

ambassador to ask you to come back and retain your position as Assistant Librarian." Whoa. Didn't see that one coming.

I stared at him in open-mouthed disbelief. It probably wasn't very attractive, but I didn't have time to worry about that right now. "She wants me to come back?"

"Yes, she does." He had a very deep voice, and it was currently laced with concern. "Between you and me, Molly," he said confidentially, "my mother has had a very difficult time keeping an Assistant. You were...are...by far the best Assistant Librarian she has ever had. Her temper and strict moral code are something that she has had a hard time compromising in favor of human personalities and social relationships."

For some reason, the comment stung a bit. "I have a moral code, too," I said, "but I believe that people should come before rules, and I simply can't work—"

He was smiling again. "I'm sorry Molly," he said, reaching across the table and placing one of his large hands over mine. "I certainly did not mean to imply that you had no morals." His eyes twinkled into mine. His hand was warm and comforting. "What I meant was that Mother was raised in a different time, and she has a hard time identifying with people. She seeks her comfort in the structure of life. That's why she needs someone like you so much. Someone who will help her see the difference between sticking solely to the rules and bending them a little for the benefit of someone else." His voice turned pleading, "Won't you please come back?" He let go of my hand and reached into his suit coat and pulled out a folded piece of paper from the inside pocket. "I have, here in writing, a formal apology and also a list of things that Mother has conceded to should I be able to entice you back."

I read through the apology quickly. It was short and to the point. I quirked my lips. It was written in typical Mrs. Goldmyer style. It was an apology, and it wasn't. While she did apologize for losing her temper, and in the process, firing me, she still believed her reasons were sound. Perhaps, in the future, we could work together on refining the Library's Handbook to better suit today's world. There was also a small list of things that she felt would make my job at the library easier and more fun (Fun? I wonder if she had to use a dictionary to find the correct meaning of the word), and these she listed at the bottom of the page. I was very amused to note that one of them was a space heater for behind the circulation desk. And an extended lunch hour once a week.

I read it twice before I dared to look back up at Nathan. Surely this was some kind of joke. I must have said something like that out loud, because he laughed and assured me that the letter was perfectly legitimate. "Mother would have come herself," he said, "but, things like this are very hard on her. She really is a deeply sensitive person, you know. She's actually a very lonely person. Ever since my father—" here he broke off and looked out the window.

Pity pulled at me and washed over my heart. I tried to see Mrs. Goldmyer as a lonely, sensitive person who covered up her loneliness with a cold, unfeeling attitude. Scared of showing her love to the world, she had put up a wall around herself so that she couldn't be hurt again. Especially after her husband...what...left her? Died? Ran off with another woman? Like I said, I tried to see her that way. Really, I did.

Mrs. Goldmyer's troubled personality notwithstanding, the question now was, did I want to go back and work at the library? My head told me that I belonged there. It was what I had wanted my whole life. My Plan on the refrigerator affirmed it. And now, I had written proof that things would be better. A heater under the desk! Toasty toes! What more could I want or expect? If Mrs. Goldmyer really wanted to change, perhaps it was God's way of telling me to go back and help her.

I looked around the yarn store with new eyes. Did I really want to stay here and sell...yarn every day of every week? Not only did I not know what I was doing, but I was petrified of the customers. Besides that, what kind of future was there for me here? Mrs. Goldmyer was no longer a young woman. In a couple of years she would be thinking about retirement. And who better to take her place than the Assistant Librarian? A little thrill ran through me. And then, I would have my own assistant. Wow. Just think. Me. I would be in charge. And have an assistant.

I thought, then, of Carolyn. I thought of her sweet little Mother Goose face and the way she had taken me in, given me a job and a place to live. Something niggled at the back of my head. Oh yeah...why had she done that? Why would a complete stranger do something like that for anyone? I reminded myself sternly that something strange was going on here at Crabapple Yarns. My presence here seemed to serve some sort of purpose. Did I really want to be used? Was I really any better off here than I was at the library? At least there I knew where the battle lines were drawn.

I don't know at what point I put both elbows on the table and held my head between my hands, but I must have, because I eventually realized that Nathan was no longer sitting across the table from me. He was crouching next to me, patting my shoulder. Did I mention that he was very handsome?

"I know it's a lot to think about," he said, "and I know it would be really hard to go back and work at the Library with my mother right now." At this point, he grimaced. "Believe me, I know how intimidating she can be." I lifted my head just a little. I could only imagine, well, actually, I couldn't imagine what it would be like to have her for a mother. "But, she truly, truly would like for you to come back." He smiled again.

Joy flooded my heart all the way to the bottom and bounced back up to the top. This was for real. I could go back. I could go back. I visualized my friends, the books, wiggling with anticipation on their shelves, happy and grateful to welcome me back. I pictured myself sitting behind the circulation desk with toasty feet as Mrs. Goldmyer came out to greet me with a mug of streaming hot chocolate...uh...okay, so I couldn't quite picture that. I could, however, picture my life back in its nice, orderly routine. Everything would be back on track. My Life's Plan had only taken a week's vacation. My family would be so happy – being people who were 'denying their inner knitter' they hadn't quite grasped the concept of a yarn shop either. Everything would be perfect. Isn't it amazing the way life works? Isn't it wonderful?

With a smile, I sat up straight. "Thank you so much, Nathan," I said warmly. "Thank you for speaking to your mother and for coming out here to see me. The offer is more than I had ever dared to dream of. Mrs...err... I mean, your mother, is a very complicated person, and I hope in the future, we will be able to communicate more effectively together." His smile threatened to split his face, and he began to speak, but I cut him off. "But, I'm afraid that I cannot accept your offer."

Oh rats. Did I really just say that? From the look on his face, I guess I did. My mouth seemed to be doing that a lot lately. I was going to have to start thinking of what I could do to control it. Someday, it could get me in real trouble.

He cleared his throat. "Perhaps a raise in pay?" he offered.

I shook my head. "No, I don't think so." See, there goes the mouth again. What was I thinking?

"More vacation time?"

I shook my head again. "It's really not about money or vacation or anything like that," I said slowly, working out my feelings as I spoke. "It's about what's good for your soul." It sounded a little cliché and trite, but I realized that I really meant what I was saying. I didn't want to go back to my boring but safe routine. I wanted to stay here and work with Carolyn. There may not be much future for me, but did I really need those things? I thought of the little charming apartment upstairs. Money? Promotion? Suddenly, they didn't seem quite so important anymore. With a sigh, I realized I was going to have to re-write The Plan.

The doorbell jingled as if on cue, and I stood up to greet whomever was coming in. Nathan had no choice but to stand up as well. "It's been a difficult week for you," he said slowly. "Why don't you take some time to think it over?" He straightened his tie. "I'll check back with you in a couple of days." And, with one last smile, he was gone.

"You must be Molly," the lady who entered said as she came forward, holding out her hand, "I'm Rachel."

I felt like I had been through a tornado and back again. I tried desperately to remember. Did this lady know me from somewhere? "Excuse me?" I said weakly.

She was a short, petite lady with (unlikely) blond hair that was short and curled perfectly around her small head. She had dark blue eyes that were wide and full of life. Her fashionable jeans and sweater looked like they were made for her, and she wore a scarf in her hair that perfectly matched the white in her sweater. I had always wondered how people got scarves into their hair like that. I had tried it a few times, and somehow always managed to look more "Prairie Girl" than "Vogue."

I'm never very comfortable around people who match perfectly and never wrinkle, but she smiled again, and I felt at ease. "I was in here watching the store for Carolyn when she first brought you in." She laughed, "You looked like you had just fallen down the rabbit hole. I don't think you even noticed me."

I sat slowly back down in my chair again and offered her a tentative smile. "Sorry," I said, "it's been a crazy morning."

Rachel, smiled knowingly and looked towards the door through which Nathan had just left. "Hey, don't apologize," she said with a wink. "If I had a visitor like that, I would be a little flustered too." She grinned and plunked herself down in a chair next to me. She threw a large quilted bag up on the table. "I just thought I'd hang out in here for a while today," she said.

I heard the back door open and Carolyn came walking out. Finally. "Oh, I thought I heard your voice, Rachel," she said welcomingly. "How are you today?"

To my complete surprise, Rachel leaned back in her chair and threw her feet up onto the table. She looked like she was sitting in her own living room. "Great Carolyn," she said, "I've had the worst day ever, and so I thought I would come in here and let you cheer me up."

I later found out that Rachel was a nurse at Springgate Memorial Hospital. She also loved to come in and sit at

Crabapple Yarns and knit. Quite a few of Carolyn's customers also enjoyed the same thing. Well, I guess that explained the seating areas. Rachel volunteered from time to time at the store when a big order came in or Carolyn was doing inventory or getting ready for the monthly Sit & Knit.

Sit & Knit, you ask? One night a month, Carolyn threw open the doors to the store and ladies from all over town would come just to...yep, you guessed it...sit & knit. Hence the name. Creative, huh? Why they did that – I have no idea. I mean, one can knit at home just as well as hiking all the way to Crabapple Yarns. Can't they? But, according to Rachel and Carolyn, it was a very well-attended event, and if they had any more ladies they would have to stand & knit. But that doesn't really have the same ring to it, does it?

Thankfully, the rest of the day passed without fail, as did Wednesday. It was soon Thursday afternoon. Tomorrow things were going to change. Tomorrow, Louise was coming back. And, do you know what's funny? I thought that was the worst thing that could happen.

Chapter 14

Winter Returns – Sanity Flees

Last night it had started snowing. Seriously. Snowing, in the middle of spring. Did I mention that it was also freezing cold and the snow was already up to my waist? Well, alright, it wasn't quite that high, but it was a good thing that I still had my winter clothes fairly accessible. Today I dressed in a long, wool grey skirt with a turtleneck and a sweater that was the color of frosted cranberries. I really didn't think that I would be wearing this again before next Christmas. It was only 7:30 a.m., but I decided to go to the store early. I had accidentally left my knitting at the store yesterday, and I had a sneaking suspicion that Carolyn just might be there early, too. And besides that, being tucked away at Crabapple Yarns sounded like just the thing on this cold, snowy morning. I wondered how early the bakery was open.

I trekked and sloshed my way to Crabapple Yarns. The wind bit at my face as I walked. I was only halfway there, and already quite tired of fighting the weather. I should have taken a taxi. I looked up the street hopefully, but of course there was no happy taxi sign motoring its way through the slush. My long, winter coat was good protection against the cold, but I'm afraid that the hem of my skirt was going to be completely soaked before I got to the store. A passing car threw up a combination of slushy snow and mud at me, and I jumped out of the way to avoid it. That was not a good idea. I slipped and had to grab at a convenient, sturdy, blue mailbox to steady myself. Is that a federal offense? I can never remember the rules about mailboxes. Oh well. Jail, at least, was sure to be warm and dry. The snow had already changed from the large fluffy flakes to the icky-sleety-rain type of snow. Great. Now everything was slippery in addition to being wet and cold. Yuck. Would someone please get out the balloons and throw me a pity party?

I could hear another car approaching from behind, and so I pulled myself closer to the buildings, away from the edge of the sidewalk. Ha. They'd have to find some other poor, unlucky, walking soul to splash. I had had enough. Slipping again, I caught myself with a hand against the brick wall of the toy store. The toys in the window display were completely oblivious to my discomfort. The little robot raised and lowered his hand, but I don't think he was waving to me or I would have waved back. I waited for the car to pass, but to my surprise and consternation, the car had slowed.

Looking up and down the sidewalk, I realized with a rather uncomfortable feeling, that I was pretty much alone on the street. How did I not see that before? Weren't buses running today? I picked up my pace and risked a glance at the car. It was still snowing heavily. The vehicle must have been parked outside, for it, too, was fairly covered in snow. It wasn't exactly a car – it was an unmarked van of some kind. At least I didn't see any kind of sign in the window, and the color was most likely a tan or brown. Oh good, an unmarked van is following me. No worries. I'm sure it's nothing. The engine revved, but still it did not pass. The van slowed to crawl behind me. My heart picked up speed as did my feet. My mother had always warned me about vans like this. Now, I knew why.

I was beginning to get a little bit scared. Just a tiny bit. Why were none of these stores open? Where was everybody? It was almost 8:00 in the morning, for goodness sakes. People should be getting their stores ready for the day. Where was their sense of duty? Keeping my eyes forward, I walked even faster.

I'm sure there was a simple explanation. Perhaps the driver was looking for a specific store. He could be lost. Maybe he was just an extremely safe driver – the roads were icy, you know. My heart leaped as I checked behind me; it was still there. There was a corner coming up, perhaps I could simply go the other way, and he wouldn't follow.

This was not a nice feeling. Still, none of the stores I passed were open. The sidewalk was covered in snow and was slippery. Am I repeating myself? Sorry. Allow me to summarize –

I was trapped. How could I be so stupid? If I tried running, I would probably slip and fall. Besides, where would I run to? Down the street? Ha! The van would certainly get there ahead of me.

This was ridiculous. Of course the van isn't following you, I told myself fiercely. My knees were beginning to shake. Were they waiting for an opportunity to grab me? Just driving slowly because of the weather? Why didn't they do something? And if they did something, what would they do?

I was almost at the small clothing store for children on the corner. Wouldn't you think that they would be open by now? My heart jumped. The van was speeding up. What was it going to do? More importantly, what was I going to do? This situation was rapidly becoming surreal. This was a nice, peaceful town. Surely one was not chased down by vans in Springgate. Especially not in front of a children's store.

Without realizing it, I began running. The van picked up speed to match mine. That couldn't be a coincidence. Could it? It remained a few paces behind me. My breath was coming in shallow pants. I had a pain in my side. I didn't know what to do, but I was at the corner, and I didn't dare cross the street because the van might be waiting to run me over. A hysterical laugh bubbled up in my throat. Run me over? Run me over? What was I thinking? This was Main Street. People don't get run over on Main Street.

Surely, surely, there would be someone walking outside here. I looked up and down the street again, but no one was in sight. Turning the corner, I continued my flight down Main Street with the van still following. All reasonable thoughts were gone from my mind. My only instinct was to get away and get away fast. Either that or dive into the nearest slush pile and pretend to be slush.

As I passed the next building, I heard a shout behind me. Had someone had jumped from the van and started chasing me on foot? I chanced a glance back. There was a blur of movement behind me and another shout. The van accelerated and passed me in a flurry of snow and ice and mud. My skirt was hopelessly splashed. I scolded myself for thinking about my skirt at a time like this.

The threat of the van had gone, but I kept running. Someone was chasing me. That was reason enough to keep moving. My feet lost their traction in the slush, and to my complete and utter horror, I found myself slipping. I don't care what anyone says about it not being possible, I know my heart stopped. I felt it stop. Arms reeling, I tried to catch my balance and keep running. The only thing I knew was that I had to keep running. I had to keep running. My feet refused to obey, and I found myself falling.

I closed my eyes in anticipation of hitting the sidewalk, but it didn't come. Strong arms caught me around the waist. If I thought that I couldn't get any more scared, I was wrong. Struggling, I tried to get away, blindly striking out at my attacker. But I was held fast.

"Hey, hey," a voice said, "calm down. It's just me." Something felt familiar. The message repeated and the words sank in. I stopped struggling. I was gasping for breath. My vision was still blurry from my panicked run. My heart was pounding like a freight train. But, at least it was beating now. I wasn't cut out for athletics. I was athletically challenged.

Hands turned me around. I breathed in a smell that was somewhat comforting and again, vaguely familiar. "What in world are you doing, Molly?" the voice asked. Something finally clicked, and blinking, I looked up into the face of my new best friend in the whole world. The baker.

Ten minutes later found me safely sitting in the back room of the bakery. I remember absolutely nothing of the trip here, but I imagine that I walked. Do you know that in all of our conversations I had never known his name? Looking back, I find that very strange. It was Ryan, by the way. Ryan Smith. An unimaginative name perhaps, but all the same, the most wonderful name in the whole world at the moment.

The back room of the bakery was a lot like the front of the bakery. Neat, clean, but lacking in atmosphere. Not that I cared at the moment. Right now, it looked like heaven.

Ryan knelt in front of me and handed me a cup of something that was steaming. At his urging, I took a tentative sip. It was coffee. I hate coffee. I took another sip. It was warm and comforting. Ryan had taken my soaking coat from me and hung it by one of the large double stoves, which was letting out promising smells and warm, blessedly warm, heat. My shoes were no longer on my feet. I hoped that they were somewhere warm too. I wrapped both hands around the mug and looked up at him.

He smiled, but I could see the concern in his eyes. "You look terrible," he said bluntly.

"Thanks," I croaked. I couldn't stop shaking. He frowned at me. I didn't think he looked so swell, either. His normally shaggy hair was sticking to his head from the snow outside and he looked tired and cold too. How in the world did I get here – sitting on a chair at the bakery in my stocking feet, with my skirt soaking wet and my heart shaking with a cold that even my feet couldn't match? It doesn't take long for life to go from one extreme to the next. A lot can happen in a not a lot of time. You would think that I would know that by now. Was this what adventure felt like? It actually felt very similar to the time I had food poisoning. Had I really longed for this? Perhaps it would be smarter to go back to the library.

Ryan stood up and took a step back. I wondered what time it was and what was in the oven and what would have happened if the van... I took another sip of coffee and sniffed.

"What do you think you were doing out there?" he demanded suddenly. His voice was actually quite harsh. It was so totally unexpected that I jumped in surprise, gaping up at him. I must have looked quite pathetic.

In a way, it was a good thing because tears were threatening. His abrupt tone of voice helped me push them back. I blinked at him. "What?" I asked.

He was frowning and the freckles were standing out in sharp contrast to his skin across the bridge of his nose. It was rather adorable. "You were running down a slippery sidewalk in the snow. You could have broken your neck or your leg or your arm or—"

I held up a hand. "Okay, okay, I get it," I said. "You don't think I was running on the sidewalk in the middle of a snow storm for fun, do you?" I dropped my gaze to the spotless floor. "I was scared."

He pulled up a kitchen chair so that he could sit across from me. "Anyone could see that," he said, "but what were you scared of?"

My eyes were betraying me again, and I had to sniff very hard, before I could answer his question with one of my own. "Did you see the van?" I asked in a small voice, daring to peek up at him again. I wanted to see his reaction.

"Van?" He stared at me for several long seconds. "Was someone following you?" his voice had taken on a new and serious note.

"You didn't see a van?" Panic pulled at me again. Was it somehow possible that I had imagined the whole thing? What in the world was happening to me? My head was spinning, my eyes were blurry, and my heart still beat like it was doing the tango. This never happened when I was a librarian. Was this was what a nervous breakdown felt like?

Ryan was shaking his head. His hair was beginning to thaw, and red strands were now sticking up at odd intervals. "I had already opened up at the bakery here this morning when I realized that I had left the snow shovel at home. I knew I needed it. I live in the apartments on Main Street. I was coming back out of my apartment building when I saw you running past. I recognized the scarf on your coat. Actually," he said with a small smile, "I recognized the scarf that was flying out behind you. I called out, but you didn't stop. I knew that that the sidewalk was slippery, so I yelled again. You still didn't stop, so I ran after you. There may have been some kind of vehicle going down Main Street, but I was so busy watching you trying to break your neck that I didn't notice what kind it was."

He watched me wrap and re-wrap my still shaking hands around the coffee mug and reached for a cordless phone sitting on the table. "I think we had better call the police," he said.

I almost dropped my coffee cup in my haste to stop him. "No," I said, "please don't do that. I'm fine, really. They're going to think I'm crazy or something. I don't have a description of the van or anything. Maybe this was all just my imagination." He hesitated, but set the phone down again. I put a hand to my head, my hair falling in my face. I didn't even notice when he took the cup from me and set it gently on the table.

Pushing my hand against my eyes, I tried to think. "More coffee?" he asked. I refused politely.

Had that van been chasing me or had I merely read too many mystery novels? I certainly did not want to involve the police over something as silly as being chased by a man trying to make a delivery. It was a strange occurrence though... And I had been scared. Very scared. But had I been scared for a reason? I'm sure it was all just a coincidence? If abduction had been the goal, whoever was in the van certainly would have had the time to do so. Since he hadn't done so, if he was indeed following me, the only other thing that happened to me was that I had been scared. But that's not exactly a criminal offence, is it?

"Would you like a cinnamon roll?" he asked, trying again. I shook my head miserably and tried to think harder. My brain was running overtime and spinning circles, but I could not come up with one single reason that anyone would want to scare me. I didn't have anything worth stealing, and I didn't do anything worth... Espionage with yarn – the thought came unbidden to my mind. I remembered back to my first meeting with Louise. She had stared at me as if I were a threat. Carolyn had tried to hide me from her. Could...?

"I never thought I would see the day when you turned down one of my cinnamon rolls," he said teasingly. Had I been feeling better, I would have been grateful for his attempts to distract me. However, I was not feeling better. I studied him for a moment and felt a pang of sympathy. Poor guy. He didn't quite know what to do with me. With a great deal of effort, I tried to pull myself together.

"What do you put in those cinnamon rolls anyways?" I asked. "It must be something addicting."

"Sorry," he said. "Top secret." But, he said it with a little smile.

I was starting to feel a little self-conscious about this whole situation. I wasn't too sure about the proper procedure for sitting in the back room of a bakery without shoes and a wet skirt. "Thank you," I said, suddenly feeling very shy. "It was very nice of you to bring me here."

I think he was feeling a little unsure of himself too. He got up to pull a tray out of the top oven, and set it on the cooling racks.

I tried to pull myself together. "I know you're really busy," I said, looking around for my shoes. "I'll get out of your way."

"I wish you'd let me call the police," he said again, not looking up from his tray where he was frosting the tops of what looked to be coffee cakes.

I shook my head again, and little ringlets of water splashed across the table. "There wouldn't be anything to report," I said firmly, wiping the droplets up with a corner of my sleeve.

He looked up from the frosting process. "Then at least promise me that you'll be more careful. No more walking through town before there's more traffic. Take a taxi. And if you see anything suspicious, you should—"

"What's your favorite color?" I asked him.

After that, I think he was glad to see me go.

Chapter 15
Do Knitting Fairy's Exist Even If You Don't Believe In Them?

Back out in the cold again, I stood in front of the bakery. For two brief seconds, I debated with myself whether or not I should go home and change, but it didn't take me long to abandon that idea. The thought of walking across town again completely freaked me out. Maybe the van had not been all in my imagination, maybe there was someone out to get me. Maybe Carolyn was a foreign spy who sent out secret coded messages in skeins of yarn. Maybe.

Heaving a heavy sigh, I tucked my hands into my coat pockets and pulled them out again with a start. There was something in the left pocket. It crinkled. I pulled it out. It was a bakery bag. It was a warm bakery bag. Peeking inside, I saw a juicy cinnamon roll. It was slightly squished, but it warmed my heart. He really was a sweet baker. Ha, get it? Sweet? Never mind.

Looking up and down the street, I checked to make sure that there were no vans in the vicinity. It's like they always say, just because you're paranoid, doesn't mean they're not after you. They were probably right. I headed towards the yarn store. I was right about one thing, Carolyn was there already. Perhaps now would be a good time to have a talk.

Walking in, I went to hang up my coat. Carolyn took one look at my rumpled hair and wet skirt and pointed at the sofa. Still clutching my bakery bag, I sat. She sat next to me.

"What happened?" she demanded. She looked so cute wearing a red and green plaid jumper. Her white shirt underneath had a large collar that lay over the jumper becomingly. Her silver curls glinted in the lamplight and her glasses hung on a silver chain around her neck. I just couldn't find the words to tell her that a van had almost chased me down this morning, and I suddenly didn't have the heart to have a little talk with her either.

"I got a little wet on the walk over," I said.

She didn't look like she quite believed me, but she didn't say anything. I held up my bakery bag. "Would you like half a cinnamon roll?" I asked.

***

Well, so far working with Louise was a piece of cake. I don't know what I had been so worried about. She simply refused to acknowledge my existence. Therefore, it wasn't hard at all to get along with her. If I asked her a question, she would make her reply to the air around her. I wasn't complaining. She still wasn't as bad as Mrs. Goldmyer. At least not yet. But, she was watching me. Waiting. Just waiting for me to slip up. She had the eyes of a hawk. And I was the poor little gopher she wanted to gobble.

On the positive side, though, I had abandoned my idea that she was somehow behind the Great Van Conspiracy. In the warm light of day and the cheery ambiance of the yarn store, I found it very hard to believe that my adventure this morning was anything more than imagination and a little bit of coincidence. From now on, no more scary books before I went to bed.

It was mid-afternoon, the snow had stopped falling, and sunlight was filtering in through the windows. Rachel was there along with some of her knitting friends. They had taken over the front seating areas. Louise had parked herself behind the counter. I was a little resentful of that. I think she knew that I liked to be behind the counter in my own little sanctuary. But maybe that was just me, being paranoid again. Carolyn floated here and there, telling funny little knitting stories, helping customers, and smiling her warm smile at everyone. It was very cozy. Did you ever in your life think that spending time in a yarn store would make you happy?

Helen and Lacey came in together just after lunch. Lacey was proudly wearing her scarf. She waved it at me as she came through the door. I saw Louise bristle as Lacey came closer and hugged me – yes, that's right – hugged me right in the middle of the store. "I just can't thank you enough for recommending this yarn," she said. "I just had so much fun." I noted with amusement that Louise's lips pursed like she had just had a good chug of lemon juice.

"You did a beautiful job," I said, ignoring Louise and examining Lacey's scarf like a person who knows what they are looking at. "I love it."

"You wouldn't have loved it on Wednesday," she said. "You should have seen me Wednesday. Something happened and I lost a stitch or it ran (or whatever it's called), and it was an absolute mess."

"Wow," I said, even more impressed, "you would never guess it. However did you fix it?" I grinned at her. "I know – you had to start over again, right?"

"Oh no," she said, shaking her golden curls. "No, I didn't start all over again. I put it down in a fit of anger and went to bed. When I woke up, it was fixed." She beamed at me. "Isn't that great?"

Helen was standing behind her grinning madly. I surely wished that I had the capability to raise one eyebrow. It would have been so appropriate right now.

"When you woke up, it was fixed," I repeated slowly. "Who fixed it?"

"I don't know," she replied innocently, "but I'm guessing that it was the Knitting Fairy."

I groaned, "Helen!" I should have known that she wouldn't lose a minute telling anyone and everyone about the Knitting Fairy.

"It wasn't me," she said, holding up her hands, her eyes wide and honest. "I was away that night, visiting my mother. You can call her, if you don't believe me."

"Then how did you know about the Knitting Fairy?" I asked Lacey.

She bobbed her head back at Helen, "Why, Helen told me about the Knitting Fairy," she said, "how it knitted Carolyn's scarf for her. It must have known how much I needed help and came to visit me." She said it as if that were that. Maybe it was.

We stared at each other for several long seconds. Unfortunately, her face didn't crack into a smile and she didn't say anything like, "Just kidding." So, I turned my stare into my best intimidating librarian stare. Who was I kidding? My intimidating stare has never worked on anyone in my entire life. Not even little Lucas Heath. Lacey, however, was a stare-down professional.

"Alright, Lacey," I said finally, "give it up. Who really fixed your mistake for you?"

"The Knitting Fairy," she replied. Helen and Lacey exchanged mischievous looks.

"If Helen hadn't told you about the Knitting Fairy, then who do you think fixed your mistake for you?" I asked. Let's see her come up with an answer to that.

"Just because you don't know what something is doesn't mean that it still won't work for you," she said.

My brain hurt trying to think that one through. I put a hand on her arm. "But surely you don't really believe in a Knitting Fairy?" I asked gently. "I mean—"

She looked at me in horror. "You mean you don't believe in fairies?" Her voice went up in volume.

I risked a quick glance around the store to make sure that there were no small children in the store. I didn't want to traumatize anyone.

She raised her voice further, "But you were the one who said it was a Knitting Fairy in the first place. Helen told me."

"But Lacey," I objected, "surely you don't believe that there is a fairy that goes around knitting for other people."

Her smile was tolerant, "Oh Molly," she said gently, "it's really the only explanation."

Oh boy. Here we go. I knew it. Knitters are crazy. It was probably yarn fumes. It must mingle with your brain chemistry and mutate your logic sensors. Or something like that.

I took a deep breath. It would be best to handle her as carefully as possible. If she were this delusional, there's no telling what she was capable of next. "Who else was at your house that night?" I asked. "Another knitter could have done it. Fixed it for you and didn't tell you or forgot to tell you or wanted to surprise you or—"

"Now, you listen here, Molly," Lacey said firmly, "I think you—"

"Whoa, whoa, whoa," Helen held up her hand with a laugh, "I have to admit that when I told Lacey about the Knitting Fairy I thought it was a bit of a joke. I thought someone must have knitted Carolyn's scarf when no one was looking, but now I'm not so sure." She sent a joking look at Lacey. "One thing I know for sure is that Lacey did not pick up a dropped stitch by herself."

"Hey!" Lacey protested, turning her ire on Helen.

I rolled my eyes, and left them to their shopping. There was just no talking to some people. I wished that I knew Helen and Lacey a little bit better. Were they just teasing me? Or, did Lacey really believe that a knitting fairy had fixed her knitting? It was hard to tell. I shrugged. Crazy knitters.

Carolyn was standing by the counter alone. Ha! Louise had abandoned her post. I knew she would have to eventually. After all, you should have seen how much coffee she drank. Maybe now, I could sneak in and sit behind the counter for a while. "Carolyn," I said in a low voice, "did you hear that? Lacey thinks that she was visited by the Knitting Fairy."

Carolyn was smiling. "I heard," she said. She twirled her scarf with one hand idly and watched the customers across the room with a fond eye.

"But what do you think?"

"I think someone fixed her mistake for her," Carolyn replied.

"Me too," I said. "But who?"

Carolyn took a step away from the counter. "Maybe it was the Knitting Fairy," she quipped playfully.

Louise came back from the kitchen area, and I let the conversation drop. There was no way I was going to humiliate myself in front of Louise by talking about fairies.

Helen and Lacey wandered back up to the counter, and I watched in amazement as the little twig woman, err...I mean, Louise, came to life. She greeted them warmly. I'm serious. Warmly. Her thin little face cracked and creased and folded up into an actual smile. A smile! It was an amazing thing to watch. Of course, once she saw me watching, the smile dematerialized again into her usual scowl. But the damage was done. Now I knew she could smile. With a sudden surge of goodwill, I stepped aside and allowed her to resume her post behind the counter with a sweet smile of my own.

"You sure are happy," she said instead of thanking me. "I hear tell that some people smile because they don't know what they're doing."

Ouch.

A roar of laughter came from the front of the store. The knitters up front were certainly having a good time today. Of course, they probably always did. I decided to leave the counter to Louise and investigate the current source of their hilarity. A couple of the women were laughing so hard, it looked like they might be in danger of falling off of the sofa. Actually, I felt a little bad for the poor little loveseat. It was bouncing up and down with their laughter. It's a good thing Carolyn's store was at the end of the street. Innocent passers-by might think it was an insane asylum.

And then I saw it. Lacey was trying on someone's sock for them. The sock was a little... large. The knitter responsible for the monstrosity had a red face and was torn between howling with laughter and covering her face in embarrassment. "Take it off!" she kept shouting. But, Lacey wouldn't. Lacey had both feet stuck into one sock. With a wicked grin, she flipped the sock up and down like a mermaid flipping her tail through the water.

"I love it," she declared to the delight of the other knitters. "It's a mer-sock, perfect for those times when you just want to hop."

The knitter in question ceased yelling, "Take it off," and switched to, "Why didn't I notice it sooner?"

"We tried to tell you," Sarah said. "Anyone could see that it was going to be too big."

"Yeah," the knitter said, "but I do have big feet."

"It's just too bad you don't have a fin," Lacey said.

Helen snatched the sock off Lacey's foot. "Give Nicole her sock back, you big bully."

I looked around at the little group. At least half of them were knitting socks. What was it with these sock knitters? I smiled to myself – without trying to look obvious, each one was surreptitiously inspecting the size of her own sock.

There was also a lady was working on a sweater, one lady was working on a hat, and Rachel was knitting fair-isle mittens. How much knitting they were actually getting done, though, was a good question. As I worked, I heard bits and pieces of their conversations. Let me tell you something folks – I've heard soap operas with less of a plot. Funny.

The one thing that I like the most about the knitters, is the way in which they all sit together. These ladies were perfectly comfortable with each other. When Sarah dropped her knitting in dismay, I watched as the lady who was working on a hat (I think her name was Ann) reach across the sofa and calmly show Sarah what was wrong. Sarah's smile returned, and the knitting and talking resumed.

Every time the front door opened, the knitters sitting up front let out little squeals as the cold air hit them. I'm not sure if the cold air really upset them or they just enjoyed squealing. One thing was for certain, we didn't need the doorbell when we had knitters on the sofa.

Strangely, it was both busy and calm this afternoon. Louise, despite being surly and sarcastic to me, was a great help to Carolyn. Between the two of them, they handled the customers with deft efficiency. I felt a little bit left out. But, I was determined that it would not be for long. Someday, it would be me floating around the store. I could see myself now. "Oh," I would say airily, "that mistake is easy to fix, let me show you how...Louise told you to ask me? She's just the sweetest little thing, isn't she?" or "I know just what you need. We have the perfect blend of goat and turtle right over here—" It was a beautiful little daydream.

The knitters squealed again, bringing me to reality. A customer burst through the door in a clear state of agitation. She stomped her feet clean of snow – not on the rug that was meant for such things, but right on the hardwood floors. I think it was right then that I decided that I wouldn't like her.

"Carolyn! Louise!" she gasped, "you won't believe this. You just won't believe this."

Unfortunately for her, Carolyn did not look too upset.

"Let me guess, Mary," Carolyn said dryly, "the Knitting Fairy came to visit you."

Mary stopped in her tracks. Confusion was evident on her face. I saw Carolyn valiantly trying to suppress a little smirk. "What?" Mary demanded. "Knitting fairy? What's that? Don't be silly. I have serious news here." Louise leaned over the counter as Carolyn leaned back against it. I stood right where I was. We were the picture of casual interest. Not at all the look Mary was going for, I'm afraid.

The lady continued with great excitement mixed with something else. She had the look of someone who was going to deliver bad news – and didn't exactly hate doing it. In other words, a real Drama Queen. "Oh Carolyn," she cried, "I have the most dreadful news." Here she paused to wring her hands, and make sure that she had the attention of everyone else in the store too.

Half of the knitters on the sofa were wide-eyed and breathless with anticipation. The perfect audience. The other half of them looked distinctly annoyed at having their knitting interrupted. Sarah was muttering something that sounded like, "Can't stop. Wait till I finish the round. Can't stop. Almost there—" She finished her row in due time and looked up at Mary with an expression that definitely said, "This had better be important."

Mary continued to squeeze her hands dramatically. She shifted her weight from foot to foot. Once she decided that we all looked appropriately attentive, she finally continued, "There's another yarn store opening across town."

It must have been hard to deliver news like that and try to gauge everyone else's reaction at the same time. I hope that she got the reaction she was hoping for. The knitters on the sofa were amazingly quiet. Louise was amazingly expressionless, and Carolyn was amazingly ...well...Carolyn.

"Isn't that nice," she said. "Where will they be located?"

Clearly, clearly not the reaction Mary was hoping for.

"But Carolyn," Mary wailed, "you don't understand. It's a huge store. I mean huge. They've got so much yarn, and they're going to have classes every night of the week and...and...oh Carolyn, what are you going to do?"

"Do?" Carolyn repeated blankly. "Whatever do you mean?"

"But you can't go out of business, you just can't," Mary cried.

I narrowed my eyes. Mary was really starting to annoy me. Wouldn't it be terrible if she slipped and fell in her own little puddle of melting snow? Just awful. A low murmur was beginning to be heard from the general area of the seating area. "Now just wait a minute," Carolyn said, she didn't exactly raise her voice, but she had the attention of everyone in the store. I could literally feel the tension. Thanks a lot Mary. "Just because another yarn store is opening in town doesn't mean we're going to close. We have been here for over 20 years; we love our customers and our customers love us. We wish the new store well, but we are not going to close." I had an urge to clap.

"What's the name of the new store?" I heard myself asking. I realized, too late, that this was just the question Mary wanted someone to ask.

"Happy Knits," Mary replied soberly, her little mouth drawn downwards in terrible grief. Her eyes gleamed.

111

Chapter 16

Is Now A Good Time To Hide Under The Counter?

We were standing in the kitchen whispering so that the customers wouldn't hear. Mary had left. Apparently delivering the bad news had been her only goal. She could have at least pretended that she was going to shop. But, she didn't. She just stomped right back out of the store in her wet boots.

"You mean to tell me that you don't think it's a bit strange that your store is called CRABapple Yarns, and they named their store HAPPY Knits? You don't find that the least little bit strange?" I hissed as loud as I dared.

"I agree with Molly," Louise said. (Yeah. You could have knocked me over with a feather too.) "This store is going to be trouble."

Wow. Louise was agreeing with me. A little fluttery feeling of happiness was beginning in my stomach. Perhaps this was the beginning of a new and beautiful friendship. Sometimes that happens, you know. Adversity has been known to do some pretty strange things. Perhaps this new trouble would band us together, and we would become the best of friends. I looked into the twig's beady, little eyes and searched to find a bit of camaraderie. Hmmm, perhaps this would take longer than I was thinking.

"Please don't get so upset," Carolyn said, looking back and forth between us. "Let's just wait and see how things go."

"But Carolyn," Louise and I parroted each other.

"No more 'But Carolyn," Carolyn said firmly. "The only thing I am going to do about this is pray, and I hope that you'll join me. Other than that, we'll just wait and see." And with that, she swept out of the kitchen, back into the store. We both stared at her retreating back. Carolyn was clearly in denial.

Louise's momentary truce with me ended as soon as Carolyn left the room.

"What do you think, Louise?" I asked, feeling quite brave for daring to address her.

She looked up at the ceiling as if she was expecting rain. "I think this is none of your business," she said, without looking at me. I escaped.

There was no more squealing from the sitting area. A few more customers came and went, but the knitters sat sobered and subdued, their knitting needles made more noise than they did. I wonder how often that happened. Rachel had even taken her feet off of the coffee table. She looked troubled.

The beautiful peace of the knitting store had been disrupted. One by one, the knitters left, each muttering some excuse. There was not a doubt in my mind that in a matter of minutes, each one of these knitters would be halfway across town, checking to see whether Happy Knits did indeed exist.

I was feeling restless and anxious. We didn't have enough customers to keep us all busy, but I couldn't sit down either. I didn't feel like knitting. I didn't feel like sitting. I didn't even feel like going to the bakery, if that tells you anything.

Carolyn, on the other hand, did not look as if she were troubled in the least. I admired her poker face. Then again, maybe it wasn't a poker face. Maybe she really was at peace. But that was just silly. Her livelihood was at stake here. Could you be at peace when your way of life was about to change forever? If that was the case then I wondered where that kind of peace came from. It was something I would have to think more about later.

I tried to imagine myself in Carolyn's shoes. What would I do? It didn't really take much thought. I would be hiding under the counter eating chocolate right about now. I looked at her closely. She was standing by the novelty yarn, re-arranging the fuzzy yarns by color. Did she look a little pale? What if the new store really was bigger and had more yarn? Would she close? Would customers still come here? Would it break her heart? What would I do? What would Louise do?

I transferred my gaze to Louise. Was she nervous? Louise was...well, with Louise, who knew? She remained stubbornly behind the counter, her knitting needles clacking noisily and a look of intense concentration on her face. It looked like she was knitting another one of her tentacle hats. Yikes. Did one really need more than one tentacle hat? Did anyone really need one?

I was glad when the UPS man came and delivered a small box full of baby yarn. Putting the yarn away gave me something to do. Of course, as soon as I was done, Louise came out of her hole behind the counter to re-arrange it all. Oh the joy of it all.

It was almost 6:00 when the doorbell rang for hopefully the last time during the day. I was so ready to go home. I was exhausted, both emotionally and physically. The last of the customers had long since deserted us, and the store was almost empty with the exception of Rachel. For some reason, I didn't really count her as a customer. I looked up. "Hi Ryan," I said. Carolyn was in the back cleaning up, and Louise and Rachel were by the counter discussing Rachel's cabled sweater pattern. Louise, for some strange reason, did not look exhausted. She looked almost happy. It was so interesting to see Louise when she was animated. The dry, little twig had come to life again. Was it only knitting that brought her to life or were there other things that woke her up? I wonder what would happen if we watered her.

Ryan leaned his tall frame against a study bookcase. He looked me up and down, "You look better."

I nodded. "I feel better too. Thanks for everything you did for me this morning. I'm really sorry that I was such a mess. The more I think about it the sillier I feel." I ran a self-conscious hand through my hair. I still felt like a mess.

"You know," he said slowly, "I was thinking just the opposite. The more I think about it the stranger I think it all was."

"No," I said firmly, "it was just a coincidence." The last thing I needed was for my paranoia to affect others.

Carolyn came out from the back room. "Well, Ryan," she said pleasantly, "what do we owe this pleasure?"

Uh-oh. I hope he wasn't going to mention "the incident" to Carolyn. He smiled warmly at her. "Hello Carolyn. I was on my way home and saw your lights. I just thought I would drop in to say hi to two of my best customers."

I almost wilted with relief. Carolyn laughed, but she tilted her head as if she expected something else. It was almost eerie the way that she saw through people.

"Actually," he continued, "I ran into Molly here on her way to work this morning." Uh-oh. "And I was going to ask her if she would like a ride tomorrow. I think it's supposed to snow again."

Carolyn beamed at us maternally. What was I supposed to say? If I said no, he would...well, let's just say I didn't say no. I was being blackmailed by the baker. Espionage with yarn and blackmail at the bakery. And just think – I used to think that an overdue book was exciting.

Chapter 17
In Which I Am Rude On Purpose

The next morning dawned bright and sunny. Not a snowflake in sight. But, I didn't mind missing my walk through downtown. I think it would be a long time before I wanted to walk downtown by myself again. The snow was still thick and muddy on the sidewalk. Ryan was pleasant and, for the most part, silent. He did not mention "the incident" again. He dropped me off right in front of Crabapple Yarns. I thanked him for the ride. I felt bad for making him leave the bakery to come and pick me up, and I told him that next week I would take a taxi. I was very firm. He listened very nicely and then said, "I'll see you Monday." I sighed. It looked like I had a new chauffeur. I gave up and told him I would be in for my daily fix later.

It was still fairly early in the morning when a customer came rushing through the door. They do that a lot here, which was actually a change because people very, very rarely rushed into the library. As usual, there were several other customers in the store, and everyone looked up in concern. Because, you know, knitters have a sixth sense about these kinds of things. I mean, if someone came rushing through the door and yelled, "Hey, there's an elephant in the street playing a tambourine and walking a kangaroo," no one would even look up. However, when a fellow knitter runs into the store, carrying their knitting – not in a bag but in their bare hands and with a frantic expression on their face, every knitter within walking distance comes running. Even if they can't see her face. They just know.

Laurie (I later found out was her name) was very upset. She was not thinking clearly. How could I tell, you ask? Well, for starters she only had one sock on. The other clue was that half of her hair was up in a ponytail. The rest of it she kept brushing out of her eyes and trying to tuck behind her ears. Her hair was a brilliant shade of red and it matched the brilliant shade of blood currently creeping up her cheeks. Someone should warn her of the harmful effects of high blood pressure. Perhaps she should take up something that lessens stress. Maybe she should try knitting. Hee hee. I decided to keep my little knitting humor to myself. This was clearly not the audience for it.

She threw her knitting down onto the counter. Her expression could be classified as somewhere between intense panic and frustrated hysteria. Louise actually looked mildly alarmed. I shared her emotion. A crazed knitter was the last thing we needed. I hoped she would stay away from the sock yarn. I had just gotten that reorganized, again.

A small crowd of customers surrounded her. Knitters share a bond that defies explanation. As I looked around, I was not surprised to see sympathy and understanding on each face. They might not know what exactly was wrong, but that didn't stop them from identifying with her on a deeper level. It was really quite touching. And yet very weird at the same time.

I was proud of myself that I recognized a few of the faces in the little crowd. It's strange how many times one can visit a yarn store in a week's time. Why would they come so often? It's not like we get new yarn in all the time. If you saw it yesterday, why in the world would you want to see it again today? You'd think that they would buy their yarn and not come back again until they were ready for more. Maybe they did knit it all, you say? That's doubtful.

Carolyn hurried across the floor over to the mob by the counter. She greeted Laurie with her usual warmth. "What's the matter, Laurie?" she asked, "is something wrong with the sweater?"

Not the brightest question I have ever heard.

Laurie half-sobbed. "Is there something wrong?" she asked, her voice rising on each word. "Is there anything right?" She looked around the little group with wild eyes.

Personally, I thought she was being a little over-dramatic.

Carolyn placed a reassuring arm around Laurie's shoulder, and the crowd sighed in collective relief. They knew that Carolyn would fix it.

"Let's just take a look here." Carolyn carefully separated the pieces of knitting. To be honest, it didn't look like much to me. As a matter of fact, it was pretty sorry. The pieces looked limp and humiliated. She had not yet tucked in her ends, and pieces of bright pink yarn stuck out everywhere. "Well, here's the back," Carolyn said, picking out one of the pieces of knitting and smoothing it out with her hand. I wondered how she could tell. At least the yarn was very pretty. A variegated pink. Maybe it would be a cute sweater someday. "And here's the left front," Carolyn said. Her hand paused as she smoothed out another piece of knitting. "Uh-oh," she said.

The crowd gasped.

Clearly, something was seriously wrong.

Helen exchanged a grim glance with her neighbor in the crowd. Whispers floated through the air. People nodded knowingly at each other. I was frustrated. I couldn't tell what was wrong. I couldn't ask either. Asking would clearly blow my cover as an experienced yarn person.

Louise was watching me. Her small eyes were trained on my face. I quickly tried to match the expressions of those around me – knowingly sympathetic. She wasn't fooled. She didn't believe that I was an experienced yarn person.

Two tears rolled down Laurie's cheeks. "Look what I did," she said. "Look at that. How stupid can I get?" She hit herself on the head with a balled fist. "Who knits two left fronts?" She was pulling at her hair. "Who in their right mind knits two left fronts?" She was still pulling at her hair. I hoped she didn't pull any out. I hoped it didn't fall on the floor. I could just picture little tufts of her hair blowing across the polished wood floors like miniature tumbleweeds.

Ahhh...now I got it. Yikes. And she still needed to knit the sleeves. And, sew it all together. And put a collar on.

Things surely did not look good for Laurie. Apparently, this was the sweater she was knitting for her daughter's birthday. When is the birthday, you ask? Well, my friends, of course, the answer was tomorrow.

Suggestions from the crowd were plentiful. They ranged from "knit real fast" to "sleeping is over-rated" to "if you don't drink anything you won't have to take the time to go to the—" well, you know. Helen suggested that she forget the sleeves and make it into a vest. That sounded like a good idea. My favorite suggestion was from another well-meaning knitter who told her that she could flip one of the left fronts over so that the front was mis-matched and then sew in one of the sleeves in reverse as well. I thought that sounded like a good idea too. Personally, I would have just gone to the store, picked out a nice pink sweater, cut out the tag, and called it good. It was a little sweater. A little person wouldn't know the difference.

Laurie looked hopefully at Carolyn. I think she was waiting for Carolyn to wave her magic wand and make it all better. When Carolyn shook her head sadly, two more tears spilled down her cheeks. "I'm sorry, Laurie," Carolyn said, "the only thing you can do is take out one of the fronts." Laurie began shaking her head frantically. Carolyn spoke in her most soothing voice, "Just down to the armhole, dear. And then knit it according to the right front directions. It really won't take that long."

Laurie was not consoled, but she was counseled and advised. By the time she left, I think she was feeling better. She was still very determined, however, to finish the sweater for her daughter's birthday tomorrow. We all wished her luck. I don't think anybody thought that she would actually do it. Denial: another attribute of the knitter.

The store was surprisingly not too busy today. So we took advantage of the quiet time to do a little dusting. As I dusted the top of the acrylic yarn shelf, I thought about how strangely quiet it was today. I hoped that it had nothing to do with Happy Knits. I hadn't told Carolyn, but last night, I had gone (don't worry, I had taken a taxi) across town and peered into the windows of Happy Knits. My heart had literally dropped to my toes. It was huge. I mean HUGE. Not all of the yarn was out yet, but it was still humongous. The sign on the door said that they would be opening in two weeks. I had gone home feeling depressed. One could only hope that there were enough crazy knitters in Springgate to support two yarn stores. I guess it was possible. I was beginning to think that anything was possible with knitters.

My stomach was just beginning to make rumblings about lunch when Nathan Goldmyer came striding into the store, his smile wide. I was a little annoyed. That surprises you, doesn't it? I mean, I've told you how handsome he is and what a good lawyer he is and how he had gotten my old job back. So, why was I annoyed, you ask? I have absolutely no idea. I just was. Maybe it was because I had just now decided that he smiles too much. For some reason, I have a hard time trusting people who smile too much. He offered to take me out to lunch. That cheered me up a little.

Not ten minutes later, we were comfortably sitting at a little restaurant about three blocks away from the store. It was a little Italian restaurant. Perfect for a lunch date with a handsome lawyer. Had been any nicer, I would have been insanely nervous. For some reason, the crumbling wallpaper reassured me. It was only too bad that I didn't care for Italian. He had never asked. We ordered spaghetti and made pleasant small talk until it arrived. I wondered when he would ask me again about the library. I wondered what I would say. Maybe it would be for the best to go back to the library – especially with Happy Knits opening. If Carolyn lost business because of it, maybe she wouldn't be able to pay me anymore.

"So, Molly," he began, "have you had a chance yet to reconsider?" That was quick. He twirled his spaghetti onto his fork with beautiful grace. I didn't even try it.

"I have," I said, "and my answer remains the same." Well, that took care of that. I wondered what we would talk about for the rest of lunch. I slurped up a noodle that was slipping off my fork. From the look on his face, I don't think slurping was proper spaghetti procedure.

"You studied Librarianship at college," he said, stoically ignoring my unfortunate slurp. "You have a degree. I'd hate to see you throw that all away." His smile was pleasant, as was his voice. Was I imagining that there was an edge to it?

"I'm not throwing it all away. I'm trying something new." My smile was pleasant. As was my voice. He really would have to be dense not to hear my edge.

Why was I finding him so irritating all of a sudden? Especially when he wasn't saying anything so far that I hadn't already thought. This was all very strange.

"Trying something new is always a good idea," he agreed easily, "but don't you think you should try something new on a smaller scale? Knitting is all well and good, but it's better suited to a hobby rather than a career. You have to think about your future. Surely you would rather have a recognized career with goals and promotions. Don't you want a job that other people will understand?"

I don't think I was imagining the condescending tone now.

"The only reason I'm working at the yarn store is because I was fired from the library," I pointed out. "And I happen to love it at Crabapple Yarns. Life is more than picking a career that is socially approved of. For once in my life, I'm following my heart instead of my life plan, and I don't care what other people think." I cheered myself on mentally. It wasn't very often that I allowed myself to speak so bluntly. It felt good. I could tell that he was a bit surprised.

"I wasn't trying to lecture you," he said soothingly. "I can see that it's a lovely store. I just think you can do more with your life."

"More with my life," I repeated slowly. "Which implies that if I continue working with Carolyn I'm wasting my potential?"

"You can't possibly want to spend your days sorting yarn."

"I'm not spending my days sorting yarn." I said. "I also ring up purchases and wind yarn and—"

He didn't think it was funny. I could tell by the way he wiped the corner of his mouth with his napkin and set his napkin down on the table with a little more force than was really necessary. You'd think he would have stopped at that, wouldn't you? I mean, it was clear that we were not going to agree about this. Why should he care, anyway? He was taking his duties as her only son a little too seriously.

But, he didn't stop. He got worse. "At least as a librarian, you're helping people. It gives some validity to your life. If you continue on this path what do you have to look forward to? When it's time to retire, you're going to look back at your life and realize that you spent it winding wool." His voice and eyes turned gentle. "And, really," he said slowly, "knitting may be a fun, little hobby, but there's really no point is there? It doesn't make the world a better place. No one is helped by it."

I opened my mouth to object, but he held up one hand. "It's not like you can knit anything that you can't buy at a store for a lot less work and probably less money too. It does nothing other than give women who have too much time on their hands a way to sit and gossip and look like they're doing something important with their own silly lives. If you think about it that way, it's a little bit like a self-perpetuating circle. Don't you see? You're better than that. I know you are."

The spaghetti tasted like sawdust in my mouth. What was I doing here? Why had I come? Why, oh why, was I sitting in an Italian restaurant eating spaghetti that I didn't like and trying to justify my choices to someone I really didn't even know? Someone whom I could clearly see had no idea of the concepts of friendship and love, which I already knew were at the core of all true knitters. Why did I need affirmation from an arrogant lawyer? And, come to think of it, when had I started thinking of Nathan as arrogant? Was it when he had insulted yarn? Was yarn something that needed to be defended? Why had I been so excited to go out to lunch with him? What had I thought was attractive about him? What did he really want? That was the biggest question, wasn't it? Why was he going through so much work to try to convince me to go back to the library? So many questions, so few answers. Maybe he was more like Mrs. Goldmyer than I had initially thought.

Lunch was nowhere near over, but I was ready to leave now. There was no point in arguing with him. He would not be able to see things from any viewpoint that wasn't his own. He had no concept of what knitters were, and what a yarn store was all about.

The sad thing is, it wasn't that long ago that I would have agreed with him. But, I couldn't think about that right now.

I put my fork down very slowly and laid my napkin next to my plate. I was going to do something I had never done before in my whole life. I was going to be rude on purpose. As my feet prepared to push my chair back, his cell phone rang as if on cue. He answered it without even bothering to look at me to see if I minded. I wished I had left before the phone rang. Now, I was stuck. I wanted to be rude, but not that rude.

I waited. For two minutes. He was still talking. I stood up. He looked up at me. I met his gaze evenly and calmly pushed my chair under the table and walked away. He was not talking anymore.

It was cold outside. But, that was okay. I was cold inside too. Looking at my watch, I realized that I had only spent about 20 minutes of my lunch hour. I couldn't possibly go back to work so early. Louise would know that my lunch date had not gone well. That would never do.

I stopped in the diner down the street for a bowl of soup. Spaghetti and rudeness had left a bad taste in my mouth. Chicken noodle soup always makes you feel better. I sat by the diner with my feet up on the rungs of my bar stool and slurped my noodles as much as I wanted. I have to admit that I was starting to feel just a little bad for my behavior with Nathan. He probably had not meant to insult the yarn. If Carolyn had been there, she would have said that he was just a person who was denying his inner knitter. I don't think she would have walked out on him. He couldn't help it that he didn't understand. I should have been more sympathetic. When would I learn to stop taking everything so personally?

"Hello, Molly," a happy little voice said.

I looked up from my gloom and doom to greet the friendly faces of Helen and Patrick. He was smiling too. What on earth did everyone find to be so happy about?

"Hi," I said, forcing myself to bend my own lips into what I hoped resembled a smile. "How are you guys?"

"Oh, we're just great," Helen said. "We're actually sitting over there. We saw you come in. You look miserable. So, we just had to come over and ask you to join us."

My protests were waved aside, and soon I and my bowl of soup were sitting with Helen and Patrick. I slurped a noodle experimentally. Both of them grinned. I liked them even though they seemed to smile a lot. Strangely enough, their smiles didn't annoy me. Maybe it's because I'm pretty sure that they were holding hands under the table.

Even though I didn't feel like talking, I found out a lot of things about both Helen and Patrick. They had only dated for three weeks before they got married two years ago. Patrick loved to ride motorcycles. Helen thought that they were death traps. He owned his own very plumbing business and enjoyed hunting and fishing. Helen enjoyed shopping and knitting. He was a woodworker and had built their kitchen table. Helen enjoyed cooking. This worked really well because Patrick enjoyed eating. I've never seen a couple so different and so the same and so perfect for each other. Their differences didn't split them; they both loved each other more for them. Helen started knitting about six months ago because Patrick had so many hobbies that she thought she was going to go crazy all by herself while Patrick was out tinkering. "After all," she said, "there is only so much television that one can watch."

In less than ten minutes, I knew their entire life history. My head was reeling, but it was a happy kind of reeling. I had eaten almost all of my soup.

They were the kind of people who made you feel like you were life-long friends. I could have sat and chatted with them all afternoon. Or at least until the end of my lunch hour. Then, Helen had to go and say the worst thing that she could have ever said. "So, how long have you been knitting, Molly?"

It was a very legitimate question. I should have expected it. It was the knitter's equivalent to "So, how about the weather?" But I wasn't prepared. And this was unfortunate. I could feel a blush creeping up my cheeks, and I knew that I looked guilty. They, of course, would have no idea why I was feeling guilty. This made me feel even more so. The red blush crept higher.

I tried to think of an answer. What was I supposed to say? Later, when I would look back on this conversation, I would see all of the perfect answers I could have given. But at the time, my mind was blank.

"What's the matter?" Helen asked. Patrick was staring at me strangely. They looked confused, which was not surprising.

"Was that a bad question?" she looked alarmed. "I'm sorry, I didn't mean to—"

It's always best to tell the truth. However, I didn't want anyone else (especially Louise) to know how little I knew about knitting. Would everyone know if I told them? Would the cat be out of the proverbial knitting bag? My feeble little brain was getting sick of all these questions, so I decided to throw caution to the wind. Forgetting about good manners, I put my elbows on the table and lowered my voice. "Can you guys keep a secret?" I whispered. I felt like a spy passing on top secret information.

They both leaned forward over the table, too. Helen's eyes were shining with excitement. Two heads bobbed in tandem. "I only learned how to knit last Wednesday."

Helen's eyes and mouth popped open at the same time. Patrick threw back his head and laughed.

I grinned at them. "Please don't tell," I said, "I'm trying to look like I know what I'm doing."

Helen grinned back at me. "You sure had me fooled," she admitted. "I thought you had been knitting for years."

Choosing my words carefully, I explained to them that Carolyn had hired me rather spontaneously. I actually felt a little relieved about confessing. I wasn't cut out for a life of secrets.

Helen's next words reassured me that I had done the right thing, "Well, Molly," she said, "if you ever need any help and don't know who to ask, feel free to ask me. I haven't been knitting for that long either, but I'd be happy to try and help you. Don't worry, I won't tell anyone." Her eyes were sparkling.

"Your secret is safe with me," Patrick said, "not that I'm trustworthy, but I don't know anyone who would be interested—" He was joking and winced dramatically as Helen's elbow came in contact with his ribs. His face sobered. "I have to say, though," he said, "I am very impressed. It takes a lot of courage to do what you're doing. I know Helen has absolutely loved knitting, and at first, she was really overwhelmed by it all," he paused to look at Helen, "you never know that you can't do something until you know you can't."

My head hurt trying to think that one through.

Helen rolled her eyes. "And that's why he has so many hobbies," she said.

127

Chapter 18

Molly Stevenson – Great Big Fraidy Cat

Carolyn had given me a key to the back door of the apartment (not the yarn store). Carolyn said that she was having one made for me, but in the meantime, I was welcome to enter and exit the apartment anytime I wanted through the back door. Today was Sunday. I had gone to church this morning, but found that I could not settle down at home afterwards. So, I had decided to start cleaning.

I had to go around the side of the building to get to the back door. There was a small alleyway back there with enough room to park a car. I wondered whether Mr. Morrie lived over his store, and if he did, what kind of car he drove. The only car currently residing in the small alley was a little blue one. I knew someone also lived over the bakery. So, it could be either of their cars. Three separate staircases led up to the three small landings that would let each tenant into their own apartment. They rather reminded me of an exotic iron vine crawling up the back of the building. Like the staircase on the inside, the staircases outside went in one direction and then switched back to go the other direction. I was very happy to see that they were built sturdily. I hiked up the first flight of stairs and took a break on the first landing to survey my new kingdom. I wasn't catching my breath. Really, I wasn't.

Two hours later, though, I found myself catching my breath from cleaning. It was dusty. Definitely dusty. But, it wasn't dirty. In my humble opinion, the two most important rooms of the house to be clean are the kitchen and the bathroom, so that's where I started. I had finished the bathroom and was starting to clean all of the cupboards when I heard a noise downstairs.

"Stop it," I told myself, "you're going to hear strange noises sometimes." The window next to the fireplace rattled in its pane as I heard a muffled thump from the room below. You're probably getting tired of hearing this, but I had to wonder, once again, about how smart I was being. Maybe I didn't want to live in this apartment after all. It might be too scary here. Perhaps I was going to have to go and meet my new neighbors. Maybe that would alleviate my jitters. Then again, if the neighbors were weird, it wouldn't help at all. I heard another thump, and I went to check the deadbolt on both the door that led outside and the door that led downstairs. That would make me feel better, too. There was a little crocheted curtain over the window on the outside door. Hugging myself to the wall, I crept up to the door and peeked cautiously around the curtain. No one was there. Did I feel a bit foolish? Yep.

Did I open the door that led downstairs to check to make sure that no one was down there either? No. No way. Are you crazy?

I consoled myself with the thought that it was probably the heater, creaking and groaning. Yeah, that's it, the heater. Another little creak had me skittering for the door handle. Perhaps one could overdo the whole cleaning bit. Perhaps I should leave some for another day.

Two minutes later, my feet were splashing through the slush in front of Crabapple Yarns. You have never seen someone lock up so fast. I was immensely relieved to be back outside away from the spooky noises. I was feeling a little panicky. Would I be able to find the courage to live up there? I guess it really didn't matter since I had already given my landlord notice and could no longer afford to live in my current apartment anyway.

Now that I was safely on the street, I decided to sneak up on the front window and see if there was, indeed, someone in the store. For all I knew, it was just Carolyn. But, if it wasn't Carolyn but instead a yarn-crazed burglar, I should call the police. With moves that would make a seasoned marine proud, I slithered and slunk my way up to the front window. Keeping to the left of the window, I stood with my back to the stone wall. I gathered my courage together with one deep breath and struggled to remember what I knew about how to spy properly. I turned and ever so carefully peered through the front windows of Crabapple Yarns. I tried to only let the parts of my body that were necessary for spying get in the view of the window. This was a lot harder than it looked on television. I was a little off-balance, and I tried to imagine how it would look to the bad guy in the store to see a girl, arms flailing, topple over in front of the window. I tried to imagine how it would look if it was just Carolyn in there.

The little lights that Carolyn left on when the store was closed revealed that the store was completely empty. No shadows ducked behind the baby yarn. Nothing slithered under the great oak table. No one was stuffing yarn into bags. No one was doing anything because no one was in the store. I hadn't really expected there to be.

With a shrug, I walked back to the street. The bakery, unfortunately, was not open. I had checked when I came in. No sugary snack to alleviate my jitters today. But, what was that? There was a light on in the hardware store. How strange. What luck! I should go and introduce myself. Meeting Mr. Morrie would surely alleviate the last of my jitters. It would be nice to know the person I would be living next to.

I was sure that he would also love to meet me as well. Being his new neighbor, he would be very happy to know that should he ever need to run over to my apartment because he heard spooky noises coming from below, he could now do so. Oh wait, maybe that was me. Anyways, it would be nice to know whose apartment I would be running to. Not, of course, that I ever really would. It's good to be prepared, because, you just never know.

You know what's funny? I used to say stuff like that to other people a lot. "Never say never," I would say cheerfully. "You just never know," I would say wisely. Now, it was coming back to haunt me. Because, now, it was really true – I really didn't know.

I didn't even think about what I would do if the door were locked. And it was. Bummer. Undaunted and feeling very brave, I peered in the window. I didn't, however, use my top secret spy techniques; I just stood in front of the window, put my hands around my eyes to block out the sunlight and stared inside. Two eyes were peering back at me. A tiny little scream came out of my throat and hung mockingly in the air. As screams go, it was rather pathetic. More of a whimper, actually. I jumped back away from the window so fast that my feet got tangled together and I fell to the sidewalk. Great. Now my jeans were nice and wet. A perfect ending to my great adventure. This never happened to the spy on television either.

By the time I had struggled back to my feet, the door was rattling in its hinges. I am not kidding you when I say it creaked open. Literally. Creaked open, loudly. Have you ever heard of a hardware store with a creaky door? Isn't that a little like a plumbing store with a leaky sink or a...What? What did you say? It's not any stranger than a knitting store with an employee that barely knits? Yeah, yeah, yeah. Maybe you should just be quiet for a little while.

The man who opened the door was quite something to behold. He had red hair. Lots of red hair. His beard, however, was grizzled grey. There was a lot of that, too. It hung down almost to his chest. His hair stood up wildly in every direction possible. His flannel shirt was rumpled and it looked like he had slept in it. From his expression, I seriously doubted that I would be welcome to run to his apartment if I were scared. Ever.

Perhaps a moment of reflection is in order. Had I really lived such a sheltered life up until now? Being a librarian, I thought that I had met almost every type of person possible. I had met tall people, short people, grumpy people, and happy people. But, ever since that fateful day when Mother Goose stood in front of me with hypnotic fruit swaying on her hat, I had never, ever, in my entire life, met such a crazy cast of characters – Mother Goose, the skinny baker, the twig woman, happy little Rachel, the lady in the pink sweater. The list just goes on and on. And now, to top it all off, I was standing in front of a hardware store faced with a man who looked like he had just come back to civilization after living for 20 years in the

132

wilderness eating bark and berries. Is it possible to live such a sheltered life that you don't even know you're sheltered? Clearly, it is.

He didn't speak. I didn't speak. I was incapable of speech. So we stood there. The sun was shining down on us. You would think that the last thing on my mind was Mr. Morrie's windows. But, at the moment, the only thing that I seemed capable of doing was watch the sun glare off the dirty windows of his shop. I have no idea why, but I had the sudden desire to wash them. Don't worry. I squelched it. I do that a lot when I think about washing windows. After that, my mind went blank. It was Mr. Morrie who broke the silence.

"Can I help you?" his voice was surprisingly soft and well-mannered.

"Uhhhh—" Well, that was certainly intelligent. Maybe he thought I looked like a crazy person, too. That was certainly something to think about. A bird tooted happily from somewhere overhead. I looked up, but there were no trees in sight. It must be on the roof.

Have you noticed that your thoughts tend to wander the most when you're insanely nervous? I pulled myself together with a stern mental scolding. "Hi." I smiled at him. "My name is Molly Stevenson. I work at—"

"Yeah, I've seen you at Carolyn's," he said with a frown. "I figured you must be new there."

Well, at least he wasn't biting my head off. "Yep," I said with another bright smile. "Just started last week. I love it. Actually, I'm also going to be living on top of the store. I just thought I would stop by and introduce myself. I was thinking that I had never seen your store yet."

He stepped aside. "Well," he said somewhat gruffly, "then come on in and see it."

Uh? Go in? Whoa, let's just wait a minute. I didn't exactly want to go in NOW. I wasn't even so sure that I wanted to go in at all anymore. But, what could I do? I had sort of committed myself.

I glanced around behind me to see if there was anyone else on the street. Someone to hear me scream, someone to come to my rescue when I didn't come back out. There wasn't anyone. I wonder how many people have gone into this store never to be heard of again. Perhaps he used an axe to chop... Oh, stop it Molly. Swallowing the dread rising up in my throat, I went in.

Chapter 19
My Nice New Neighbor?

It took me a few minutes for my eyes to adjust to the light in the store. It was quite a change to go from the glaring sunshine to the dimly lit store. A few brave rays of sunshine managed to find their way in through the front window. Dancing in each ray were thousands and thousands of dust particles. It was actually rather pretty. He let the door fall behind us. He did not lock it. Believe me, I was watching.

Tools hung on every surface. I don't know a lot about hardware stores, but from what I could tell, there was a certain order to the store. I don't know why, but that surprised me. Hammers hung on the far wall. Other types of tools hung everywhere else. There were drawers and drawers and drawers filled to overflowing with almost every kind of nut and bolt imaginable. Upon closer inspection, I noticed that, strangely enough, they went from little too big, regardless of type. Dust hung close in the air, but I could imagine that tools are a naturally dusty thing to have in a store. I think the store was smaller than Carolyn's but every square foot of space was being used. Vacuum cleaners, brooms, mops, pails, cleaning utensils of every sort, and the chemicals that went with them. I noticed that there weren't any of those pesky modern mops or brooms. Just the good old-fashioned kind. Despite the dust, everything was very clearly in its place. Strange.

I walked all the way to the back of the store. "What a nice store," I finally managed.

He grunted. Either he didn't agree or he was being humble. It was hard to tell which.

"Well, I surely don't want to take up anymore of your time, Mr. Morrie," I said. "Thank you for the tour of your store."

Instead of answering me, he walked past me to the back room. There was no door to separate the two rooms, just a curtain. A flowered curtain. Which was another strange thing because he didn't really strike me as being a flowered-curtain kind of guy. I wonder what he expected me to do now? Follow? Leave?

I decided to peek my head around the curtain and say goodbye. He was standing by a little table with a great big gleaming knife in his hand.

Chapter 20
This Is Getting Out Of Hand

If you're thinking that that wasn't a very nice place to end a story, you're probably right. Sorry. I couldn't help myself. Once in a while, it is important to indulge one's own flair for the dramatic. Try it yourself sometime.

Then again, it really was a good place to end things because nothing much happened after that. And that's really the truth. I had clearly interrupted the socially-challenged Mr. Morrie's lunch, and as he was done giving me the grand tour, he went back to chopping his luncheon meat. I have no idea what it was, but it was a big roll of some kind of sausage that curled all over the table. I left very, very soon after that. And that was the end of my great adventure at the hardware store.

I wish I could say that the knife-wielding, crazy man who owned the hardware store next door was the strangest thing that happened for the rest of the week. But, that would not be true. I wish I could say that things at Carolyn's smoothed out a little bit, but that wasn't true either. I wish I could say that Louise was finally warming up to me. But, that would not only be untrue – it would be a miracle. And, I didn't really expect a miracle, at least not this week.

Unfortunately, the only thing our knitters could do was talk about the "other" yarn store opening. Funny, isn't it? Less than two weeks of working at Crabapple Yarns, and I was already referring to them as "our" knitters. The atmosphere could only be described as a disconcerting mix of apprehension and excitement. I watched them with a wary eye and wondered what I would do if I were in their shoes. What made it worse was that they talked about it at Carolyn's store. Oh, don't get me wrong – they didn't exactly say anything to her face, but it was very obvious in the way everyone would stop talking as soon as Carolyn was within hearing range. I don't know which was worse, the gossiping or the sympathetic looks. It was like everyone had already decided that Carolyn was going to have to close the store. I couldn't stand it.

On a stranger note, the Knitting Fairy was also stepping up her game. Old Mrs. Harrison (seriously, I'm not being rude; that's what everyone calls her), came in on Monday with a very perplexed look on her face. She headed straight for the sock yarn, picked up a ball and plunked it down on the counter. I ventured forth with a timid greeting. She stared at me for several seconds. "What does everyone call me around here?" she asked in voice that was surprisingly strong for a little old lady. Her frail hands were paper thin, each vein clearly visible. Her wispy hair didn't even pretend to be set in a hairstyle, and her mouth was set in a grim line.

"Excuse me?" I asked.

"What does everyone call me around here?" she said again, clearly impatient with me.

Oh, boy. This could get ugly. "Err...Mrs. Harrison?" I said with some hesitation. I heaved a sigh and wished that Carolyn would come and rescue me. Most people think that heroes ride white horses and dress in chain armor. I knew that they didn't. They were about five feet tall with white hair and long noses. Where was she, anyways? Getting coffee? Couldn't she tell that I needed her?

She snorted and one hand banged on the counter. "Nonsense, girl," she said. "Everyone calls me 'Old Mrs. Harrison' don't they?"

What was I supposed to say? What would you say? "Well—" I said, "If they do call you that I am sure that it is only done in kindness...or jest—"

She snorted again, this time in laughter. "I don't care that they call me that," she guffawed. "It was always kinda funny before."

"And now it's not?"

She turned serious. "No, it's not. It's not funny at all. I think I might be losing my mind."

Finally, a knitter who realized that she was crazy.

She leaned as far across the counter as her bent back would allow. "Something has been knitting my socks," she whispered. Her wizened little face peered up at me from behind her spectacles.

"Something has been knitting your socks?" I dropped my head as well holding her eyes with mine. "What do you mean?"

Her voice dropped even lower. "Three days ago, I noticed that the sock I was working on suddenly had a turned heel." She paused for emphasis. "And then, on Saturday, I realized that the toe on the other sock had been kitchenered." She looked over her glasses at me. "And, honey, I know that I didn't do that, because I always save the toes and kitchener both socks at once."

Could there really be a Knitting Fairy? Had the Knitting Fairy struck again? I couldn't help but frown at the thought. Was there really something to the idea? Why on earth would someone be going around knitting on other people's projects? It was really almost unthinkable. No, it was ridiculous. Mass hysteria, perhaps.

"Perhaps you just don't remember turning your heel," I began.

She made a sharp gesture with her hand. "If I am that old that I don't remember turning my own heel, then I must be getting too old to knit." Oopsies. Unofficial Rule #1: Don't offend customers so that they never come back. Check.

I chewed my lower lip for a moment. "Perhaps a visitor—"

She cut me off again. It was an annoying habit. When I get old, I will make sure I don't get rude and cut people off mid-sentence. "Shucks, girl," she said, "if I had a visitor, I certainly wouldn't be neglecting them long enough that they could knit a whole heel and then kitchener a toe together. What kind of person do you think I am, anyways?" Unofficial Rule #1 was a real pain sometimes, because, clearly, she found me annoying as well.

Well, that was just fine with me. Maybe then she would just go away and leave me alone. It takes forever to knit socks anyways. If she was really losing her mind, she wouldn't

139

remember she was mad at me by the time she was done. Ha! Take that Unofficial Rule #1.

She paid for her sock yarn, and I could have just let the conversation end right there. I could have thrown her sock yarn into a bag and wished her a nice day. And, I don't think that there would have been anything wrong with that. But then, she would have left feeling pretty low, and I would have felt guilty. And I hated feeling guilty. I could see that she didn't believe that she had knitted her socks, and there was no way she was going to believe that someone had knitted her socks for her. And, really, I wasn't too keen on pushing the idea either. I didn't really want her to think that someone had snuck into her house to knit on her socks. You didn't have to be an old lady to be afraid of thumps in the night. This I knew all too well.

I took my time tucking her sock yarn into the brightly colored plastic bag. There really was only one option. If it were mass hysteria, then what was one more person? "You know," I said slowly, "it sounds to me like you've been visited by the Knitting Fairy."

She blinked at me. "Excuse me?"

"I know it sounds a little strange, but odd things have been happening around here lately. Someone or something has been knitting other people's projects for them. We think it may be the work of the Knitting Fairy."

One frail hand tucked an errant strand of hair behind a wrinkled ear. She opened and closed her mouth several times. "You don't say," she finally said.

I bobbed my head. "I'm serious. We were the first vict-err...recipients. The Knitting Fairy knitted almost a foot on Carolyn's mohair scarf last week. Since then, she also picked up a dropped stitch for a beginner knitter. It's really strange. We have no idea how it happened."

A slow smile was spreading across her face. "The Knitting Fairy," she repeated, "how nice." She paused thoughtfully. "It's hard saying if you're serious or not. And I can't rightly say that I completely believe you. But, it does explain who's been knitting on my socks. When you get to be as

140

old as I am, even something as strange as the Knitting Fairy won't surprise you anymore." She patted my hand affectionately, "You're a sweet girl," she said. "Perhaps I will leave my sweater out tonight. I hate sewing seams."

There was a little glint in her eye, and I knew that from now on she would be on the lookout for the Knitting Fairy. Good. Maybe she could catch it and put it in a jar and bring it in. We could set it out on the counter for everyone to see. I bet Happy Knits wouldn't have a Knitting Fairy on their counter.

A loud honking startled us both apart. "Oh my goodness gracious," she said, "I forgot all about Harold."

Ah, perfect. A way to steer the conversation away from her knitting. "Someone is waiting for you?" I asked, looking out the front window. I could see a large pick-up truck with its lights on.

"Oh," she said, waving her hand in dismissal, "that's just Harold. I swear that boy has an internal clock like nothing you've never seen before. He can get so annoying sometimes. He only gives me five minutes when I visit here before he starts honking the horn. That was just the warning toot."

I could understand that. I had seen several men waiting outside for their wives last week. I wondered if they were afraid of catching yarn cooties. I smiled. "Harold is your husband?" I asked.

She guffawed and smacked her hand on the counter again. "Shucks, no, girl," she said, grabbing her bag of sock yarn, "Harold's my golden retriever."

Golden retriever?

The horn honked again – this time with a little more emphasis. With a surprisingly quick step, she hurried towards the floor. "Thanks for your help, honey," she yelled back to me. "I'll let you know if the Knitting Fairy sews up my seams for me."

The ladies sitting on the couches all looked up in amusement as Old Mrs. Harrison stopped to say goodbye to them.

Had she really said golden retriever?

I rushed towards the window. I had to hop over a knitter to get there (which was a little bit dangerous because she was knitting with a really long needles.) It's a good thing I'm a good hopper. That could have ended very badly.

I looked out into the street. It was somewhat startling to see a canine face peering intently out of the front window over the steering wheel. I don't know if dogs can get annoyed or not, but Harold did not look pleased. His great head swiveled one way and then another. Both paws were on the dashboard, and I watched as he slowly lowered one paw to the steering wheel. The honking was loud, insistent, and seemed to go on forever. I choked back a laugh. He looked very serious. Harold was staring at the door, almost as if he were willing her to come out.

"Lands sakes alive," Old Mrs. Harrison said, with her hand on the door handle, "I'm gonna leave that dog home next time."

From the tone of her voice, I don't think that would ever happen. Old Mrs. Harrison shuffled outside and clambered into the driver's side of the old pick-up truck. Harold practically attacked her, giving her dog kisses as if they had been apart for years. She patted Harold roughly on the head a few times, and his eyes rolled with happiness. With the air of someone who is rewarding an obedient child, Harold put his nose up in the air and scooted over to the other side of the truck where he sat at attention in the passenger seat. I was actually a little bit surprised that he did not put his seat belt on. Seeing me in the window, Old Mrs. Harrison gave the horn a farewell toot and, engine roaring, threw the car in reverse and out into the street.

Hopping back over the knitter once more (she very kindly laid her needles down this time), I made my way back to the counter where Carolyn was standing. Without warning, she threw her arms around me and gave me a bone-cracking hug. Carolyn did not have personal space issues. I patted her shoulder uncomfortably.

"What is this for?" I asked.

She pulled away from me and wiped a tear from her eye. "That was just the sweetest thing you said to Old Mrs. Harrison," she said.

My mind was still on the car-horn-honking dog. "What do you mean?"

"Why, telling her it was the Knitting Fairy that finished her project for her. That was very, very sweet of you."

I shrugged, still uncomfortable. "It wasn't really anything."

"Oh, but it was," she said, "you probably don't know about this yet, but once you get a certain age, you start realizing that you've lived most of your life already and you start thinking about the fact that you're getting too old. And then, little things start happening, and you start wondering how much longer you can do everything you've been doing up until now. And then, something happens, and you think maybe you are getting old and senile. And just when you think you should give it all up, someone comes along and smooths the way. And you think that just maybe, you can keep going."

Were we still talking about Mrs. Harrison?

She patted my cheek. "Thank you, my dear," she said, "you made Old Mrs. Harrison feel a lot better."

Whew. Life at the library sure had been boring. With a sigh, I went back to what surely would be my destiny in life – re-sorting the sock yarn.

Louise chose that moment to come out of the back room, blowing past me so fast, that, as I was already halfway bent over, I finished my descent to the ground a bit faster than I would have liked, knocking into the sock yarn shelf and causing every skein to fall off. I gaped at her galloping back. That was rude. And she wasn't even supposed to be here. It was her day off. The Rat. Either she felt the weight of my stare or else she wanted to survey her handiwork, because she turned around with a large scowl of her own.

"Is something wrong Louise?" I asked timidly. What? I think you should know by now that I'm a little, tiny bit weak around aggressive people.

She snarled. "You'll be sorry to know that it didn't work."

"What didn't work?"

"Don't play stupid with me," she hissed, "you know very well what I mean. It's just a good thing I stopped by and figured it out before everyone else had a chance to die."

The nice little burst of righteous indignation was rapidly dying, only to be replaced by a feeling of impending doom. "I'm sorry, Louise," I said, "but I really don't know what you're talking about."

She licked her lips as if she were tasting something bad. "Well, then... I guess you didn't make the coffee this morning either."

"No," I said, "I did make the coffee this morning. I'm sorry. Did I make it the wrong way?" Carolyn's coffee pot was an extremely complicated little sucker. And sometimes I forgot to put the coffee grounds in.

"I could take it to the police, you know," she said, stepping forward threateningly, "and have it analyzed. Then, we'd know for sure what exactly you were trying to poison us with."

Poison? Poison?

"Now Louise," Carolyn said sharply, coming out of the back room quickly, "I told you not to mention this to anyone."

"Was something wrong with the coffee, Carolyn?" I asked, bewildered and just a tiny bit afraid.

"It had a funny taste," she admitted, looking down her long nose at me still sitting on the floor, "but I'm sure you had nothing to do with that. It was a new container of coffee. Perhaps there was something wrong with it."

Louise snorted. "Yeah. Like it was poisoned."

"It was not poisoned, and we will not talk about this anymore," Carolyn said firmly. "The coffee grounds were bad, and I've thrown them away. Everything will be fine. Good bye Louise," she said. "Enjoy the rest of your day off."

Louise snorted again and headed out the door while waving to the ladies up front as she left. Good riddance. My thoughts returned to the coffee. Poisoned? Could it be?

Carolyn placed her hand on my head. "Everything will be fine," she repeated, "don't worry. Louise is a little high strung sometimes. I'm sure if you were trying to poison us you'd have the sense to make it taste a bit better so we'd actually drink it."

That was very reassuring.

Not ten minutes later, Jean, one of the knitters sitting up front, gave a great shriek, startling me from my sock sorting. I jumped to my feet. Thank goodness I had the sense to jump backwards to my feet and managed to miss knocking over the sock yarn for the second time today. Carolyn also came rushing out from the back of the store. The other knitters sitting around the circle were staring at Jean with open mouths and wide eyes – their own knitting forgotten. That doesn't happen every day.

"Jean!" Carolyn exclaimed. "Whatever is the matter?"

Jean was holding her knitting bag on her lap with a sheet of paper in one hand and a circular needle with some stitches on it in her other hand. She looked back and forth from her paper to her needle. Then she looked accusingly at the other knitters.

"Alright," she said, "who did it?" Wow. There was an actual snarl at the end of that.

No one replied. I think we were all in shock – either from the snarl or the shriek. Strange. Jean was usually such a nice, little knitter.

Rachel made a small movement and looked like she was about to speak. Jean turned on her in an instant, holding her circular needle like a weapon. "Rachel! I should have known it was you. How could you do this?" She shook the circular needle violently in front of Rachel's face.

Rachel closed her mouth. She looked helplessly at Carolyn and then back at Jean. "I-I—" She started scooting backwards on the sofa. I didn't blame her. For just one second, sweet, little Jean looked pretty dangerous. What is it that they say? Every person is capable of murder given the right circumstances? Perhaps knitting was Jean's boiling point. I wondered whether any of the women here knew any self-defense moves. Instead of knitting classes, perhaps Carolyn should

145

teach people how to defend themselves against irate knitters. It was definitely something to think about.

"What exactly is it ·that you're upset about, dear?" Carolyn asked. "Let's just—"

Jean dropped her circular needle to her lap, and the knitters around the circle breathed a sigh of relief. It was hard to tell if they were relieved that she wasn't going to hurt anyone with her needle or they were worried about her dropping stitches. With knitters, it's also hard to tell which they think is worse.

Jean's face crumpled and she looked like she was going to burst into tears. When she spoke, it was in a halting voice, choked with emotion. "My...my...you know I wanted to...I can't believe...I didn't get the chance—" She picked up her circular needle again and twisted it around and around in her hands.

With a graceful motion, Carolyn shooed Rachel from her seat next to Jean and put a motherly arm around the other woman. "Now, Jean," she said, "calm down. What has gotten you so upset?"

I looked around the store discretely. Thankfully, there weren't any other customers right now. We wouldn't want to scare anybody away.

Jean took a deep breath and tried to meet Carolyn's sympathetic gaze. She gulped and could not quite stop the little sob building in her throat. We probably should have all stepped back and let her have some space, but we didn't. We stayed. And stared. We were mystified and couldn't have cared less if we looked rude.

Abbey didn't even put her knitting down. She just sat there with her hands poised in mid-air, right in the middle of a row of knitting. I couldn't help but wonder if, when all of this was over, she would remember where she was in her pattern. I hoped it wouldn't take too long. She was going to get a cramp sitting like that.

Taking a deep, shuddering breath, Jean calmed down enough to look a little embarrassed by her outburst.

"I apologize for getting so carried away," she said, "but I'm just so upset." Her hands were still twisting the circular needle in her hands. "I was saving this," she said, "and I was so looking forward to casting on, and now everything is just...just...ruined." It was quite a good wail.

Hmmm. We all looked around the room at each other. I still didn't have a clue, and by the looks on the other faces, no one else did either.

Carolyn very carefully took the needle away from Jean and inspected it closely. Jean was reluctant to let it go, but Carolyn gently pried her fingers away. She was such a brave woman. "Well," she said in surprise, "Jean, I didn't know you were planning on making a moebius."

Well, that did it. Jean burst into tears. And, figuring that as long as Jean was crying, they wouldn't miss anything, the other ladies also burst into speech.

"I remember my first moebius," Abby said, "I had a terrible time trying to cast on."

"I love my moebius shawl," Rachel said, "I wear it all of the time. It's just right for spring weather."

I wondered what the heck a moebius was. It sounded like some kind of medical condition. Like something that might itch. I would have to look it up on the internet tonight. I wonder how you spell it?

And then, bless her beginner-knitter, little heart, Sarah spoke up. "What's a moebius?" she asked innocently. Perfect. Now I would know too. I waited expectantly for the answer and looked naively around the little cluster of knitters. Then... reality sank in.

Uh-oh. Were they all looking at me? Oh dear. My heart began pounding in my ears. Oh dear. They were waiting for me to answer, weren't they? Weren't they? Oh dear. They were.

The jig was up.

"A moebius is a circular piece of knitting with only one edge," Carolyn said calmly. "Like a twisted circle, a never ending loop. It's quite amazing."

147

My heart leapt with relief. Once again, Carolyn had saved me. Of course, I still had no idea what a moebius was (I mean – what kind of explanation was that anyways?), but hey, at least everyone stopped looking at me.

Jean tried to pull herself together again. "That was the yarn I bought in England last summer. I was saving it for something special. And then, when I saw that moebius pattern this winter, I knew that's what I was going to make with it. I have just the right amount of yarn. I wanted to try and learn the cast on so badly, but I had promised myself that I would finish my cabled sweater first. So many times I almost started it, but I didn't. I waited. I finished my sweater yesterday. I was going to start it today. And now it's all ruined." It was the wail again. A person with a howl as good as that one must spend a lot of time practicing.

We were staring again.

"But why is it ruined?" Carolyn asked gently. "Your cast on looks perfect."

Jean covered her face with her hands, "Because it's not my cast on," she sobbed. "Someone else did it."

I met Carolyn's eyes. I knew what she was thinking. The Knitting Fairy. This was getting out of hand.

Chapter 21

I Am Not One Of "Those" Knitters

By the time Carolyn had gotten Jean settled back down, it was well after lunch. Granted, Jean was still very upset that someone (or something) had taken her beautiful yarn and stolen her cast-on fun. But Carolyn had very calmly taken the stitches back off the needle and wound the yarn back onto the ball. Jean was still not happy. The yarn was now "wrinkly." She was going to go home and iron it. Carolyn quickly talked her out of this and began teaching her the moebius cast on. She explained to Jean that when you are learning a completely new technique like this, it's better to do it several times in a row anyways to really get it into your head. "So," Carolyn said, "it doesn't matter if someone else did it first because you would probably do it over again a couple of times yourself anyways." That smooth-talking Carolyn. At least Jean had stopped crying.

Carolyn and Jean were almost through the moebius cast on for the second time when Helen burst through the door. "Sorry I'm late, ladies," she said cheerfully, unwrapping her scarf from around her throat. "Did I miss anything?"

Everyone quickly looked down at their knitting. I had to turn away to hide my smile.

I loved life at Crabapple Yarns. Especially on days when Louise wasn't working.

Oddly enough, besides our knitting friends and the drama that came in the door with them, we were really quite slow today. I decided to take advantage of the slowness and knit a little more on my...ummm... Alright. Before I go further, I should explain something. Now, let's just take a step back here. Don't be jumping to conclusions and get the wrong idea. I am not one of THOSE knitters. Really, I'm not. I still firmly believe in one project at a time. But, you see, what happened is that I really wanted to re-pay Ryan for his kindness, and being the experienced knitter that I am, I thought that the nicest thing I could do would be to knit him something. That's not a crazy idea, is it? The only problem is that I had already started my sweater. By the time I got that done it would be way past scarf-wearing time, and so it was imperative that I start the scarf even though I wasn't done with my sweater. Doesn't that make sense?

Let's just be perfectly clear. I didn't have two projects going at the same time because I wanted to – it's because I had to. See, there's a big difference between me and those other knitters. You're not laughing, are you?

Anyway, like I was saying. I decided to take advantage of the slow day to do a little work on Ryan's scarf. It was a beautiful yarn. It was alpaca. Yeah, sigh, alpaca. Whenever I worked on it, the only word that I could think of was "delicious."

It sure was working up nicely, too. I was doing it in a pattern called seed stitch. It was easy, but I still had to concentrate on each row so I didn't get the pattern wrong. Believe me, un-knitting was a real pain.

The doorbell did not ring to let another customer in for the rest of the day. On the bright side, Jean had caught on to the moebius cast on quite nicely and was making good headway on her scarf. At least it seemed that way. It was hard to tell since it really didn't look like much. But the wailing had stopped, so that was progress.

It must have been close to 2:00 in the afternoon when Rachel approached me, her footsteps hesitant across the plush rug. She leaned against the counter, looking thoughtful. Today she was wearing a crocheted spring tunic of lavender over a white turtleneck. It was still cold outside. Her golden hair shone under the lights of the store, and her face was calm, but there was an expression in her eyes that didn't match her bright clothes.

"What's the matter, Rachel?" I asked. "You look troubled."

Her face cleared instantly, and she looked like her old self again. "Do I?" she asked. "Maybe." She hesitated again.

"Actually," she said, "I am a little bit troubled. I heard something from another knitter, and I don't quite know how to say this."

My fingers were itching to begin another row of knitting. It would be rude to start another row when someone was talking to me, wouldn't it? Or, would it? After all, she was a knitter too. She might think it was strange if I didn't. Perhaps it was a knitter's rule that you should talk and knit at the same time. Would she realize that I wasn't a real knitter if I didn't? But, could I even handle knitting and talking at the same time? Perhaps now might be the perfect time to find out. Or, perhaps I should have been listening to Rachel. She had been talking for quite a while now.

"I'm sorry, Rachel," I said. "My mind was wandering. What did you say?"

She gave a little huff. "I knew you weren't listening."

"I was listening," I protested. "I just didn't hear what you said." I gave her a little grin, and she couldn't help but grin back. "Please tell me what you were saying."

Pushing a strand of hair out of her face, she said, "Well, if you're going to listen this time, I'll tell you again." She leaned over the counter. "I was trying to tell you that I've been hearing things."

"What kind of things?"

She frowned, "That's just the problem," she said. "It's nothing that I believe, mind you, just things that I have been hearing."

"What kinds of things?" I asked again.

"Things about Carolyn," she admitted. "People are saying that she's going out of business."

"That's just ridiculous," I said indignantly. "She is not going out of business just because there's another yarn store opening in town. There are plenty of places with more than one yarn store, and they seem to get along just fine." That wasn't entirely true. Well, it might have been true, but then again, I really had no way of knowing. Since Crabapple Yarns was the first yarn store I had ever seen, I really had no idea if other towns had more than one or not. But, Rachel seemed to believe it. So, I guess it worked.

She nodded, "I know. But, that's not what I was talking about."

"Then, what kinds of things do you mean?"

"People are saying that Carolyn is doing something—" she laughed nervously. "This is so ridiculous. I can't believe that I'm even telling you."

"Well, now that you've started, please finish."

"They say that she's involved in something illegal."

I stared hard at Rachel. Waiting for her to say, "Ha, ha, just kidding." But she didn't.

"Something illegal," I repeated softly, "what exactly does that mean?"

"I have no idea," Rachel admitted with a shrug. "That's the only thing I've heard. People tend to clam up when I'm around because they know how close I am with Carolyn." There were tears shining in her eyes.

"But, that's just ridiculous," I protested. "Carolyn isn't...she wouldn't—"

Rachel made a quick gesture to keep my voice down. "I know that," she whispered fiercely. "But, I just thought you should know. So you could keep your ears open too."

We both looked at Carolyn, sitting over on the couch with Jean. In the sunshine filtering in through the front window, she looked a little pale. "Who did you hear this from?" I asked quietly. I don't know what a shy librarian could possibly do to a rumor-spreading knitter, but I was determined to go and do it. I did have long pointy needles after all.

Rachel shrugged her shoulders and backed away from the counter. "I really don't want to say," she said quietly. "But I am going to keep my ears open from now on. I'll let you know if I hear anything else."

"You do that," I said.

Chapter 22
In Which We Are Almost Squished Like A Bug

On Tuesday morning the only snow left on the ground was the stubborn snow that lingered in the corner of the parking lot at the grocery store. I hate that kind of snow. It's depressing. Why does it have to look so dirty? Why doesn't it just melt with the other snow? It's unnatural how long it can last. Isn't it strange how something that fell to the earth in great sheets of white downy flakes ends up shoved to the side, grey with grime? At one point, they had been eagerly anticipated and welcomed, and now they were now shunned and isolated. It didn't even look like snow anymore. It didn't even look cold anymore. Like I said, it was depressing. I hoped it wasn't a life lesson.

My thoughts were not exactly cheerful as Ryan skillfully navigated our path to the store. Yes, he was still my self-appointed chaperone. He didn't say much. He just showed up at my door in the morning and waited for me to hop in.

Despite the fact that I did enjoy not being chased through the downtown area by rampaging vans, I was a little bit resentful of the fact I had lost my freedom. Yet another reason to be glum.

And, did I mention that Happy Knits would be opening early? Yeah, that exciting news reached us just before we closed yesterday. Apparently, the grand opening would be on Saturday. Rumor had it that they had classes already lined up for every day of the week.

Perhaps another one of the reasons for my cheerful mood was the fact that Louise would be joining us at work today. A truckload of spring yarn was expected to arrive, and Carolyn said that she could use all of the help she could get with putting it all on the shelf. I couldn't help but wonder how many times Louise would re-arrange the yarn that I arranged. Luckily for me, Rachel would be there, too. At least I would have someone else to talk to if Carolyn was too busy. Then again, I would also have another pair of eyes on me, too. I would have to be very careful.

By mid-morning, we were all worn to a frazzle. I didn't even have time to go and get my morning cinnamon roll. What a terrible day. You know how sometimes when you get up in the morning and you just know that everything that could possibly go wrong today will, and you really wish you could stay in bed? Next time I have that feeling, I think I will – stay in bed, I mean.

I was a nervous wreck. Working with Louise was turning me into a quivering bag of anxiety.

The big order had come in, just as Carolyn had predicted. And since we were so slow yesterday when we had nothing to do, it only made sense in the grand cosmic scheme of things that today we would be hopping busy – which we were.

The customers were giddy with excitement to see the new yarns and everyone rushed at the boxes, trying to pull this and that out at the same time. Apparently, this was a yearly tradition. How (and why) Carolyn let this happen was completely beyond me. It was utter chaos. To make matters worse, Louise talked Carolyn into letting me put the price tag labels on the new yarn. Carolyn had waved her hand in agreement and went to help a customer. Louise turned to me and said that she didn't think that even I could screw this one up.

Well, apparently I could.

And did.

It was only one bag, but still, with the amount of fuss that Louise made over it, you would have thought that I had committed a terrible crime against humanity or something. I honestly don't know how it happened. It was the bamboo yarn that did it to me. The funny thing is that all of these years, I thought bamboo was just something that pandas ate. Who knew it could be turned into yarn? What in the world possesses people to turn something like that into yarn? Who even thinks of things like that? It's not like there's a shortage of sheep in the world so that knitters need to seek alternate sources. One could only hope that there weren't starving pandas out there crying because their bamboo had been turned into yarn. It's not like you could give it back – as I seriously doubt that the bamboo yarn was suitable for eating anymore.

Anyway, like I said, the bamboo yarn came in five different variegated colors. It was just gorgeous. And very, very, very soft. It was also hypoallergenic and antibacterial. Rachel had said that to me like I should be impressed. But, I couldn't really see how important that could be. It's not like you were going to eat off of your sweater. Or perform surgery with it. I could see Doctor Louise now, "Nurse, pass me the 07 bamboo...No, not color 05, I said color 07, who labeled these, anyway?" But, now, I am getting ahead of myself.

To the inexperienced eye, the colors all looked very similar. Allow me to clarify – to *my eye*, they all looked alike. And, since various customers had pulled the poor innocent skeins from their packaging and not put them back properly, I accidently stuck a color 07 label on a color 05 skein. Yeah. The horror of it all. Louise probably wouldn't be able to sleep tonight.

After that, I was demoted to cash register duty for as long as there were customers in the store. She was actually quite rude about it. It was very embarrassing. After the last of the customers had left and Carolyn flipped the closed sign over, I was once again allowed to join yarn duty. My new job was putting the yarn on the shelf. Don't worry – I couldn't possibly goof this one up. Louise had very kindly put little sticky notes on all the shelves of what went where. She was so sweet.

Darkness was already upon us by the time we were done with the last bag of yarn. We were all drooping with exhaustion. Carolyn called for take-out, and we all crammed into the back room with our plates heaping. We shut the door. We were tired of looking at yarn. I looked yearningly at the door that led upstairs. If I was living here, I would be almost home. That sounded really good.

I had my feet up on the rungs of Carolyn's chair. She had her feet up on the rungs of Rachel's chair. Rachel sat with her feet tucked under her Indian-style, and Louise sat straight up in a very ladylike manner. It couldn't have been more crowded with all of us, but yet, it felt very homey. Well, except for Louise's presence.

We were full. Stuffed, actually. Lethargy had set in. I yawned and wondered where I would find the energy to get up and go home. Rachel was the first to move.

"Oh, my goodness," Rachel exclaimed out of the blue, "I almost forgot. I have a gift for you, Molly."

My ears perked up a little. "A present? For me?" I asked. "What is it?"

She grinned. "If I told you then it wouldn't be a surprise, now would it?"

"Is it your empty plate?" I asked with a smirk. "Do I get the gift of doing dishes tonight?"

"Don't be silly," she said, "it's my turn to do dishes. Why do you think we're eating off of paper plates?" Rachel patted her pockets. "Darn," she said. "I left it in the car." She unfolded her legs with a groan. "Well, it doesn't look like you guys are going anywhere soon, so I'll be right back." She was serious. She really did have a present for me. Nice. Strange, but nice.

Walking on stiff legs, she headed for the door that separated the back room from the front room.

Carolyn also swung her legs off of the chair rungs with a small groan. "Oh dear," she said, "I think I left the extra labels on top of the sock yarn shelf."

I put my hand out. "Don't get up, Carolyn," I said. "I'll go and get it." That sock yarn was going to be the death of me.

I had no idea how right that statement would almost prove to be.

I pushed open the door between the front room and the back room, letting it swing shut behind me. That was funny. I didn't remember turning the overhead lights off in the store. Carolyn had probably done so when we went in the back room. Too bad the light switch was all the way across the room. With a shrug, I decided that there was enough light from the little twinkle lights that were still on so that I could make my way over to the sock yarn shelf with little effort. It's not like I didn't know where that stinking little display was anyways. For the hundredth time, I wondered why on earth anyone would want to go so much work to knit socks.

I was halfway across the room when I felt a prickling at the back of my neck. Have you ever read that statement in a book and wondered what it felt like? Let me tell you – it is not a nice feeling. I paused and stood still for a moment, listening and straining my eyes in the darkness. Nothing. Maybe it was time to turn on the overhead lights.

Keeping one hand on the shelving against the wall, I made my way as fast as I could to the front of the store and the light switch.

A sudden crack pierced the air. I jumped, my breath catching in my throat as there was a great groaning and the sound of creaking wood. It was hard to tell where the sound had come from, but as I looked around, it seemed like everything was happening in slow motion. The great massive bookcase to my right was shifting in its tracks. It almost looked alive. Like a great black bear shaking off its winter sleep. It was falling over.

Horrified, I realized that it was coming towards me. I had nowhere to go. It was too late to go back, and there was no way I could move forward quick enough. Thankfully, my body seemed to know what to do even when my brain was frozen. I threw myself down on the floor as close to the wall as I could get. Yarn poured over me like rain. I covered my head with my hands. It sounded like the world was caving in around me. The bookcase crashed into the shelving on the wall behind me. Wood splintered. Something hard hit me behind my shoulder blade, and I let out a little cry.

There was the sound of running feet. Through the chaos, I felt a blast of cold air hit me as the front door opened and closed.

More running feet came into the room, and I heard Carolyn cry out. The lights came on, and they were blinding in their sudden brightness.

"Molly!" Her voice was filled with shock and concern. "Where are you?"

I didn't dare move. I could feel the bookcase literally inches away from my body. Even talking loud might move it.

"Molly!" Carolyn called again, and this time she was joined by another voice.

"Good Heavens. What happened?" That was Louise.

"Oh my goodness!" I could hear Rachel come back inside and there was another cold blast of air. "What on earth happened? I heard a crash—"

"Molly!" Carolyn said, her voice becoming frantic. "Please!"

I managed to find my voice. "It's alright, Carolyn," I said with as much calm as I could find buried under the skeins of fallen yarn, and a bookcase that just might crush me like a bug. "I'm alright."

I could hear Rachel's sharp intake of breath. "Molly's under there?" she asked, her voice shaking. "Oh my goodness, we have to get her out."

Louise's voice was sharp and dry as usual. "Rachel," she said, "get a hold of yourself and grab the other side of the bookcase."

"Be careful, girls," Carolyn warned.

They tried shifting the bookcase, and I let out a little scream as I felt it slide a little farther down the wall. My triangle of free space was getting smaller. If it came down any more, I would be squished.

"Stop!" Carolyn yelled, "This is not going to work. Rachel, run out and see if Mr. Morrie is home. Then see if Ryan is still at the bakery."

From my limited vantage point, I could crane my neck and just barely see the bottom crack of the door. I watched it open and Rachel's tennis shoes run out. I could hear Carolyn and Louise moving around in the room.

The dust from the floorboards was tickling my nose. I willed myself not to sneeze. It would be very unfortunate to have been spared from being crushed only to sneeze and crush myself. Very unfortunate, especially for me. There was a skein of mohair right by my forehead. It really wasn't helping. Mohair is beautiful and gorgeous and incomparable when life is normal, but when you're trapped under a bookcase, it's itchy and makes you want to sneeze and rub your eyes. I pictured its fibers snaking its little tentacles of adorable fuzz over the ground to my nose.

I sneezed and then held my breath in horror. But nothing moved.

I craned my neck again to look out the little triangle that was now the center of my universe. I could see Carolyn's shoes. For some reason, that made me feel better. She knelt down and peered under the bookcase without touching it. "Molly, dear," she said, "are you alright?"

I managed to give her a small smile. "I think so, Carolyn," I said, "but I'm a little bit scared."

"I'm scared too," she confided. "If it makes you feel any better, I'm praying as fast as I can."

I tried lifting my foot experimentally and only went up a couple of inches before I encountered the bookcase. Not much room. If it moved again - I gulped. Then again, the sneeze hadn't shaken anything else loose. I wondered if I could somehow slither out. I tried shifting my body to the left a little, and above me, the bookcase gave a little shudder.

"For heaven's sakes," Carolyn cried, "lay still!"

Sometimes, she is just so bossy. But, for this one time, I decided to listen.

It seemed like forever and there was still no sign of Rachel, or anyone else, for that matter. Now that I knew I could sneeze without punishment, the urge was completely gone, which left room for a new emotion. Claustrophobia. It was beginning to set in, and I could hardly resist the urge to move. I just wanted to get out. Please God, I prayed, please let me out of here.

Mr. Morrie came running in first, followed closely by Ryan and Rachel. How could I tell? I could see their shoes too. He let out a word that shall not be re-printed here, and then said, "That little gal is under there?" in a voice that clearly didn't believe it.

"Molly?" Ryan said hoarsely, "call an ambulance. I can't believe you didn't—"

"I'm fine," I said as loud as I could, "But I would really, really, really like to get out of here."

Mr. Morrie's shoes went past me and I heard them go to the other side of the bookcase. "Ryan," he said and then more firmly, as if to get his attention, "Ryan. Grab a hold, right there and Louise, you stand here. Rachel," he said, "you stand by Ryan." His soft voice was surprisingly authoritative and everyone obeyed without question. Even Louise. If I ever got out of here, I would have to practice talking in that voice and see if Louise listened to me. "All right, Molly," he said, "don't move. We're going to get this off of you in no time."

I couldn't help the waver in my voice, "Alright."

"Carolyn," Mr. Morrie said in a softer undertone, "you just stay there and let us know if it's moving the wrong way."

Did he really think that I wouldn't hear that? My eyes shot up to Carolyn's concerned gaze, which was again peeking at me through the crack by the floor. Her eyes were steady and reassuring. If I live to be a hundred years old, I will always remember Carolyn's calm eyes.

"On the count of three," Mr. Morrie said, "One, two...three." The bookcase creaked and groaned again – so did the four people trying to lift it. And then, the bookcase was standing up straight again.

It was a miracle.

I struggled to my knees and Carolyn was next to me in an instant. Yarn tumbled off of my back in a little waterfall of fiber. I felt a brief twinge of regret. We had spent so long getting the shelves perfect. Now everything was a mess again. At least we didn't have to put the price tag stickers on again. Carolyn's hands were surprisingly strong as she helped me to my feet. She was watching my face anxiously. To my utter humiliation, my knees wouldn't support me, and I was very grateful to Mr.

160

Morrie as he whipped a chair from around the oak table and slid it under me. I wilted onto it.

"Are you alright?" Rachel asked. I looked up at her. Her face was white and drawn. "Oh my goodness, Molly, I was so scared." She was scared? I didn't see her under the bookcase.

"I'm fine." I was getting a little tired of saying that. But, it seemed that it was about all I could say. My throat was incredibly dry. I felt like laughing and crying.

Carolyn put her hand on my shoulder, and I winced before I could stop myself.

"You are hurt," she cried.

Every head in the store spun to stare at me. I hastened to reassure them. "Really, it's nothing. Something hit my shoulder when the bookcase fell. I'm fine."

"Probably the lamp," Ryan muttered, kicking it over with his foot.

"Oh, Molly! I am so sorry. I just can't believe that the bookcase would tip over like that." Carolyn was wringing her hands.

"Maybe it didn't," Ryan said darkly. He was still standing by the bookcase, surveying the damage with a critical eye.

The bookcase had stood toward the middle of the store and when it fell, it had fallen onto the shelving standing on the wall, breaking the shelves as it fell. Thankfully, the wall had stopped it from falling all the way to the ground. Although, had it moved backwards at all, it would have finished its great orbit to earth – and I would not be sitting here on the chair with only a bruise.

Mr. Morrie went to join Ryan. He pointed to something on the floor. Their heads were close together, and we could not hear what they said.

The good news was that my knees were no longer shaking. The bad news was that the rest of my body was. Louise went to the back room and returned with a cup of steaming tea.

"Drink this," she said curtly, "and maybe you'll stop shaking like a leaf." Somehow, even when she was being nice, it felt like she was criticizing.

I reached for the cup and found that it still shook slightly even when I was holding it with both hands. Carolyn rested her hand underneath mine for a moment, and I felt a little steadier. I looked up at her, but she had her eyes closed. "Thank you, Lord," she said softly.

Rachel was still pale, and she pulled some chairs out for the rest of them before sinking onto one herself. "You could have been killed," she whispered. Her eyes sought out Carolyn's. "I just can't believe it."

"I just don't know how something like this happened," Carolyn repeated. "It's just too hard to believe."

I don't know how to say this, Carolyn," she said, "but when I was outside by my car, I thought that I saw someone run out of your store."

Carolyn frowned. "Run out of the store?" She sank into one of the chairs that Rachel had retrieved and accepted a cup of tea from Louise as well. Her face was set in a grim line. "Then that means that someone did this on purpose."

"I'm afraid you're right," Mr. Morrie said. "There's a mark on the floor that looks like it was made with some kind of pry bar. A huge bookcase like that doesn't just move on its own. The mark doesn't look too fresh, though," he said thoughtfully, "but I would bet that it was done sometime in the last week."

"You're right," I said suddenly. "It had to be this week because I saw Ryan lean on it just last week, and it didn't move at all." Oops. Maybe I shouldn't have mentioned that right now.

Ryan met my gaze. "That's right, Molly," he said, "I remember that. It was last Friday." He ran a hand through his red hair and sighed. "And I was wrong for not saying something then."

Oh, rats. I knew it. Couldn't he see that now was certainly not the right time to go mentioning "the incident"? I shook my head warningly at him, but his expression was determined.

"What do you mean?" Carolyn asked.

"Do you want to tell them, Molly," he asked, "or should I?"

"There's nothing to tell," I said stubbornly. "There's absolutely no reason to upset everyone because my imagination got away from me."

"Do you think it was your imagination that made this bookcase tip over?" he shot back, looking angry. What he could be angry about, I had no idea. I wished everyone would just go home. I wished I was home. Right now. I wanted nothing more than to put my pajamas on and hide under my covers.

Rachel was looking back and forth between us. "I can't stand it," she cried, "will someone please just tell us what's going on? Molly, what happened last Friday?"

Instead of answering, I took a sip of my tea. It was very sweet. Just the way I liked it, actually.

Carolyn put her hand over mine once again. "Molly," she said softly, "I knew something was wrong last Friday morning. Why didn't you tell me then?"

My knees were shaking again. Was it possible that someone was actually trying to hurt me? Who would want to do that? Why would anyone want to do that? I looked over at the bookcase. It had shattered and splintered the shelves on the wall. It was so out of place in Carolyn's little peaceful store that it almost hurt your eyes to look at it. If I had been a little slower – or the bookcase had been sitting one foot farther away from the wall – it would have fallen right on top of me.

I couldn't see anymore. Not through the tears that had sprung to my eyes. What on earth was wrong with me? Now was not the time to cry. I sniffed and wiped them futilely with the back of my hand. Rachel handed me a tissue. I looked around the little group. They were still waiting for me to talk about the van, weren't they? "I didn't want to worry anyone," I said, "I was so sure that it was just my imagination." I looked up at Carolyn. "I was walking to work and I thought a van was following me." Her eyes widened, "But that's all that happened." I finished firmly. Perhaps the tears trickling down my face were not as reassuring as I would have liked.

She looked to Ryan for confirmation. His face was still grim. "I was coming out of my apartment and I saw Molly

163

running down the street. It was slippery, and so I called out to warn her. She didn't stop and so I followed her. She slipped and almost fell. I caught her. She was so scared that she didn't even realize it was me."

I stared at him. The tears stopped abruptly. The nerve of him. He made me sound like a big chicken. How dare he tell everyone? Especially in front of Carolyn? And Louise. I looked like a moron. I sent him a look, but he stubbornly refused to meet my gaze.

Rachel looked back and forth between us. "That's terrible," she said, "you could have hurt yourself."

I shrugged. "But I didn't. Everything turned out fine." I put on my best happy face and made a move to get up. It was time to get this mess cleaned up and get everyone out the door. Unfortunately, Rachel's hand on my arm set me back on the chair all too easily.

Carolyn put one hand to her head and sat back in her chair. Her beautiful face was lined with wrinkled concern. She looked old and worn and tired. Tears glittered in her eyes. "I just don't know what to do," she said.

I glared at Ryan. I didn't know why, but I was suddenly sure that this was all his fault. Why did he have to mention the van incident now? Talk about having bad timing.

Ryan didn't seem too upset by my glare. He merely glanced at me and turned his attention back to Carolyn. "Molly is right about one thing, Carolyn," he said softly. "Everything did turn out fine. If someone had wanted to hurt Molly on Friday, I think they would have had plenty of time to do so. But they didn't. Nobody got hurt. On Friday or tonight. Well," he amended with a small smile, "the bookcases are a little worse for wear, but we can fix them. And then we're going to get to the bottom of this."

"I for one don't see any possible reason why anyone would want to hurt Molly," Louise said sourly. "She doesn't do anything special."

For once I was happy to agree with her. "That's right," I said quickly, "I don't do anything special. The van incident was just a weird thing. I let my imagination get the best of me."

"But it doesn't explain the crowbar marks," Mr. Morrie said. Rats again. Men could really be a pain in the rear end sometimes. It was definitely time for him to go home, too. I just couldn't handle any more of this craziness.

Rachel looked down at her feet. "It could have been—"

"What?" I asked.

"What?" Louise asked.

"Who?" Ryan asked.

You'll notice that both Louise and I said, "What?" and Ryan said "Who?" That should tell you something about our state of mind.

"Well, you have to admit that some pretty weird things have been going on around here lately."

I rolled my eyes as did Carolyn. Louise just stared at Rachel. "You think that the Knitting Fairy tipped over the bookcase?" I couldn't help the sarcasm. "What do you think it used for a pry bar? Circular or straight needles?"

"I'm just saying that some weird things have been going on around here," Rachel repeated stubbornly. "And I don't think we can forget the fact that another knitting store is opening across town."

"Oh, please," Louise said crossly, "now we're going to blame the new yarn store?"

For some reason, this brightened Mr. Morrie's face. "Of course," he said, "your competition is trying to dishearten you."

Dishearten? Who talks like that? But...in some way, it did make sense. It was possible, I suppose, that evil knitters trying to take over Springgate by opening a super mega yarn store felt threatened by a little store named Crabapple Yarns and were trying to put it out of business by scaring their new employee half to death. Then again, maybe not.

Carolyn pulled herself up with a visible effort. "Well," she said slowly, "clearly we won't have any answers tonight." She glanced around the room firmly. "And we are certainly not cleaning up this mess tonight either."

I took a deep breath. "I think it's time I went home," I said, "I'm really tired."

"Me too," Rachel said. And, she did look exhausted. So did Carolyn.

Mr. Morrie stood up. "I'll be over in the morning to fix your shelves," he said. "We'll have it back together in no time."

"Thank you, Mr. Morrie," Carolyn said. "I don't know what we would have done without you and Ryan." She smiled at both of them. "Thank you."

Ryan drove me home. As I opened my front door, I realized what had been bothering me since I left Crabapple Yarns. Strangely enough, no one had suggested that we call the police.

Chapter 23
My Scandalous Thievery?

Carolyn had told me that she didn't want to see me until after lunch. I was only too happy to oblige. I didn't think that I would be able to sleep, but after a hot bath, I fell right into bed and didn't wake up until mid-morning.

I passed Louise going past the bakery. She glared at me so hard that I could only stammer a feeble good morning. She didn't reply. She just stalked right past me. I don't know what I was expecting, but for some reason, I had hoped that our situation yesterday would have bonded us a little. Hope springs eternal, they say. But hope is not always justified. And it looked like the hope spring was but a mere trickle today.

When I got to the store, there was evidence that Mr. Morrie had already been hard at work on the shelves. The broken ones had been taken away, the yarn neatly stacked in piles on the floor. There were no customers, and the sign did not say "Open". I had to use my new key to get into the door. I wondered about that. Surely customers would have no problem working around a little re-construction. I would have thought that we could use all the money we could make.

"... you don't have a choice," Mr. Morrie was saying, "you have to—" They stopped talking when I walked into the door. Rats. It sounded just like it was getting good. He nodded his head curtly at me and left quickly.

"Good morning Carolyn," I said as cheerfully as I could. "It looks like Mr. Morrie has been busy already."

Her smile was a little strained. "Good morning, dear," she said. "How are you feeling?"

"I'm alright," I said. I gestured towards the bookcase., "Last night seems like some sort of dream."

Walking over to me, she put her arm through mine and gave a squeeze. "More like a nightmare," she said. Her

167

expression turned mock serious. "I thought I told you that I didn't want to see you until after lunch?"

"I just couldn't stay away. I wanted to see how the progress was coming and to make sure that the customers weren't too freaked out by all of the damage."

She glanced uneasily at the counter. "Yes, well, we won't have customers today," she said.

"Why not? I'm sure that they don't mind working around a little mess."

She sighed. "Well, my dear, we couldn't find the cash register money this morning."

"That's terrible," I gasped in surprise. "Someone stole your money?" I tightened my grip on her arm. "Do you think that's why someone tipped over the bookcase? Because they were stealing?"

That made more sense than the Knitting Fairy theory or the vengeful new yarn store.

But, she was already shaking her head. Her snowy hair was pulled up into a tight bun this morning. Little tendrils were already falling out. People who look like Mother Goose shouldn't have to deal with things like this.

She sighed again, "No," she said, "we found the money."

"Oh!" I said, "that's wonderful. Where did you find it?"

"That doesn't really matter," she said.

"Did you just misplace it, then?" I asked.

"No, we didn't misplace it. Louise couldn't find it this morning, and so we looked all over the store. I was sure that someone had stolen it, but then we looked some more, and we found it." She managed a small smile, "All's well that ends well, as they say." She sighed. "But between that and the shelving repair, I'm afraid that I just decided I couldn't handle customers today."

It was a very strange story, and one thing still bothered me. "But wherever did you find the money then, Carolyn?"

She smiled sadly. "I'm afraid we found it in your knitting bag, my dear."

168

When the world stopped spinning, I found myself sitting on the same chair I had sat in the very first time I had entered Crabapple Yarns. Just like that time, my head was spinning and my heart was pounding. I literally felt sick to my stomach. I let my head drop forward into my hands. I stared at the rug under my feet. It was actually quite a lovely rag rug, all done in jewel tones. It had seen a lot of wear but it was still beautiful – and why on earth was I thinking about the rug right now?

Because it was easier to think about than the fact that the cash register money was found in my knitting bag. My knitting bag. After the commotion last night, I had left it at the store. I had forgotten all about it until now. Maybe I wasn't cut out to be a knitter after all. One simply didn't leave their knitting bag lying around unloved and forgotten. It was like leaving a child or one of your own limbs behind.

Something was pounding on my arm. That was odd. Usually my heartbeat pounded in my chest. It had to be the stress. I wondered if my job was still open at the library. Hopefully I wouldn't need a reference from Carolyn.

"Molly, dear," a soft voice was saying, "just take deep breaths."

I did, and I felt a little bit better. But my arm was still thudding softly. I lifted my head. Oh, it wasn't my heart. It was Carolyn, patting me on the arm sympathetically. She was perched on the arm of the chair. I couldn't look at her.

"Now Molly," she said firmly, "you can't possibly think that I believe you were trying to steal my money, do you?"

Oh.

"You don't?" I asked in a small voice.

"Of course not," she scoffed. "I'm shocked at you. Really, I am."

Oh.

"But you hardly know me. How do you know I didn't do it?" I finally lifted my eyes to meet hers. They were twinkling at me.

169

"When you get as old as I am," she said, "you'll be a good judge of character, too. Besides, if you had wanted to steal the money, you would have taken your knitting bag home with you."

My heart soared back into my chest. "I don't know," I said jokingly, "I've got a long ways to go before I'm as old as you."

"Hey!" she said.

My mind was churning as fast as it could, trying to bring the pieces together.

"Louise thinks I tried to steal the money, doesn't she?" I asked, remembering the scowl on her face.

Carolyn nodded soberly. "I'm afraid so," she said. "She thinks that after the commotion last night, you forgot about your scandalous thievery and left your bag by accident. But, don't worry – she'll come around."

I doubted that. I seriously doubted that. Which brought to mind the very disturbing question of who put the money in my knitting bag?

I decided that it was time to get firm with Carolyn. "Carolyn, what is going on here?"

She patted my arm again. "As soon as I figure that out, I'll let you know," she said.

"Two heads are better than one, Carolyn. Maybe if we—"

But she was shaking her head. "My problems are not going to be your problems," she said firmly. "Everything will be fine. Just wait and see. You're helping me a lot just by being here."

She walked away to answer the phone leaving me to gape at her back. Didn't she see that her problems were already mine? As a matter of fact, her problems just might be the death of me. She was going to get my help whether she wanted it or not.

The days passed slowly. Louise was barely civil to me. She made a point of standing over my shoulder every time I rang up a sale. It was annoying. And insulting. I was sick of it about half way through the first day.

I finally cornered her coming out of the bathroom. In case you ever need to corner someone, take my advice – get 'em when they're coming out of the bathroom. That's when they least expect it. "Louise," I said, getting straight to the point, "you can't possibly believe that I was trying to steal from Carolyn."

She rolled her eyes.

I tried talking to her, but she looked right through me. I tried explaining, and she rolled her eyes. I pointed out that if Carolyn had thought that I was trying to steal, she would have fired me.

At this point, a strange look came over Louise's eyes. "She'd never fire you," she hissed. "She thinks you're some great, saintly, sweet person. But I know who you are."

"Who am I?" I asked curiously.

Louise took a threatening step closer. I couldn't help myself. I stepped back. Perhaps I shouldn't have approached her. Especially not when she was coming out of the bathroom. Keep this in mind – never corner someone when they're coming out of the bathroom. There's just not enough witnesses around. "You're not a knitter," she whispered fiercely. "You're just a pretender. You've got Carolyn fooled into thinking that you're nice and sweet, but I see through you. I see how manipulative you are. I see the trouble you're causing here."

"Trouble?" I said feebly, "I'm not trying to cause trouble. I love Carolyn. I would never—"

But Louise was already stalking away.

Hmmm. That went well.

Unfortunately, I don't think she was content to just be angry with me by herself. I never saw her do it, but I do believe that she shared her exciting news with every knitter she could get her hands on. I have never felt so terrible in my entire life.

It didn't take long before people started looking at me out of the corners of their eyes and avoiding me at the same time.

Abby and Sarah, whom I was just starting to get to know, were suddenly cold to me. Abby didn't even show me the progress she was making on her hat. I tried to approach what few knitters there were sitting by the window, but they all became very quiet and concentrated hard on their knitting. I felt like crying. It was awful.

Even Rachel was different to me. She was subdued and quiet – something that she normally wasn't. She didn't quite meet my eyes when she talked to me, either. I finally gave up trying.

To make a bad situation even worse, I didn't dare go to the bakery. Not even for a cinnamon roll. Ryan had not picked me up for our daily commute all week. It was nice weather, and I didn't mind the walk, but he didn't even pick me up once. Louise had spread her poison to the bakery. I just couldn't go there and see the condemnation in his eyes too.

When Friday rolled around, Mr. Morrie was putting the finishing touches on the new shelves. They blended in perfectly with the other ones around them. He had also bolted each bookcase and shelf to the floor. Carolyn said that she felt much better knowing that nothing else would be tipping over.

And tomorrow? Tomorrow, Happy Knits would open.

Chapter 24

In Which We Are Not Happy At Happy Knits

It was Saturday afternoon. We were deader than dead. Slower than slow. No customers. Nada. Zip. Zilch. Yes, my friends, Happy Yarns had opened.

The only ray of sunshine in the day was that Louise wasn't working. There was no point. There was nothing to do.

"Everyone just needs to check them out," I said to Carolyn. "They're just curious."

"Naturally," she replied from the couch. "I don't blame them a bit."

"Your customers absolutely love you. They'll be back."

"Of course they will," she said. Then she sat her needles down and looked over the rim of her glasses at me. "This is the fifth time we've had this conversation today, Molly," she said. "Don't worry so much."

"How do you not worry Carolyn?" I asked, crossing the room to sit next to her. "Surely there must be some part of you that is scared that this monster store is going to put you out of business."

She paused thoughtfully. "Well, my dear," she said, "the Bible says that we shouldn't worry about anything because the Lord will take care of us no matter what we are going through." She smiled gently at me. "And if God is with us and taking care of us, then what is there to be afraid of?"

"Carolyn," I said, "that's a really nice thought, but what if—"

She didn't let me finish. "Molly, God has a plan for everyone's life. We may not always know what it is, but we can know that nothing happens that He has not planned – the good and the bad. And, sometimes, what we think is the bad turns out to be one of the best things for us. Think about it... The worst times in your life are awful to live through, but in the end, you're a stronger person – especially if you've learned that your strength comes from God and not from within your own self."

"So, you don't care whether or not you stay in business?" I was incredulous. I thought she loved this store.

Her eyebrows shot up. "Oh no," she said, "don't get me wrong. I'm going to do everything I can to stay open. But, if God says no and has something else for me in mind, I'm going to go along with that, too." She squeezed my hand. "Will it make you feel better if I tell you that I am sure that we're going to be open for many years to come?"

"How do you know?"

"I don't know," she answered, "but I can tell you that I feel a real peace about it. We're going to be just fine." She picked up her knitting again. "Don't you want to go and get a cinnamon roll?"

I shook my head. "I'm not hungry." And, it was true. I wasn't hungry. I was... in turmoil. I believe in God. I had always known that God had a plan for my life, even when The Plan on the refrigerator held my attention more. But, I have to admit – I didn't know God the way that Carolyn did. She spoke so confidently. And comfortably. Like they were friends. It made me feel hollow and wanting.

Two hours later, I was still feeling restless. And there were still no customers. And no knitters sitting on the sofa. And no one drinking the coffee. And no one starting a new project even when they had three going already. It was really sad.

Carolyn set her knitting down and flexed her arms. "I've got an idea, Molly," she said, "let's close early and go and visit Happy Knits."

I gaped at her. "Are you serious?"

"Sure, why not?"

"But...but...what would they say?" I stammered. "Won't they think it's strange? Are we allowed? What if we see some of your customers there? What—"

"Whoa," Carolyn said laughing, "first of all, it's a free country. They can't kick us out." Man, she almost sounded sassy. "Second of all," she continued, "it would be rude not to welcome them to the neighborhood, and, since it's pretty reasonable to assume that we will see some of our customers there, when they see that it's fine with us that they're there, maybe they won't act so oddly about visiting another yarn store in the future."

Confusing... but somehow logical.

"Ohhh, alright," I said slowly. "Let's go."

And, in all honesty, I was dying to see what the store looked like. So, we closed up the store, turned off the lights, and headed downtown towards Happy Knits.

Knitters were swarming over the new store like bees on a hive. From the outside, there was nowhere near the character that Carolyn's charming little building had. It was modern-looking. Very modern. Happy Knits also had the benefit of being right on Main Street. That meant they would naturally be more visible. Bummer. Their huge glass windows looked right out to the world and proudly shouted that a knitting store resided here.

We walked in and the lady behind the counter gave a gasp and immediately dove for the back room. Clearly our reputation (or at least our identities had preceded us). I snickered to myself, but Carolyn's expression did not change. Serenely calm and in her element, she floated through the store, fingering yarns and eyeing patterns.

I remembered standing outside of Happy Knits and peering in not so many days ago, and my initial impression remained. It was huge. With a sinking heart, I realized that she probably had double the amount of inventory that Carolyn. Needles of every shape and size hung neatly on peg boards along the side of the store. I peered closely at them. Some I was familiar with. Some were completely foreign. One brand of needle even proclaimed that it was made out of milk protein. Milk protein!!??!! Why on earth...Never mind...I wasn't going to think about that right now. There had to be a reason – maybe there were people out there who were allergic to wood and metal needles, and milk protein was the only thing that they could handle.

175

The overhead lights were very bright. Very bright. I squinted. They were quite fluorescent. You could see the colors very clearly, but it was giving me a headache.

There was a lot of yarn. Did I mention that already? Carolyn's little store looked sparse in comparison. I glanced at Carolyn to see what she was feeling, but as always, it was impossible to tell.

We headed towards the back of the store where there was a small table set up with a folding chair on each side. On the table stood a little odd-shaped clock with little cards next to it. I leaned over to read the sign.

Need help?

Our Master Knitter, Gretchen Goodsmith would be happy to assist you. Fees: $20/hour for the first hour and then $15 for each hour thereafter, prorated. Please fill out a time card below. After your lesson, please take your card and pay at the cashier's station.

Bewildered, I looked toward Carolyn. "What does that mean?" I asked.

"Just what it says," she said. "If you want some knitting help, Gretchen would be happy to help you for $20 for the first hour and then $15 for each hour after that?"

"They charge for help?" The concept was staggering. Mind boggling even. What kind of knitter charged somebody to help them?

"Apparently they do," Carolyn said calmly.

"Yes, we do," a cool voice behind us said. I whirled around guiltily. Carolyn turned calmly.

"Hello," Carolyn said, "My name is Carolyn Crabapple, and I own—"

"Crabapple Yarns," she interrupted, "of course you do. My name is Susan Holmes, and I am the owner of this establishment."

Hmm. I didn't like her tone. I didn't like the looks of her either. Her eyes were too close together, and her hair looked like it was lacquered to her head. She wore so much makeup that it was hard to tell how old she was, but I guessed her age to be in the mid-40's. Although she probably told everyone it was in the 30's. Alright, alright, I know. That's not very nice. I'm sorry. I guess she didn't look that bad – but before I go back to being polite, I would also like to add that her clothes looked like they fit her very nicely – when she was two sizes smaller. There. I'm done being mean now.

She was staring at us like a farmer stares at the grubs on his potato crop. I smiled sweetly at her, but her face didn't thaw. Perhaps, if she smiled, her makeup would crack and fall off. That might be fun to see. Then again, do you think it would it peel or simply crack? Now I just had to figure out how to get her to smile.

"And to answer your previous question – Molly, isn't it? – Gretchen is a Master Knitter." and the way she said it, I knew that master knitter was capitalized. "She has studied in France and England and has gone through rigorous training. Her advice is well worth the small fee that we charge."

Well la-di-da, I thought to myself.

Carolyn also smiled sweetly, but I knew she did it without the malice that I felt. Sigh. What can I say? She was a better person than I was. "We weren't implying that there was anything wrong with charging for advice," Carolyn said soothingly. "Molly was only a little bit surprised because it's not something she has seen a lot of."

The woman smiled depreciatingly. "Yes," she said, "I'm sure she hasn't. I understand that you give your advice away freely." Her nose lifted a few more centimeters towards the ceiling. "I'm sure your customers appreciate that. Here, we feel that our clientele would appreciate something more professional."

"More professional?" Sorry, I couldn't help myself.

"Yes, we believe that thoroughly teaching people the correct fundamentals of knitting enables them to successfully accomplish whatever task they set before themselves. We strictly adhere to the rules and guidelines of The National Knitting Association. We do not deviate."

Yeah, use that as an advertising campaign, I thought, they'll be lining up around the block.

I contemplated the horrors of deviation for a few minutes before trying to lighten her up a little. "You do realize that the word fun is in the word fundamental," I said with a small smile.

She did not reply. Her stare was enough of a statement.

"Well, I'm sure we all try to do things in the way we think is best," Carolyn said.

Susan sniffed. "We don't have to try," she said. "We know which way is the best. Real knitters know the value of self-discipline and vigilance in pursuing their skills. Here at Happy Knits we hire only the most capable and proficient knitters that are available."

Hey...was that a reference to... me?

"I've never known a knitter who wasn't a constant learner," Carolyn said pleasantly. She took my arm as if for support, but I felt the warning squeeze. "Well," Carolyn continued, "we really came over to welcome you to the neighborhood and to bring you a little welcome gift."

Ah. My cue. I held out the pot in my hands out to Susan. She took it gingerly with both hands, holding it between her thumbs and forefingers. I guess she didn't like it. I thought it was adorable. It was a small plant in a little planter that had been shaped to look like a ball of yarn. Clever, huh? We thought it was the perfect store-warming gift for a knitting store.

"Ah," she said, examining it, "thank you. I'm sure we have a nice place for it in the back room."

Alright. Now she had crossed the rudeness border. There was another warning squeeze on my arm. I didn't say anything, but there might have been some sort of strange look on my face because she further clarified her statement. "We don't believe in cluttering the store with excess paraphernalia," she explained. "It's a lovely planter, but we want the clients to see the yarn and not let other things get in the way."

My arm was going to be bruised. I could see that now. I scanned the store again. How could anyone see knitting as something so cold, clinical, and formal?

In the back of the store, I could see a class was already underway. Six people sat around a table while one lady paced around them, talking. No one was knitting. They were all listening – some with consternated expressions on their faces. I recognized one of the faces and waved at Abby. She didn't wave back. She quickly looked down at the table. Maybe they weren't allowed to smile during class. Maybe it wasn't in the Knitters National Association Handbook.

We tried to walk the rest of the way around the store, but Susan remained determinedly on our heels. Every time either Carolyn or I reached for a ball of yarn, she visibly tensed.

Finally, Carolyn turned to her. "Does it bother you that we're here?" she asked kindly. "We came over to welcome you and we both enjoy knitting and yarn so much that we just wanted to make friends with your yarn as well."

We were up front again. The cashier stood by her little counter with her arms over her chest, glowering. Susan was, of course, right next to me, practically breathing down my neck. And it wasn't pleasant breath either. I'm guessing some sort of garlic had been in her lunch.

"I hope you're not implying that we're afraid of you as competition," she said with a tight smile. "Of course you're welcome here any time. I wouldn't believe for one minute that you were trying to compare prices or intimidate your former customers who now shop here."

We left soon after that. Walking arm in arm down Main Street, neither of us said a word for several minutes. It was a beautiful spring day, and as the gentle breeze played with my hair, I let out a long breath.

"That was a big sigh," Carolyn remarked. "What was it for?"

I squeezed her arm. "I'm just so glad that you found me," I said honestly, "and taught me how to knit and enjoy the beautiful things in life. I feel really sad for the people who will learn how to knit at Happy Knits. They seemed so cold and strict. I just can't imagine learning to love knitting in a clinical environment like that."

She sighed too and squeezed my hand. "I'm glad we found each other," she corrected me, "and we'll just have to wait and see about everything else. Time has a funny way of putting everything right."

Chapter 25

The Knitting Fairy Is Not Being Nice

On Sunday morning, as I was coming out of church, I ran straight into Helen. We both grabbed onto each other for balance before we even realized who each other was. She was carrying a beautiful felted purse over her arm. It had a flap closure with a gorgeous vintage button on it. I had helped her pick it out, and couldn't help but feel a little surge of pride seeing it all completed.

"Your purse turned out beautifully, Helen!" I exclaimed, "I love it."

Her smile was wide. "I love it too," she said, "and thanks to you, the button looks great too." Sticking her tongue between her teeth, she scanned the crowd around us before standing closer and lowering her voice. I could tell she was excited. "Guess what?" she said breathlessly. "The Knitting Fairy visited me too! Can you believe it?"

"No," I shook my head, "I don't."

She rolled her eyes. "I'm serious. It felted my purse for me."

Was it possible that Helen was the Knitting Fairy? I narrowed my eyes at her and regarded her seriously. Nah, I don't think she possessed the appropriate amount of deviousness to be the Knitting Fairy.

"Helen," I said patiently, "do you really think that someone snuck into your house and felted your purse?"

She nodded.

"Don't you think you would have heard the washing machine?"

She shook her head. "I wasn't home. When I came back, it was lying out to dry."

"Was Patrick home?" I asked. Although, I have to admit it was a little hard to picture Patrick felting his wife's purse.

181

"No," she said, "he was at work. He didn't get home until late, actually."

"And you think this is a good thing?" I asked.

"What?"

"You mean to tell me that the thought of someone or something felting your purse inside your own home doesn't make you just a little bit uncomfortable?"

She looked at me uncertainly. "Well, when you say it that way," she said.

"Did it use your washing machine?" She was beginning to look worried, and shrugged her shoulders helplessly. "Maybe you should check your washing machine for fuzz," I suggested. "I don't know about you, but the Knitting Fairy is starting to get a little too close for comfort."

Her eyes were large, but not with delight anymore. "You could be right," she said.

Monday morning rolled around all too soon, as most Monday mornings do. Monday afternoon was not far behind. We were still quite slow, although I was heartened to see some of the knitters returned to the sofas. That had to be a good sign. There were no comfy sofas or chairs at Happy Knits. They were probably considered frivolous. They probably weren't in the handbook either. The nice comfy cushions were probably detrimental to regulation knitting posture.

Helen was one of the knitters sitting on the sofa. She still carried her felted purse, but I didn't see her tell anyone about the Knitting Fairy felting it for her. Every once in a while, she glanced uneasily at it.

Jean came in around mid-afternoon, very upset, again. I just don't know what had gotten into that girl lately. You may find this hard to believe, but she really used to be such a nice, sweet, QUIET person.

"Alright," she said, "I don't know which one of you did it – but I want to know and I want to know now," she said without the preamble of "Hi, Hello, or Good Afternoon". I wondered which was the real Jean – the quiet person we had almost

182

always seen or the woman who kept demanding to know who messed with her stuff.

Since it looked like it could get ugly again, Carolyn and I both went up front to protect the other knitters and make sure that no one got hit by a stray knitting needle.

"Did what?" Abby asked from the sofa.

Jean pulled a sweater out from her quilted knitting bag. It was the sweater she had just finished (before the moebius incident). It was quite lovely. Very pretty. Which we all quickly remarked upon. "Oh," she said with the snarl we were all coming to recognize, "you like it, huh?" Every head bobbed in tandem. No one wanted to upset her further. She tossed the pale plum sweater to Abby. "Try it on."

Abby caught the sweater with both hands reverently. It was a lovely lace and cable pattern that looked deceptively fragile. Abby was about the same size as Jean, and since the sweater was so pretty, she didn't seem to mind trying it on. Besides, why would she do anything that would further upset Jean? She swung it around her body and went to put her arm though the sleeve. And stopped halfway down the sleeve. A confused look came over her face. She pulled her arm back and tried again.

"What did you do to the sleeve?" Abby asked, trying to put her arm through the sleeve again.

Jean snatched her sweater back with an angry look. "I didn't do anything to the sleeve," Jean said, "but someone else sure did. Someone sewed the sleeves shut."

I had to pretend that my sudden outburst was actually a cough. What? It was kinda funny.

Carolyn reached over Jean to examine the sweater. "And they certainly did a nice job of it too," Carolyn said. "You can hardly see the stitches."

"Well," Jean said sarcastically, "that's just great. Thank you so much for the approval of the workmanship, Carolyn. Now, I want to know who did it."

We all looked back and forth at each other. "I think I can say with confidence that no one here would do something like this," Carolyn said. "It's clearly someone's idea of a joke. A very mean joke," she quickly added.   She examined the sweater again. "But I would be happy to help you fix it, dear."

Jean, however, was not finished. "Someone did this," she said stubbornly. "I don't know anybody else who knits that isn't from here. And so I seriously doubt that anyone else would know how to sew the sleeves up this well. It has to be someone from here," she repeated again. Then, she glanced around the group at us, "And what's this I hear about a Knitting Fairy?"

Oh brother.

Helen let her head fall into her hands. It was hard to tell whether the noise she made was a laugh or a sob.

"What have you heard about the Knitting Fairy?" I heard myself ask.

She turned her glare onto me. "I heard that someone is going around knitting on other people's projects. Could be that someone is someone who doesn't like me."

"The Knitting Fairy only helps other knitters," Helen protested. "It would never sew someone's sleeves together."

I was still trying to process Jean's last sentence when Carolyn said, "Don't be ridiculous, Jean," she said, "there is no one here that doesn't like you. We love you, you should know that." She tried putting her arm around Jean, but Jean shied away, clearly unhappy. She was most definitely not feeling the love.

Carolyn sighed. "There have been a few unexplained knitting occurrences," she admitted, "but I'm sure that there's an explanation for each one. No one is trying to hurt your knitting. There is no Knitting Fairy." She said it firmly and very convincingly. A few unexplained knitting occurrences? I didn't believe her either.

Jean's narrowed eyes were once again scanning the small gathering of knitters. "I shopped at Happy Knits," she blurted out.

"O-okay," Carolyn said slowly, "that's nice."

The rest of the group stared at Jean like her marbles had fallen out of her ears and were rolling around on the floor.

"I just find it kinda strange that I shop at Happy Knits and then my sleeves get sewn together," Jean said suspiciously, turning on her heel to glare at each person around the group. "Don't you?"

I couldn't believe my ears. Was she accusing one of us of sabotaging her knitting? How rude could you get? I think my mouth might have been hanging open. Even Carolyn didn't know what to say.

Abby let out a little puff of disbelief, "Now, you've really crossed the line, Jean," she said. "You had better apologize before they kick you right out of here."

A flicker of doubt crossed Jean's face. "I-I," she began, "I didn't mean to imply that Carolyn, or you Molly, or anyone from the store did this," she said, almost looking repentant. "I'm just so upset. I don't know what to think." She ran a distracted hand through her hair. This time, she allowed Carolyn to put her arm around her. "I'm sorry."

Abby wasn't done scolding Jean. "Carolyn and Molly both saw me taking a class at Happy Knits," she said, "and they weren't upset at all about it. And no one has sabotaged my knitting." She held up the mitten she was working on. "And if anyone wanted to cause some damage, it would be pretty easy to pull one of these double points out." She was right – it would be easy and pretty tempting to someone who wanted to cause trouble.

Apparently, Abby felt that she was on a roll, as all of our heads were bobbing in agreement with her. "And, see," she said, reaching down into her knitting bag, "my class project is a beaded shawl, and it's just fine." And, with that, she unfurled her shawl for us all to see. It was a very lovely shawl. She had done a beautiful job. "It took me almost an hour to string all of the beads and then you have to follow the chart to see where you should put each one." She looked around at us expectantly. "It was a lot of work, but don't you think it's worth it?"

Jean peered over to inspect it. I, too, leaned closer. Carolyn looked, frowned, and went for a double take. The other ladies inspected it as well. Abby's smile was proud and triumphant as she held out her almost finished shawl. She must have worked night and day over the weekend.

I felt like I was going to be sick.

Helen and Sarah exchanged horrified looks before staring at their feet. The lady whose name I keep forgetting quickly went back to knitting. The other ladies just stared, their mouths hanging open like little codfish all in a row.

Jean took a step away from Carolyn and looked at Abby pityingly and with a little bit of triumph. "You know what I've always thought a beaded shawl should have, Abby?"

Abby looked at her strangely, "Nooo—" she said slowly, "what?"

"Beads."

I don't think I need to tell you what happened next. I'm sure your imagination is more than sufficient to fill in the blanks that I am leaving here with the appropriate amount of tears and semi-hysteria. There were still little pieces of beads stuck in her shawl and the yarn was frayed wherever a bead had been. Someone had cracked out all of the beads.

Chapter 26
The Great Knitting-Fairy-Catching Plan

Mr. Morrie had outdone himself matching the new shelving to the old. The new summer yarns were sitting happily on their shelves. The bamboo yarn had survived its horrifying ordeal of being mislabeled. The new baby yarn was soft and scrumptious. And, the silks were amazing. You simply cannot believe the intense colors that silk can have. It defies description. Apparently, these yarns were purchased to tempt the summer customers. Carolyn had told me that spring and summer were her slowest time. Apparently, people didn't have as much time for knitting when the weather was nice. I thought that was a little strange. I seriously doubted that nice weather would keep me from knitting, but what did I know? I also didn't think that the customers stood too much of a chance when they saw the new yarns. The only flaw in her brilliant summer knitting plan was that you had to actually be in the store in order to see the yarns. And, right now, that was a big problem. I wondered how long Carolyn could go with slow sales before it started seriously affecting her.

So, here I was on a Tuesday afternoon running Crabapple Yarns all by my little old self. Strange how life goes on, isn't it? Not so many weeks ago, I had never even heard of a yarn store and now here I was running one all by myself. Well, for an hour, at least. Carolyn had an appointment with the insurance person. Apparently, Mr. Morrie needed to be paid.

Don't be thinking that my abilities as a knitter salesperson had increased so much that I was now allowed to run the store by myself. The grand opening of Happy Knits was still affecting Crabapple Yarns, and I think that Carolyn felt pretty confident leaving me alone knowing that we probably wouldn't even have any customers.

But, still. At least she hadn't called Louise in. Although, I remembered with a frown, she had offered. I had given the matter serious consideration and then declined. I did not see much hope of a future relationship with Louise.

I had been alone for almost a whole ten minutes when I realized that it was a little lonely being all by myself in the store. Not that I wished for customers. I was still not comfortable with customers. They had a nasty habit of asking questions and expecting answers.

I was starting to understand what a person felt like who had been isolated and shunned. The knitters were still short with me and stopped talking whenever I walked by. Louise's poison had spread well. It didn't help either being cut off from the bakery (although, to some extent it was a voluntary exile), and this, too, was taking its toll. My cinnamon roll addiction would need to be attended to very soon. I was starting to feel irritable and cranky. Maybe someday I would gather the nerve to go and speak to Ryan. Or maybe not.

A horrible shattering sound broke the stillness of my silent thoughts. I sprang to my feet and ran to the back of the store. Someone had thrown a rock through the little window next to the back door. Fear stuck in my throat, and I hung back, not daring to approach the door or the window too closely. I was all alone and I was scared. Something red caught my eye on the floor, and I saw the rock that had so cruelly disrupted the peace of the day. It was still dripping with bright red paint. It was probably supposed to look like blood. Actually, I thought, gripping the back of a chair to steady my shaking knees, it really did look like blood.

Giving myself a stern pep talk, I set about cleaning up the mess, sweeping up the glass fragments and taping newspaper across the window. Then I pulled the curtain across it. Why didn't I call the police? Good question. Why didn't I call Mr. Morrie? Another good question. Why not Ryan? I think you know the answer to that one.

After that, I double-checked the back door lock and reinforced it with a chair under the door handle. Once I was satisfied that no one was getting in through the door – and let's face it, no one could get in through the little broken window either – I went back out front and prayed for no customers. I felt a little bad about this for Carolyn's sake, but solitary confinement sounded pretty good right about now.

A few minutes more into my solitary confinement and Helen burst through the door. Strangely enough, I had never been so happy to see Helen in my entire life. "We have got to get rid of the Knitting Fairy," she declared.

"Good afternoon to you, too, Helen," I said, hiding my still shaking hands under the counter. "Didn't you hear Carolyn yesterday? There is no Knitting Fairy. Only some unexplained knitting occurrences."

She rolled her eyes and reached for a skein of the bamboo yarn. She ran her hand around it, rolling it over and over. In case you didn't know – knitters do this for comfort. "I found fuzz in my washing machine," she said simply. "You know and I both know that someone is doing something."

"Someone is doing something," I repeated. She had no idea. "Someone is knitting other people's knitting."

"Yeah," she said, "and I thought it was really cute at first, didn't I?"

I grinned. "Yeah, you did." I remembered the way her eyes had sparkled.

"Well," she said, flipping her hair over her shoulder, "I don't think it's so cute anymore." She leaned over the counter. "And after the fiasco yesterday, you know what people are going to be saying, don't you?"

I looked down, not quite able to meet her eyes. "People are not going to seriously think that anyone from Crabapple Yarns would be sabotaging anyone's knitting."

"Oh yes, they will," Helen said, "and you know it."

She was right. I did know it. But, I wasn't going to let her know that I knew.

"Carolyn has been here for over 20 years," I argued. "She is loved and respected by everyone who has ever come through these doors. She has given so much—"

Helen reached over to grab my hand. "I know," she said fiercely, "I love Carolyn. I love this store. I know that—" and here her voice broke a little. "But, as you well know, people are funny. And they forget. And they believe whoever yells the loudest." She grimaced. "And Jean is yelling pretty loud right now. And so are a few other people. That's why we need to find out who the Knitting Fairy is and catch her. Then, and only then, will we have something to show the other knitters."

Rachel chose that moment to walk through the door. Helen replaced the ball of bamboo yarn on the shelf and tried to look nonchalant. She didn't do the look very well, and Rachel looked back and forth between us suspiciously as she crossed the floor.

"Hi Rachel," I said as cheerfully as I could, "we missed you yesterday."

Her smile slipped a little. "Yeah," she said, "my brother broke his leg. I spent most of the day with him in the emergency room."

"That's terrible," Helen said, sympathy showing in her eyes. "How's he doing?"

Rachel rolled her eyes. "You know men," she said, "he's such a big baby. He's got a walking cast, but you'd think he was glued to one spot. I left him on the couch whining because we were out of chips. I thought I'd come down and knit for a while just to get away." She reached into her knitting bag and pulled out a small velvet pouch. "And, I can't believe that I forgot to give this to you."

She was holding it out to me. "What?" I asked, "what is it?"

Her eyes darted to Helen and then back to me. "You know," she said, licking her lips, "it was your surprise. I was going to give it to you the other night and then—"

Oh. OH. That surprise. Isn't that funny? I had forgotten all about it. "Awww," I said, "that's so nice of you. Why are you—"

She waved her hand to stop me from finishing. "Because I'm glad you're here," she said. "I can see how much Carolyn already loves you, and it makes me happy. It's a welcome gift."

The velvet pouch was smooth and soft. I untied the silk drawstring and gently tipped it over onto my palm. Something glittery fell out, a chain snaking out behind it. It was a little charm, shaped like a little ball of yarn on a silver necklace. It was exquisite and one of the nicest gifts I had ever received. I could feel tears welling up. "Thank you so much Rachel," I said. "It's beautiful."

Knitters. Completely unpredictable. They should come with a reference guide.

When Rachel wandered away to sit down and do some knitting, Helen quickly leaned over the counter again.

"I've got a plan," she whispered, "we're going to lay a trap for the Knitting Fairy." She lowered her voice further, "Tonight."

I was completely bewildered. "How? W-what?"

"Leave the details to me," she whispered, "and wait and see. Just play along. And don't plan on getting any sleep tonight."

You could say that I was a little disturbed by the almost manic gleam in her eye, but if it worked and we caught the Knitting Fairy, I guess it would be worth it.

Since there were no customers, the store was sparkling and no one had messed with the sock yarn display, I decided to join Rachel and Helen and knit. I was almost finished with Ryan's scarf, but with a pang, I realized that I didn't know when, or even if, I would give it to him.

To my complete surprise, as we knitted, more knitters came to join us. They greeted Helen and Rachel quite nicely, but had very little to say to me. I wished that I knew a good way to tell them that I wasn't a thief and... Oh, never mind. It's not like they would believe it anyway. I retreated behind my knitting and wished that a customer would come in so that I would have an excuse to get up. It wasn't until later that I found out that Helen had bribed, cajoled, and asked them to come.

When Carolyn returned from her insurance adjustor meeting, there were quite a few knitters sitting around the circle: Rachel, Helen, Abby (who despite Jean's bitterness did not believe we had anything to do with her un-beaded beaded shawl), Sarah, Laurie, Ann, and a few other regulars, including the lady whose name I can never remember. It's embarrassing. Really, it is. I can't ask her again because I've already asked her three times. I made up my mind to ask Helen later. For now, I didn't have to worry about it since none of them were talking to me anyway. An hour later, my eyes almost popped out of my head as Louise came stalking in. She didn't look at me. She didn't talk to me. She simply dropped her knitting on the floor next to a folding chair, sat down and started knitting. Helen caught my eye and sent me a thumbs-up sign.

Not for the first time, I wondered if she really wasn't crazy.

Finally, in mid-afternoon, Helen stretched lazily. "Oh my goodness, girls," she said, "I almost forgot to show you this." She reached into her bag and pulled out one of the most beautiful yarns I had ever seen. "My mother bought me this while she was traveling out west. It's hand-painted mohair wrapped with a silk twist. I'm making this little shrug." Here, she held up the pattern. It was darling, dainty, and gorgeous. And begged to be held – and knitted. I didn't think that I really was a shrug-wearing person, but I instantly coveted it. With a small inner leap of satisfaction, I could tell that everyone else felt the same. Even Ann, who clearly did not have the figure for it. Helen, Helen, I thought. Could it really be that simple?

The day wore on, and before any of the knitters began thinking of leaving, Helen stretched again. I thought perhaps she might be overdoing the casual look, just a bit. "Carolyn," she said, "would it be alright if I leave my shrug here tonight?"

Carolyn looked surprised. "Why would you want to do that, dear?" she asked. Carolyn once again looked absolutely adorable sitting on the sofa knitting. She was wearing the same dress that I had seen her wear the first day that we had met, and the same cobwebby shawl was tucked carefully around her shoulders as she closed the toe on her final sock.

"Well, because Lacey is coming over tonight," Helen replied, "and I'm giving the shrug to her. I really don't want her to see it, and my house isn't that big."

"I guess that would be alright," Carolyn replied, although she was looking at Helen a bit strangely. "You can put it in the back room if you want." With a flourish, she cut the yarn and turned her sock inside out. The colors of a Jamaican sunset, the sock was beautiful. She pulled up her dress and tried it on over the little white socks she was wearing. Somehow, Mother Goose even managed to look cute wearing loud socks with an iris-colored dress.

"Oh, no," Helen said, "I'll just tuck it behind the counter. It'll be fine there. I'll be back tomorrow when you open to pick it up. Thanks ever so much." She kicked her feet back into her sandals and stood up. Everyone watched her put the sack behind the counter, and then she left, making sure everyone knew that she would be home the rest of the afternoon cooking and baking up a storm for her friend Lacey who was coming over to have dinner tonight. I did not miss her subtle wink at me as she left.

I could only hope that she had given Lacey strict instructions not to visit Crabapple Yarns today.

We closed the store in our usual manner, and when Carolyn invited me to go out to eat with her, I had to regretfully refuse. I felt a little better when Irene poked her head inside the door and invited Carolyn to eat with her. At least she wouldn't be eating alone tonight. Although, how much company Irene would be was anyone's guess.

We locked up the store and parted ways at Main Street. Carolyn and Irene headed uptown, and I headed back home. At least for a couple of blocks.

Doing my best to act like a casual shopper, I browsed a few stores. I crisscrossed Main Street several times to make sure that no one was tailing me. Yes. That's what I said. Tailing me. You just never know. Then, as casually as I could, I entered The

Candy Store, bought a candy bar and left again. Strolling in front of the other shop displays, I doubted that any of the other shoppers realized that I was actually walking back the same direction that I had come from. Actually, I doubted whether any of them would care, either.

Feeling extremely foolish, I made my way back to Crabapple Yarns. Mr. Morrie's light was still on. There was a car parked in front of the store. Maybe he still had a customer. Deciding to err on the side of caution, I did not walk on the sidewalk. Creeping along the far side of Roberts Alley, I tried to remain in the shadows of the department store. As I passed Mr. Morrie's store, I stared at the windows anxiously, but I did not see any sign of his long grey beard. It would be a little hard to explain that I was sneaking into the yarn store that I worked in.

I hoped that I had figured out Helen's subtle wink correctly and that she would be waiting here too. I assumed that her plan was to entice the Knitting Fairy out of hiding with her irresistible shrug. Would it work? That remained to be seen.

I approached Crabapple Yarns from the side in much of the same manner as last Sunday when I had tried to see in the windows. A long arm snaked out from behind the bushes at me. I choked back a scream.

"For heaven's sake," Helen hissed, "are you trying to let everyone see you?"

I caught my breath before answering. "I was sneaking as best I could," I said indignantly.

"Well, you're just not cut out for it," she said. "Where did you learn how to sneak – by watching television?"

That hurt. It really did.

We snuck around the back of the building, climbed the steps to the apartment and then snuck back down the stairs to Crabapple Yarns. Helen had been smart enough to bring a flashlight. I hadn't thought that far. Helen had also brought snacks. I hadn't thought that far, either. When I asked her about them, she just shrugged and said that she had to do something while she was waiting to commit her first felony of breaking and entering. I pointed out that since we had a key it was hardly breaking. Only entering.

We stood huddled together in the almost-dark for a few minutes in the shadowy store. Nothing moved. It was strange how different the store looked in the dark. It was no longer the warm, comforting space it was during the day. The building creaked and groaned. Little flickers from outside made us jump. Only one light was on by the front door for security purposes. Things moved. The yarn whispered to us in a sinister voice. I had to suppress a shudder as we shuffled past the tall bookcase, very firmly reminding myself that it was now nailed to the floor. It didn't make me feel that much better.

We made sure that Helen's shrug was still in its bag behind the counter. It was. There was just one problem. We couldn't decide where to hide. The glow of the streetlight outside made sitting on the sofas impossible. The Knitting Fairy would see us before we saw her. Helen wanted to hide behind one of the bookcases. I just couldn't do it. Really, I couldn't.

In the end, we decided to hide under the great oak table. As quietly as possible, we arranged the chairs to allow for quick escape and crawled under the table. The plan was to scurry out from under the table towards the front of the store once the Knitting Fairy was safely inside. We had propped the chairs up carefully around the outside of the table so that their legs were sticking out. If the Knitting Fairy got away from us, we would simply herd her this way and she would be slowed down by the outstretched legs. Hopefully, she wouldn't fall and break her neck – that would be bad. But, no one asked her to break in, so, if she fell, it was not really our fault. It was a great plan. We congratulated ourselves on our plan and then, hugging our knees to our chest, we waited. The only sound that you could hear was our ragged breathing.

I could see Helen's profile dimly in the darkened store. Every so often, her head would tilt to one side and then back again.

We did not speak.

I wondered how the Knitting Fairy would get in.

Perhaps she had a key.

Perhaps she had a magic wand.

We strained our ears for any sound.

If the Knitting Fairy was someone that we knew, things were going to get very awkward. What would we do with her? I hoped she wouldn't cry. I hate that.

Silence.

It couldn't be someone that we knew. All of our knitters were nice knitters. Nice knitters didn't do mean things. But, it had to be someone that we knew. Otherwise, it just wouldn't make sense.

Darkness.

Maybe it was Jean. My heart brightened a little. Yes, maybe it was Jean. Jean the Troublemaker. But would she really go so far as to sew her own sleeves together? I remembered her snarl. Maybe. She definitely possessed the drama for it.

Boredom?

Wiggling a little, I developed a new appreciation for spies. The floor was uncomfortable. My rear end was starting to hurt. This could be a really long night.

Without warning, Helen grabbed my arm. She had heard something. My eyes were now used to the darkness. In the dim light, I could see that her eyes were wide and she was shaking with excitement. We both held our breath and waited. And waited. I let out a breath of disappointment. Nothing.

The sound of a car door slamming shut sent us both jumping backwards. Our brilliant plan forgotten, we scrambled to get out from under the table. Not through the front as we had planned – but out the back. Where the chairs were.

We knocked over the chairs and they fell to the ground loudly. I tried to sit up, knocked my head on the bottom of the table and tried sitting up again, clutching what I was sure would be a rising lump on my forehead. Helen was across me, her arms tangled in one of the rungs of the chairs. She must have seen them starting to fall and had made a blind grab to keep them upright. I tried to sit up, but she did not let go of the chairs. My struggles caused her to move, which in turn, caused the chair to scrape across the ground. Too much noise. We both froze. I then tried to wiggle out from under her. Maintaining her hold on the chair rung, she was trying to climb over me. Really, what did she think that the chair was going to do? Get away?

Hopelessly tangled, I hissed, "Get off of me, you crazy woman."

"You get off of me," she jeered back. It took her a few seconds to realize how silly that sounded, but she eventually let go of the chair and rolled off of me. I rolled over to prop myself up on my elbows, as she struggled to sit up. Somewhere, out in the night, an engine revved and sped away. My brain told me that it was Mr. Morrie's last customer leaving. Great, we attacked the chairs because someone was leaving the hardware store.

I looked over at Helen. She looked back at me and then quickly away. Silence descended upon us once more. It was a heavy silence this time. The darkness in the store seemed to envelop us.

"Well," she finally whispered, "We'll just consider that our dry run, shall we?" She rubbed her hands together nervously. "We should just look at it as a learning experience." She turned to me, her expression serious. "What did you learn?"

Still rubbing my head, I stared at her. We were halfway under a table. In a yarn store. Trying to catch the Knitting Fairy. In the middle of the night. With killer chairs.

I think it was me who snickered first. I couldn't help it. The serious look on her face as she said "What did you learn?" was just too funny. I slapped a hand over my mouth, but then she let out a little gasp of laughter. She, too, promptly smacked a hand over her mouth. I snickered again from around my hand, my eyes widening in consternation as noise escaped. At this rate, the Knitting Fairy would hear us before she ever saw us – hiding under the table, giggling like madmen. Who knows? That above anything else might be the one thing that did scare her away.

Have you ever tried to stop laughing by covering your mouth? Let me tell you – something has to come out somehow. Let me also tell you that it did not help my hysterical delight any when Helen began snorting. Her look of horror after the first snort sent me over the edge. My elbows began shaking and could no longer hold me up. I fell face first to the floor, overcome with giddiness. She snorted again. Eyes watering, I was laughing so hard that no sound could now come out of my mouth. My sides were shaking with the effort of trying to stop.

Watching me convulse on the floor left her too weak to hold her hand up, and when it finally slipped, she let out a loud, "Hee Ha HAW!" It was one of the craziest laughs that I had ever heard, and my sides felt like they were splitting. Choking and laughing helplessly, I knew that the image of Helen braying like a mule was forever burned upon my memory. Tears were streaming down my cheeks. I couldn't stop laughing. I felt like I was going to die.

From between my watery eyelids, I could tell by her stricken face that, for her part, she was absolutely horrified by her outburst. She had ruined the perfect silence of our stakeout. I watched the struggle for control play over her face. She firmly clasped both hands over her mouth.

And snorted.

I couldn't take it anymore. I rolled over to my back, still laughing so hard that no sound would come out.

Helen gave up and collapsed into a boneless heap on the floor next to me. We laughed so hard that it echoed back to us across the room. One could only hope that the Knitting Fairy wasn't within hearing range.

When our right minds eventually returned, we calmly wiped our eyes and sat back up to survey the damage.

"Maybe our next plan should be to exit towards the back of the table," I whispered. We were back to whispering like the professionals that we are. "Somehow, I think it just feels more natural." Helen swallowed something that could have sounded like another laugh to anyone who wasn't a professional. Like me, I knew she wasn't thinking of the both of us hurtling ourselves backwards against the chairs that we had so carefully propped up.

"We should probably move the chairs, then," Helen said in agreement, in a very prim voice. "Otherwise we could run into them and they would hinder our getting out from under the table." Hers was the voice of experience. I nodded.

Yes, we were both back to being very serious. Neither of us referred to our temporary breakdown. It was like it never happened. And, as we re-grouped and went back under the table, this time with cushions and pillows from off of the couch, it was only a little hiccup - not laughter that escaped from my throat one last time.

Helen scowled at me, and with a great deal of effort, I tried to erase the picture from my mind, of Helen, her eyes wide with horror as she let out her loud mule-like laugh. One more hiccup. There. Now I wouldn't think about it anymore. I chanced another glance at Helen and tried very hard not to picture her with pointy ears and a wide nose. I wondered if I could talk her into putting her hair up into two pony tails. She scowled at me again and passed me a cookie before I could hiccup again.

It must have been close to midnight when we lost our minds.

We had eaten all the cookies and drank all the juice. We had even taken turns crawling on our hands and knees to the bathroom after we drank all the juice.

There was nothing else to do.

"Did you bring your knitting?" I whispered to Helen.

"No," she replied, "I didn't think it was going to take this long."

"I didn't either," I admitted sorrowfully. "Besides, I don't think I can knit in the dark. I can barely knit in daylight" Helen made a sound that could have been a smothered laugh, "What's so funny?"

She grinned, and in the darkness, I could see her white teeth gleaming. "It's the perfect definition of irony."

"What is?"

"Two knitters dying of boredom in a yarn shop."

"I don't think it's that funny."

"Well, maybe you've just lost your sense of humor."

"Maybe you've lost more than your sense of humor," I replied grumpily. "Whose crazy idea was this, anyway?"

"Hey!" She protested a little too loudly. "You'll see – this is one of the best ideas that I have ever had."

I think it says a lot about me that I didn't make the obvious reply to that statement.

We settled back into quietness. I seriously didn't think we would be seeing the Knitting Fairy any more tonight. I was ready to go home. Helen wasn't.

It turned out that Helen had a pack of cards in her purse. So, we decided to live dangerously and play some cards. We set the flashlight up on its end and shielded it from being seen from the street. Like little kids at a slumber party, we soon forgot how tired we were.

"Do you have any threes?" she whispered. The light from the flashlight was shining up on her face. I wondered if she knew how funny it made her look.

"Go fish," I replied, smiling sweetly.

She scowled and grabbed a card from the top of the deck. I grinned to myself. Whoever would have guessed that Helen was so competitive?

"So," I said softly, "what made you ask me to do this with you? And not someone else?"

"You have a key."

Oh. Bummer. I thought maybe she had asked me because she wanted to be friends or something.

I don't think it was the flashlight that was giving her the wicked look this time when she added, "And I knew that there was no way you were the Knitting Fairy because the Knitting Fairy actually knows how to knit."

I rolled my eyes. "Yeah, yeah, yeah," I said. We continued playing.

"How do I know that you're not the Knitting Fairy?" I asked suddenly.

She glanced up, her cards forgotten. "What? Why on earth would I be sitting under a table with you in the middle of the night if I was the Knitting Fairy?"

"Well," I said, "It would be the perfect way to throw suspicion away from yourself, for one thing."

She looked indignant, but then her eyes gleamed. "Yeah, but you're the only one who knows we're doing this, so your theory is unsubstantiated."

"Hmmm—" I muttered, "good point."

"Hey," she said, "maybe you're the Knitting Fairy."

"Nope," I said, "remember – I barely knit."

"Maybe you're just pretending you don't know how to knit." I cocked my head to look at her. "Do you have any eights?" she asked.

"No," I replied, "go fish. And what do you mean, pretending I don't know how to knit? Believe me, I wish I did know more. Maybe then, Louise would get off my back."

Uh-oh. Did I just say that out loud? Judging from her amused expression, I guess that I did. She chuckled softly. "Okay, I believe you but I know you're lying."

"I am not."

"Not about the knitting," she said patiently, "hand over the eight."

"I don't have an eight."

"Yes, you do. I know you do. You're a terrible liar. Hand it over."

"I don't have any eights. Go FISH," I said with emphasis.

She glowered at me and swung her hand out to take a card and accidently knocked over the flashlight. The beam of light lit up the room crazily. We both scrambled for it. It jumped out of our reach and skittered across the floor. Helen dove for it with the skill of a wild game hunter chasing his quarry. She shut it off for a moment, clutching it to her chest and returned to our little cave. I could hear her ragged breathing.

"Whew," she said, "we'd better be more careful." She repositioned the light.

"You had better be more careful," I corrected her. "Now, where were we?"

"Your turn," she said grumpily.

"Oh, yes." I looked from my cards up at her. "Do you have any eights?" Hee hee. I just couldn't resist. You should have seen the look on her face.

"What?" she shrieked as quietly as she could. She narrowed her eyes at me. "I knew you were lying. Hand it over. I asked first"

I held up my hands. "I'm joking," I protested. "I don't have any eights."

The sound of something scraping at the door made us both jump. Helen was faster than I was. She shut the flashlight off and picked it up in one graceful motion, plunging us both into darkness. Perhaps we should have thought the whole card playing by flashlight thing through a little better. Our eyes were no longer accustomed to the darkness.

The door was creaking open, and we were frozen to our spots. I blinked rapidly, willing my eyes to adjust.

"On the count of three," Helen barely breathed the words. She re-adjusted her grip on the flashlight.

I had no idea what we were supposed to do once we hit three, but I nodded my head anyway even though she couldn't see me. Strangely enough, we actually had never discussed this part.

We both got to our hands and knees and crawled to our escape hatch. I swept my hand across the exit. No chairs. One could never be too sure.

"One."

My heart was thudding loudly in my chest. I couldn't believe it.

"Two."

Helen's plan had worked. The Knitting Fairy was here.

"Three"

Now was the moment of truth.

We sprang out from under the table, our knees buckling and wobbling from being cramped so long and yelled.

Helen yelled something that sounded a lot like "Gotcha sucker!" while I yelled a more sophisticated "Ha!"

Helen turned the flashlight on the person at the door.

Funny how it never occurred to us that anyone besides the Knitting Fairy could possibly show up. The person in the doorway had a large weapon that shone silver in the light from the street. It swung towards us just as the beam from the flashlight caught its body. It was a man. A man with a giant weapon.

Someone let out a blood-curdling scream. I think it was me. Helen dropped the flashlight. Thinking as one, we decided to run. Unfortunately, Helen, standing to my left, went right and I went left. We crashed into each other, screamed, and went around each other. She denied it later, but she has a much louder scream than I do.

I don't know where I was going, but I headed towards the back of the store when I was stopped by blinding lights. "Aaagggh," I said, "I can't see." I put my hands over my eyes to block the unwelcome brightness.

"Run, Molly, run!" Helen yelled desperately from somewhere to the left. "He can't catch both of us."

"When you girls are done goofing around," a calm voice said, "maybe you wouldn't mind telling me what's going on."

Oh.

The humiliation.

I turned around slowly, still blinking. I cleared my throat. "Good evening, Mr. Morrie."

This time we sat around the table instead of under it. His sledge hammer was propped up very carefully against it. We explained everything to Mr. Morrie. At least, we tried to explain. He kept shaking his head and muttering things under his breath. It's hard for non-knitters to understand something like this. As a matter of fact, I think the whole concept of the Knitting Fairy went straight over his head.

"You're not going to tell Carolyn about tonight, are you?" I asked, trying not to sound too pathetic.

"I think I should," he said. "I don't know what she's going to say about all of this, though."

I had been trying not to think about that very thing. "Mr. Morrie," I said, "despite the fact that we were a little foolish tonight, there is something going on here, and we do need to get to the bottom of it."

Mr. Morrie looked at both me and Helen. "Sometimes," he said, "strange things happen. And things still work out just fine. Despite being a mite peculiar, I do believe you ladies have your hearts in the right place. But, you need to take a step back and let Carolyn figure this out. She's a smart lady. It's her store, after all. If she thinks something is wrong, she'll ask for help when she needs it."

I felt mildly rebuked. On the plus side, it was one of the longest speeches I had ever heard him give.

"But, Mr. Morrie," I said, "it wouldn't be right not to know the truth."

Mr. Morrie stood up slowly, and for the first time, he looked like an old man. And somehow, a sad man. "The truth isn't always what's needed," he said. He shuffled slowly toward the door, one hand gripping the sledgehammer. He turned at the front door for the last time. "And next time you decide to hide under a table," he said, "don't turn on a flashlight."

I looked at Helen and then we both looked at the floor.

Chapter 27
Louise Thinks It's Time For Me To Quit

It was early morning when I got home. Helen drove me. She let me off and then grimaced. "So much for our life of crime," she said, "I guess we're just not cut out for it." She pounded the steering wheel. "I was so sure that it must be one of the afternoon knitting ladies."

I shrugged. "It was a great plan, Helen," I said. "It's only too bad that it didn't work out." I leaned back into the car. "And besides nearly being frightened to death and bored to death and then frightened to death again, I actually had a lot of fun."

She grinned impishly. "Me, too. See you tomorrow."

I waved goodbye to her and trudged back toward my apartment. Despite the fact that hiding under a table in the yarn store trying to catch the Knitting Fairy was a bigger adventure than I had ever had, I was strangely depressed. Carolyn's business was not doing well. We had barely done anything in sales today, and I knew that Saturday had not been much better. What if the trend continued?

I hoped that Mr. Morrie would not tell Carolyn about our fiasco tonight. She really didn't need another thing to worry about. Speaking of which – I had forgotten to tell her about the broken window. And now we were no closer to knowing who the Knitting Fairy was and why she was suddenly being so mean. Could it be one of Carolyn's customers? If not, who else? And why?

At 6:00 a.m., there was a terrible pounding on my door. Not having nowhere near enough sleep yet, I stumbled to the door groggily. I was awake faster than if someone had thrown a bucket of cold water over me. It was Louise. Good morning.

I invited her in. She sat on my kitchen chair with her hands folded on her knees. I felt at a distinct disadvantage in my pink pajamas with the hearts on them.

205

She was quick and to the point. Her ruthless brutality left me dumbstruck.

She didn't know why I came to Crabapple Yarns, and she did not want to know. She told me that I was a terrible knitter and a horrible salesperson. She had never seen someone so ill at ease with customers. I didn't know wool from acrylic, and I didn't know indigo from cornflower blue either.

If I didn't quit, she didn't know what would happen next. She had no idea if I were responsible for all of the things that were happening or not, but she was sure that somehow I was to blame. Coincidences on this level simply didn't happen. Before I came along, things were fine.

Carolyn may have hired me, but she now regretted that decision. Couldn't I tell that? Couldn't I see that Carolyn was too compassionate to ever fire anyone? How could I, in all good conscience, take Carolyn's money for a job that I could not do? Even I could surely see that with a new yarn store opening across town Carolyn would need all of the competent help that she could get to survive. It would break Carolyn's heart to fire me, but, in the end, she would. If I cared anything about Carolyn, I would not make her fire me. It was up to me to do the right thing and leave.

Having spoken her piece, she left. Before she went, I told her to let Carolyn know that I wouldn't be in today. I wasn't feeling well. That wasn't a lie, either.

After Louise had gone, I sat down by the kitchen table and tried to think. It had hurt, but Louise had actually made some very good points. Grabbing a piece of paper, I made a list:

1. I am not an experienced knitter. Conclusion: I can't help customers with their problems. Carolyn needs someone to assist her. I only get in the way.
2. I am not experienced at selling things. Conclusion: I don't know how to get people to make purchases. Carolyn needs someone to help her sell.
3. I'm scared of the customers. Conclusion: ...

This was getting depressing. I didn't write down any more, even though I could have kept going. The phone rang. I let the answering machine pick it up. It was Carolyn.

"Molly, dear," her voice said over the speaker, "I'm so sorry to hear you're not feeling well. Take as long as you need, and if you want anything, let me know."

Hmmm... Was that the voice of someone who desperately needed my help at their store? I didn't think so either.

The sun was shining brightly that afternoon, so I decided to get outside and take a walk. I had no idea what I should do. Perhaps Louise was right. Perhaps I should leave. My feet betrayed me. Without realizing where I was going, they took me straight to the library. It was nice weather, and the outer doors were propped open. The books were calling me, begging me to come in. I peeked in the front door. Mrs. Goldmyer was checking in books and looking pensive. I wondered if she missed me. She glanced up and I jumped back out of sight.

I wandered around town a little more, but my feet seemed to drag. I tried sitting under my tree, but there was no peace there, either. I took a deep breath, listened to the wind in the branches and the children playing on the playground, but I couldn't find the patience to linger. I lasted for five minutes before restlessness made me get to my feet again. I even tried praying. God, I'm sorry that I haven't been praying a lot lately. I don't blame You if You don't even want to listen to me right now. But, I just don't know what to do. Could You help me?

I've been alone a lot in my life. Being a librarian and a good student, I had never minded spending time by myself. Now, I realized with a sick heart, I was all alone. My college friends were all living in various parts of the country. My family was all at work since this was the middle of the week, and basically, the only people here in town that I knew were knitters or library patrons. I didn't think my heart could possibly fall any further, but I felt so alone. It was not a nice feeling.

THE KNITTING FAIRY

Chapter 28
Louise Really Is A Worm

I went home and cooked a light supper, most of which ended up in the garbage. Wrapping a blanket around myself, I huddled deep in the corner of the couch. I felt cold all over. Should I quit? Should I stay? Was Louise right? If Carolyn had a more competent employee would it keep her open longer? Was my job at the library still open? And, if so, how much humble pie would I have to eat to get it back?

I turned on the TV just to drown out the noise of my own thoughts. I watched as Lucy tried out her latest diabolical scheme, but somehow, tonight, it just wasn't funny. I watched the hands on the clock make their way around their dial. Time was running out. For better or worse, I should make a decision and stick to it. Tonight.

There was a knock on my door. With a great sigh, I pulled myself off the couch and kept the blanket around me, as I made my way to the front door. If it was Louise again, I had already decided that I would not let her in. I peered through the peephole. It was Ryan. Whoa. Talk about a strange day. I let him in.

He sat uncertainly on my recliner as I turned off the TV and thought about how I could make things look more presentable. With an inward shrug, I realized that I didn't really care and so I sat back down on the couch, curling my feet under me.

It's amazing the freedom that not caring can give you. Normally visitors make me very tense.

He leaned back in the chair, "So," he said breaking the silence, "I didn't see you today. Carolyn said you weren't feeling well."

Uhhh... So...he decided to come over? Since when?

I frowned at him. "I haven't seen you for the past week," I reminded him.

"I know," he said, "I just got back today. I was a little worried that you might still be feeling the effects of last week's adventure."

"Just got back," I repeated slowly, not taking my eyes off his face. "Just got back?"

He looked a little guilty. "I felt really bad leaving after what happened, but Mr. Morrie said he would keep an eye on the yarn store and make sure you girls were alright."

Somehow, I don't think we were participating in the same conversation.

"I don't understand," I said, "just got back from where?" I was beginning to sound like a broken record.

He stared at me. "Why, from visiting my mom, of course."

"You haven't been in town?"

A look crossed his face. If I didn't know better, I would have said it was disappointment. "You mean you didn't even notice I was gone?" he asked. "Who do you think it was handing you a cinnamon roll all last week?"

I sat up straighter, letting my feet fall to the floor. I stared at my hands. "I haven't been to the bakery all week," I muttered. "I didn't know you were gone."

"Didn't Louise tell you?" he asked, clearly confused.

I felt a weight lift from my chest. Ah-ha! The troublemaker. I should have known. "Louise?" I asked, "Louise was supposed to tell me that you weren't in town?" I might not know exactly what was going on, but I was beginning to get a pretty good idea.

He frowned. "Well, that's strange," he said, "I was positive that I asked her to tell you. I would have told you myself, but I forgot and then after that night, I had to leave early and I didn't want to wake you up. She said that she would give you a ride to work all week."

I examined my nails as if they were the most interesting thing on the planet. My head was spinning. Could it be true? If it were, Louise was more of a worm than I had originally thought.

I could tell he was studying me, but I refused to look up. "Louise didn't tell you I would be gone, did she?" Ryan asked softly, "and she didn't give you a ride to work last week, did she?"

Despite everything and as crazy as it sounds, I didn't really want to get Louise into trouble with Ryan. But, I couldn't lie either. I just stared at the ground and shook my head.

"Well," he said slowly, "what did you think when I didn't pick you up all week?" He sounded puzzled. "And for that matter, why...and how...did you go all week without your daily fix?" I heard the note of teasing, but I still couldn't look up. He waited a few seconds and then, "Molly?"

Rats. He wasn't just going to go away. I picked at the threads on the couch. "I thought you didn't want to pick me up anymore."

"Why on earth not?" he demanded, "especially after what happened with the bookcase?"

"Because of the money," I said in a small voice.

"What money?"

"Carolyn's money. From her cash register. It was missing. They found it in my knitting bag."

"Oh," he said.

I stared miserably at the floor, waiting for him to take his cue and leave.

I heard him sigh and shift in his chair. Here it comes, I thought.

"Why am I finding it hard to believe that you stole Carolyn's money?" he asked.

My eyes shot up to meet his. He didn't believe it. He didn't even consider believing it.

I was so ashamed. "I didn't," I said feebly, "but everyone thinks I did. It made sense that you would think so too. When you didn't pick me up—" I looked away, "I just couldn't face you."

He ran a hand over his face as if he were suddenly very tired. "I'm sorry," he said. "I knew Louise wasn't your best friend, but I never dreamed—"

"No," I said, "I'm sorry. I should have known better."

"Yep," he said, shooting me a small smile, "you should have."

Suddenly, I felt a lot happier than I had in a long time. I smiled back at him.

"So, what's the real reason you didn't go to work today?" he asked. "Carolyn was really worried about you."

Guilt. A familiar emotion.

For some reason, I didn't tell him that Louise had visited. Instead, I told him about the Knitting Fairy, about how someone was trying to make Carolyn look bad, about Happy Knits and about how scared I was that Carolyn's store would have to close. I told him how Helen and I had tried to catch the Knitting Fairy and how Mr. Morrie had caught us instead.

Then, I admitted to him that I was feeling like Carolyn would be better off without me. When he would have objected, I plunged ahead, describing in detail how I was fired from the library and hired by Carolyn. I told him how I could hardly knit and how I thought Carolyn needed someone who knew what they were doing. I told him that maybe there was some kind of connection between me and what had been happening.

He said that was ridiculous.

I told him that Carolyn had to spend so much time helping me that she didn't have time to do the things that she has to do to run the store. I felt guilty for taking her money.

When I was all done telling Ryan how wrong I was for Crabapple Yarns, he sat back in his chair, his brow furrowed in thought. "I think you're a little confused, Molly," he finally said. "Carolyn knew you weren't a knitter when she hired you. You're looking at it backwards. What Carolyn needs isn't another knitter, what she wants and needs from you is quite simple – friendship and loyalty. Apparently, things had been happening before you got there. Things that had Carolyn a little worried. Don't you see what she's gained by having you there?" I shook

212

my head. "She's gained an unbiased third party – someone she can trust. What you think is a terrible thing is probably one of the biggest reasons she hired you."

I still couldn't see it. "What do you mean?"

"You think it's so awful that you don't know anything about the knitting world. But, since you don't know anything about the knitting world, you are the one person at Crabapple Yarns who Carolyn can trust completely. You have no hidden motive or vendetta to put her out of business. Until a couple of weeks ago, you didn't even know she was in business. She wants an ally, not another crazy knitter."

Ha! I knew I couldn't be the only one who secretly believed that knitters were crazy.

But, was it possible? Could he be right? I stared at him with my mouth hanging open very unattractively. Was I a good thing for Carolyn?

"Go and talk to Carolyn," Ryan said gently, "but don't make her decisions for her."

I closed my mouth. He did have a point.

Ryan stood up to leave, and I walked him to the door. "Since you're not sick," he said, "I'll be picking you up tomorrow." He smiled down at me, and I wondered how a person could feel so warm from just a smile. "Don't be late." As he was leaving, he turned one last time, "I'm sorry you had such a rough week," he said. "From now on, until we get this whole thing figured out, do me a favor and keep me in the loop, alright?"

I nodded and he left. I headed straight for the phone. As the line rang on the other end, I felt a little anxious about what I was doing. But then, she answered, "Hello?"

"Hi. Carolyn? This is Molly." I took a deep breath and confessed that I hadn't been sick today. Leaving out the bits that made Louise sound like an ogre, I told her about my doubts and fears for her store and the lack of my abilities. I told her how I didn't think I was right for her store, and that if she wanted to let me go, I wouldn't feel badly so she shouldn't feel badly.

That's when she wouldn't let me talk anymore. Guess what? It turns out that Ryan was right. Carolyn did want me for more than my knitting skills (which was a good thing). With a regretful sigh, she confessed that she had received some threats as of late. She needed someone she could trust. I didn't point out to her that despite the fact that she wanted someone to trust, she didn't exactly act like she trusted me. But, that's okay. These things take time. Now, at least, everything was out in the open. I felt better. I could tell that she felt better too.

When I hung up, I promised that I would be in tomorrow, and I went to bed with a happier heart than I had had all day. Isn't it just like I always say? You just never know.

My last thought before I fell asleep was that God had answered my prayer. He had helped me. I just knew everything was going to work out – even though I didn't know exactly how. This prayer thing was really not that hard, and so before I closed my eyes, I prayed again. This time I just said Thank You.

Chapter 29

The Knitting Fairy's Dastardly Deed

Well, my dear friends, you should have seen the look on Louise's face when I walked into the store the next day. They do say a picture is worth a thousand words. To be quite honest, I don't even think a million words would describe it. They also say that there was a face in history that launched a thousand ships. This was something that I could believe. Louise's face could easily send ships sailing. I wonder, though, if anyone ever thought of the idea that they were actually fleeing in terror.

"Good morning, Louise dear," I said happily, as I breezed in the door. (I do a remarkable good job of breezing when I feel like it). "Isn't it a lovely morning?" She stared at me as if I had lost my marbles. I smiled sweetly at her, and went to put my purse away. "Oh," I said, popping my head back into the main room, "good news, Louise," I said, "Ryan is back in town. You don't have to bring me to work anymore."

Hee hee. I couldn't have been happier. I had a wonderful job. A boss who loved me. And a cinnamon roll in a paper bag in my coat pocket. Is it any wonder that I lost all sense of perspective lately? I hadn't been getting my daily fix.

Today, the Knitting Fairy struck again.

But in a good way. Laurie (you do remember Laurie – the lady who was pulling her hair out because of the birthday baby sweater) came in and said it was the strangest thing, but someone had bound her scarf off for her in the neatest way. It was really pretty, she admitted, but she had no idea what it was. Carolyn examined it, told her that her scarf was bound off in a picot stitch, and proceeded to show Laurie how to do it. Laurie was thrilled. She said she certainly never would have thought of it, and it did set the whole scarf off perfectly. The idea of being visited by the Knitting Fairy didn't seem to faze her at all.

When I dared to timidly ask her about her baby sweater, she giggled and waved her hand, "Oh," she said, "of course I didn't finish that in time. I did get most of it knitted, but not sewn together. So, I just pinned it all together, put it on my little sweetie pie, took her picture, and then took it all back off again. She never knew the difference." And with that, she swept over to the sock yarn and proceeded to ruin my display – Uh, I mean shop for sock yarn.

I stared at her. Talk about mood swings.

Tonight was sock class night. The class consisted of Helen, Sarah, Rachel, Laurie, and four other women who all, strangely enough, wanted to learn how to knit socks. Carolyn had invited me to join them, but I wasn't crazy. I did volunteer to stay, though. In case she needed help (ha ha). Actually, I was staying to make sure that nothing bad happened. Two pairs of eyes were better than one, and we were now on high alert for the Knitting Fairy.

It was another long, slow day. The only customers we had were the people coming for the sock class tonight. And, as the day rolled on into afternoon and early evening, I waited for Louise to leave. She didn't. It looked like she was staying for the class, too.

The ladies arrived right on time. When Laurie pulled out her chair, a playing card fluttered out. "Where in the world did that come from?" she wondered out loud. Helen quickly looked down at her knitting, making a strangled sound, which she quickly turned into a cough.

All in all, it was probably a good thing that Louise was there. See, I don't hold a grudge. Well, if you really must know my exact thoughts were...better her than me trying to get eight women to knit with little sticks that look like toothpicks. Carolyn needed all of the help she could get. As Helen dropped one of her little pointy sticks, I wondered once again why exactly they thought this was fun.

"But I just don't see what this is doing," Sarah protested. "Why do I have to use the empty double point to knit across these stitches? Can't I just use this one?"

Louise smiled tolerantly at her. I wondered if she really liked Sarah or whether she was just happy to show off her knitting knowledge – or maybe she pretended to be nice to the customers because this was the only job she could get. "Why don't I show you with the sock I'm knitting," she said.

I have never thought of myself as psychic, but I do have to tell you that as Louise reached into her small knitting bag, I had a distinct feeling of foreboding. Foreboding. It's a big word. And an unpleasant emotion. I wasn't even surprised when she lifted her sock out. Thanks to the foreboding I had the foresight to watch the faces around the table closely. They all looked genuinely horrified. No one in particular looked even remotely guilty. Louise, though, looked hopping mad. Of course, anyone would be. Not too many people enjoy slits cut into their socks. Her seething gaze landed on me. Uh-oh.

There was someone else watching me too, and I turned to meet Helen's eyes across the table. She pursed her lips and shook her head helplessly. If only our diabolical plan last night had succeeded.

Helen was right. The Knitting Fairy needed to be stopped before Louise killed me.

Carolyn had a little tradition at her store. After an hour of knitting, everyone was commanded to get up, stretch, and go eat snacks. It was a great idea. Especially when the snacks had been catered by our favorite local bakery. Apparently, there were others, besides knitters, who also knew of this tradition. Because, strangely enough, right on the hour, the doorbell chimed and Mr. Morrie walked in with Patrick in tow. Patrick looked a bit sheepish and Mr. Morrie looked hungry. He greeted Carolyn with a grunt and headed straight for the trays of goodies.

Carolyn smiled good-naturedly. "Hello Patrick," she said, "it's so nice to see you. What a coincidence, you came just in time for snacks."

He faked a surprised look. "You're kidding," he said. "My goodness, I had better help myself then. Wouldn't want to offend anyone." Helen rolled her eyes and he grinned at her. "Especially not after the excitement she caused around here—"

Louise glanced up, "Excitement?"

Helen stepped on Patrick's toe. He winced. "Why don't you eat something, dear?" she said, through her teeth. "Maybe with something in your mouth you won't feel the need to talk so much."

"What excitement?" Louise asked again.

Carolyn was busy filling up the trays almost as fast as Mr. Morrie was emptying them. "I think he probably meant the excitement with Abbey's shawl. Isn't that right, Patrick?"

Patrick popped a brownie into his mouth and nodded.

I stared at her. Apparently, she knew more than I thought she did. Interesting. I glared at Mr. Morrie. For a person who didn't say a lot, he sure said a lot.

On their way out the door, Helen whispered an invitation to join her and Patrick for lunch tomorrow at their house.

Chapter 30
Books Are Easier To Deal With Than Knitters

Carolyn was more than happy to let me have a few hours off to go to lunch. Patrick even came on his motorcycle to pick me up at the store.

Grinning, I fastened the helmet under my chin and hopped on the back. It was a beautiful day, and we were flying down the streets of Springgate. I couldn't help but let out a little whoop of joy. Patrick threw his head back and laughed.

I was sorry that we arrived so soon at their house. It was a cute little Cape Cod style. There was even a little garden behind the picket fence. Patrick pointed out a scrap of something growing in the corner and gave it a huge name, so I assumed that he was also interested in gardening.

We walked through the front door, and he proudly pointed out the hardwood floors, gleaming in the sunlight. I felt much better when I saw that the living room was delightfully cluttered. I let out a little sigh. These were my kind of people. Delicious smells were wafting out of the kitchen. I headed in that general direction, but Patrick stopped me. "Better not go in there," he warned. "She gets pretty cranky when people invade her kitchen."

We sat down on the sofa together. He leaned forward, lowering his voice, "So you and Helen got into a little trouble a couple of nights ago," he said quietly.

I shook my head. "Not really," I said with a smile. "We got beat up by a couple of chairs and scared half to death by Mr. Morrie, but that was about it."

"Helen tells me it was all her idea," he said, "to catch the Knitting Fairy." He looked worried. "I just want you to know that I told her that all future midnight escapades have to be approved by me."

"You were out of town," I said.

219

"I know," he said with a wry smile, "that's probably why she picked that night."

"Probably," I agreed, "Helen is a very determined person. And it was a beautiful plan. It was just too bad that it didn't work. The Knitting Fairy is really causing Carolyn problems right now." I looked up at him. "I just don't know what we're going to do." I wished I dared to confide in him about all of the other things going on at Crabapple Yarns too. He seemed like such a nice, solid man. The kind of person you could tell your troubles to and he would understand. Helen was very lucky.

He frowned, "Helen told me that strange things have been happening. Is it true what she said about someone cracking all of the beads out of some poor girl's shawl?" I nodded. He shook his head, "Man, that's rough," he said. "It's hard to believe that a knitter would do something like that."

I looked up at him in surprise. "You sound like you know knitters pretty well."

"I do. Well, at least I know how much Helen has loved getting to know other knitters. And, I haven't seen a mean one in the bunch. It's been good for her. And, if something makes her happy, then it makes me happy."

Awwww. Once again I thought about how Helen was one lucky woman. I looked down at my feet. There was a pattern peeking out from under the sofa. I grinned. Typical Helen. Pulling it out, I examined it as my eyebrows shot upwards in surprise.

Patrick grinned at me. "Now, now," he said, "don't get all excited."

"Patrick!" I exclaimed, "this is a child's pattern. Are you and Helen—"

"Typical woman," he said, holding up a hand, "always jumping to conclusions." Disappointed, I glanced back down at the pattern. "Better tuck it back under the sofa," Patrick said, "so she doesn't know that you saw it."

"But, why?"

He rolled his eyes. "Because we're not having a baby right now," he said, "but that doesn't mean we're not ever going to have one." He plucked the pattern from my fingers and flipped it over in his hands. "It looks like she's preparing. I guess she doesn't want anyone to know."

"Well, I won't tell," I said, pulling the pattern back and sticking it back under the sofa. "But I do expect to be one of the first people to know when you do decide to have a baby."

"Deal," he said, grinning again.

Lunch was hot chicken salad, fresh rolls, and fruit. It was absolutely delicious. Of course, the main topic of conversation was the Knitting Fairy. It was quite refreshing to actually discuss the Knitting Fairy with people who would talk about it openly. Helen stubbornly maintained that people still thought that the Knitting Fairy was Carolyn. I told her that it couldn't possibly be. We discussed who else it might be. Patrick suggested Louise. I rolled my eyes and told him that Louise simply did not have the imagination for it.

"It's got to be one of Crabapple Yarns most loyal customers," Helen said, "otherwise, why would she be destroying some knitting and helping with other knitting?"

"You know," Patrick said slowly, "it could be someone from Happy Knits."

"Picking on their own customers?" I said skeptically.

"Yeah," he nodded, gaining enthusiasm for his own idea, "yeah, it's actually not a bad thought. They're trying to make you guys look bad."

"It's working," I said.

Helen grabbed Patrick's arm enthusiastically. "I think you may be onto something sweetheart," she said. "It makes perfect sense. If they're trying to put Carolyn out of business, what better way than to make her look bad in front of everyone else. Not only does Carolyn lose business, but she looks mean and petty while they look like the perfect little victims."

I sighed and scraped up the rest of my chicken salad. "Life was so much simpler when I was a librarian."

"What do you mean?" Patrick asked.

"Well," I said, "books are much easier to deal with than knitters. Books have happy endings."

221

Helen rolled her eyes, but Patrick looked mildly intrigued. "So," he said with an encouraging smile, "what kind of book would this be?"

"Definitely a mystery," I didn't even have to think about that one. "Probably an Agatha Christie," I said with a bit more thought.

"We don't have a murder," Patrick pointed out.

"Thank goodness," Helen said quickly.

"I'm thinking Agatha because she's the queen of zippy little twists and surprise endings," I explained. "If we ever find out who the Knitting Fairy actually is, it's probably going to be the person you least suspect – and we'll all probably go 'ah-ha! I knew it all along.'"

Patrick rubbed his chin thoughtfully. "If we went with your Agatha Christie theory," he said thoughtfully, "then you would probably be the Knitting Fairy."

"Nope," I said with a grin, "Helen already tried that one. We both agreed that the Knitting Fairy is someone who knows how to knit."

He shook his head. "I've read a few mysteries in my time," Patrick said, "and you fit the bill perfectly. We only have your word that you only just started knitting. It could be the perfect cover. And, you're trying to figure out who the Knitting Fairy is, which is another perfect cover." He looked hard at Helen for a moment before turning back to me. "If this were a book," he said, "you'd be my first suspect. It's always the person you least suspect."

I stared at him. He stared back at me. Why, he almost looked serious. He didn't look too happy either.

It seemed like forever, but I'm sure it was only a few seconds before Helen let out a rather nervous laugh and smacked her husband on the arm. "Oh, Patrick," she said, "you're just too funny."

Yeah, he was just too funny.

222

Chapter 31

The Project That The Knitting Fairy Didn't Ruin

Saturday dawned bright and sunny. It was a lot like last Saturday, actually – slow, slow, slow. Some of the sock-knitting class participants were gathered around the seating area. Helen had almost six inches done already and was looking forward to "turning her heel." Yeah, turning her heel. I have no idea, either. Rachel was still on her first inch of ribbing.

"I can't believe you're not further than that, Rachel," I teased. "How many other projects do you have going on right now?"

She stuck her little nose in the air. "A knitter never tells," she said loftily.

"Well, then," I said, "I'll just have to see for myself." I looked around the floor for her knitting bag. "Where are you hiding your knitting?"

She grinned and then shrugged, "Ha ha," she said, "my knitting bag is in the wash. I spilled a whole can of pop over it. Luckily none of it got on the yarn. My projects are hiding in strategic locations, which you will never find."

Laurie gave a great sigh. "That's it," she said, "one can only knit with toothpicks for so long." She put little protectors on the ends of her little pointy sticks and took out something the color of blue frost.

I wondered if I was the only one who winced when she pulled it out. You can't blame me. Bad things happened lately when people pulled things out of their knitting bags.

Uh-oh. It didn't look too good. What had the Knitting Fairy done this time? As of yet, Laurie hadn't noticed. Odd. She flipped it over in her hands and began working. Very odd. It was very hard to believe that it was supposed to look like that. Would it be too obvious if I asked what she was knitting? Perhaps I was wrong. Perhaps knitters enjoyed knitting things that looked a limp dishrag that had been eaten by a gang of starving moths.

I caught Helen's eyes and she grinned at me. I raised my eyebrows questioningly and tilted my head towards Laurie's knitting.

Her grin was now lit with delight. She knew what I was wondering. "Well, now, Laurie," she said, "that's a very pretty shawl."

Ohhh...a shawl, was it? It looked nothing like the ones I had seen Carolyn wear or the ones that were hanging up around the store. I stared hard at it. Was it damaged? Helen met my eyes, and I gestured slightly once again.

"You know," Helen said thoughtfully, her eyes laughing at me from across the room, "it always amazes me how different lace looks when you're knitting it and then after you block it. It's like magic."

Laurie nodded. "It is, isn't it?" she said, turning it over in her hands. "It sure doesn't look like much right now."

She was right about that. Interesting. Very interesting. Not a dishrag after all. I sighed. There was just so much to learn.

When Patrick came in to pick up Helen, he greeted everyone warmly. Helen moved over to make room for him on the sofa next to her, "Let me finish this row, honey," she said, "and then I'll be ready to leave."

He gave a great sigh, "If I've heard that once—" he said.

"There are goodies on the counter," Rachel said. "Help yourself." Wasn't she a smart woman?

You didn't have to tell him twice. He came back to the sofa with a plate full of cookies and brownies. Catching his foot on the handle of Laurie's bag, disaster was imminent.

Being the true knitter that she was, Laurie's first instincts were to save her knitting. With the fierceness of a mother lion defending her cub, she threw her shawl as far away from herself as she could. Then she reached up and tried to catch Patrick's plate as it fell.

Recovering, he caught himself, and, as Laurie steadied his plate, he managed to save a brownie headed south.

"Whew," he said, his plate re-balanced, "thanks, Laurie, that was a close one."

"You're telling me," she said. "You had better thank your lucky stars that you didn't hit my knitting."

"Don't get up," he said, "I'll get it."

Carefully setting down his plate, he retrieved Laurie's knitting. He picked it up gently, a needle in each hand. "Err," he said, "that's a real pretty—" he glanced around the room for help, "Err...thing." Yarn was wrapped around his forefinger, and he tried to disentangle himself, getting more wrapped up in the process. "Oops," he said, turning to Laurie, "you'd better help me out with this before I ruin everything."

"Yeah," Helen piped up, "you'd better get it back from him quick Laurie," she said. "One thing I've learned is that he can turn a perfectly fine ball of yarn into a tangled mess quicker than you can say—"

"Don't listen to her," Patrick said with a smile. "Who spent hours last week helping you untangle that pink fluffy stuff?"

"Who got it in a mess in the first place?" Helen shot back.

Patrick hung his head, "I guess I'm guilty," he said, "but I can't help it. I'm not good with yarn. Men don't knit."

Shrieks of outrage filled the room. I jumped. Yikes. Clearly this was a sensitive issue. Who knew?

"Yes, they do," Laurie said, "I've seen them."

"They don't know what they're missing," Sarah said matter-of-factly.

"When I lived in Pittsburgh, there was a men's knitting group that met at one of the yarn stores," Rachel said.

Carolyn's smile was wide. "I think you might have said the wrong thing there Patrick," she said, "and I have to say that I agree with them. There are lots of men who knit." She looked at him over the rim of her glasses, her nimble fingers never missing a beat as she talked. "As a matter of fact, long ago, only men knitted. Women weren't even allowed to knit. Men had knitting guilds and were considered true artists. They had to study for years."

Patrick popped the last bite of cookie into his mouth and held up his hand. "I stand corrected," he said, his eyes twinkling, "and I apologize to all of the manly knitters out there. Someday, I may even get my hunting group to take up knitting. We can sit and knit here all day and all night with our wives."

"Whoa, whoa, whoa," Helen held up her hand, "let's not get crazy. Besides, I don't think Carolyn can afford enough snacks to feed your entire hunting group."

Chapter 32
The Wicked Witch And Her Flying Monkey

I don't think it's an understatement to say that there were many of us holding our breath all through the day Saturday, Monday, and into Tuesday. We were just waiting for the Knitting Fairy to make another move and hoping that she wouldn't.

Could Patrick be right? Was the Knitting Fairy really someone from Happy Knits? Could it really be that elaborate of a set up? Or, was it one of Carolyn's customers, defending Carolyn with her own brand of bizarre loyalty? Or, was there no correlation between the knitting disasters and shopping at Happy Knits? After all, Louise, to my knowledge, had never shopped there. And was the Knitting Fairy connected to the bookcase and the broken window?

Unfortunately, I had plenty of time to think about these things. Business was still very slow. It was Tuesday, and Carolyn was once again out meeting the insurance adjustor. Or so she said. I wished that I had the time (and the ability) to follow her. Did one really need to meet with an insurance adjustor more than once?

Rachel was with me at the store. Her brother was still laid up with a broken leg, and he was driving Rachel crazy at home. So, she came in to help me with the "customers." Too bad that there weren't any. Privately, I wondered if Louise had asked her to come in and watch me when Carolyn was away. Just in case I tried to abscond with the money again. Or broke another window. Yeah. I forgot to tell you that one, didn't I? Apparently Louise thinks that I broke the window myself – either in a fit of extreme clumsiness or a fit of inexplicable rage. And, since I had cleaned everything up so nicely, there wasn't much proof without the bloody rock to show. At any rate, one thing was for certain, Rachel just wasn't herself when she was around me anymore. She tried. But, it showed.

Today was one of those days. I was in the back room making another pot of coffee (Rachel drinks a lot of coffee) when I heard the doorbell ring. It was one of our customers that I had seen before. I didn't know her name, but I remembered her buying some yarn to make a hat last week or so. I peeked around the door to watch her.

She was currently trying to explain to Rachel that she was supposed to be decreasing for the crown of the hat.

"You should have kept better track of your rows," Rachel all but snapped at her. "You can't possibly expect me to know where you are if you don't write it down."

The other lady looked shocked and embarrassed. I quickly set down the coffee pot and walked to the front of the store.

"But...but—" she said, "that's just the thing, I don't remember starting on the decreases. One minute I was knitting the hat, and the next thing I know it's getting smaller at the top, and I was clearly in the decrease section." She wrung her hands together. "I just don't know how it happened."

Rachel rubbed a hand over her face. "It's alright," she said, "I'm sorry. Let's take a look at it."

Well, the customer left quite happy, and since she now knew where she was in her pattern, she left quickly too.

"Are you alright, Rachel?" I asked carefully, "you just don't seem yourself."

Rachel looked guilty. "I'm sorry I snapped at the customer, Molly," she said. "I'm just so tired. I can't sleep. Pete is so uncomfortable in his cast. He tosses and turns. The nurse in me wants to help him, and I end up staying awake all night. And then, I have to go to work in the morning and —"

I put an arm around her shoulders. "Why didn't you say something?" I asked gently, "I would be happy to come over and sit with Pete for a while so you can get some rest."

She stared at me, and her eyes filled with tears. "Oh, Molly," she said, "that's so kind of you. But, it's okay. Me and

Pete will manage." She wiped the tears away. "We always do." She said it so softly that I think she was talking to herself.

Poor Rachel. She obviously had a lot on her mind right now. She didn't want to ask for help, but I couldn't help but wonder if there wasn't something I could do. I would have to think about it. At least it would be something else to think about besides when the Knitting Fairy would strike again.

Carolyn came back from her appointment with the insurance adjustor, looking quite grim. "There go my insurance rates," she grumbled, "you pay and pay and pay and then make one claim and poof!"

Do you remember how at first, I thought Carolyn had looked like Mother Goose? Well, today, we got a visit from another literary character – the wicked witch of the west. Seriously. It could have been her sister, not the one that the house fell on, of course. She died. Another sister. I don't care if you say she didn't have another sister. You don't know everything. The resemblance was definitely there. No, she wasn't green. And she didn't have warts – at least none that I could see. And I don't think she was wearing striped stockings. But, she did have attitude. Lots of attitude. She marched in as if she owned the place.

It was, of course, Susan, from Happy Knits.

If I wasn't such a nice person, I could also say that it might have been easy to mistake the lady following in her wake as one of her flying monkeys.

If I wasn't such a nice person, I would tell you why I thought so.

But, I am. So, I won't. Her name tag named her "Gretchen." Ahhh...the master knitter - excuse me, the Master Knitter (let us not forget the capitalization). I suppose that her extra-long arms came in handy with the longer knitting needles. Oops. Sorry. It just kinda slipped out.

Allow me to rephrase without description: We were currently being visited by Susan, the owner of Happy Knits and the Master Knitter in Residence, Gretchen.

How nice.

The wicked witch, I mean, Susan, didn't waste time. She didn't stop to admire the store. Or make small talk. Or compare prices. She went straight for Carolyn. My eyes slid to the doorframe. Nope, no parked broom.

"Well, hello Susan," Carolyn said pleasantly. "Beautiful day, isn't it? How is everything over at Happy Knits?"

"Things at Happy Knits are wonderful," Susan replied with a tight smile. "I was hoping that I might have a few words with you." Gretchen stood behind her, bobbing her head like a nice little monkey.

"Would you care for a cup of coffee?" I asked them. See – told you I was a nice person.

Gretchen's expression softened a bit, but she shook her head. As did Susan.

"We're not staying," Susan said, "we just came over to ask you to please stop."

"Stop?" Carolyn's face and voice were both puzzled. Her hands rested calmly on the counter top. "I'm afraid I don't understand."

"I don't know how to say this nicely," Susan said, "but it seems that we have mutual customers."

No. Gasp. Mutual customers. How strange.

"And some of these mutual customers feel that their knitting is being sabotaged."

Rachel frowned at Susan, and I looked around the store to make sure that we didn't have any customers roaming the store.

"These customers feel that they are being singled out because they now shop at Happy Knits instead of shopping...here." She said it with a curl-lipped, as if she couldn't believe that anyone would choose to shop here.

"That's preposterous," Carolyn said firmly.

"You can't deny that there have been several episodes," Susan said, "of knitting disasters that cannot be explained. And they were all your former customers."

Gretchen's head bobbed again.

"Unless they shopped out of town or at the supermarket," Carolyn said gently, "most knitters were my customers until you opened Happy Knits."

"Well, there's no need to be bitter about it," Susan said gleefully. "It was bound to happen sooner or later. You didn't think you would be the only knitting store in town forever, did you?"

Carolyn opened her eyes wide. "Oh, we're not bitter at all, Susan," she said. "We feel that there are plenty of knitters in Springgate to support two knitting stores, and I'm happy for the knitters who live here. Now they have even more options to learn and grow as knitters." Susan looked like she was about to object, but Carolyn continued, "I know that there have been some unpleasant occurrences recently, but they have absolutely nothing to do with this store. No one here would ever think of harming someone else's knitting."

"Then how do you explain—" Susan began again, her face turning odd colors. Interesting. One shouldn't suppress their emotions or their facial expression like that. It can't be healthy. But, I guess she couldn't risk her makeup cracking with a big frown. Strangely enough, I think Carolyn's calmness was making her more upset than anything. Could it be that she wanted Carolyn to get angry and explode?

"I know you have come here with the best intentions of trying to figure out what's wrong," Carolyn said calmly, "but, it sounds a lot like you're accusing me of something, and if I were you, I would think very carefully before making any statements of which you have no proof." Carolyn paused, "It might come across to people that the new yarn store is trying to make the old yarn store look bad."

Susan sputtered, and Gretchen looked like she wanted to crawl through a hole in the ground. Apparently, this was not going the way they had planned.

It didn't take them to long after that to make their grand-sweeping exit.

I had no idea that Carolyn had it in her. Although, I guess being in business for five hundred years had given her plenty of experience in dealing with all kinds of people. But, still...talk about turning a situation around.

Rachel had tears in her eyes. "Carolyn," she said, "I...I—"

Carolyn patted her on the arm. "Don't fret about it, my dear," she said. "I'm sorry you had to hear that. Everything is going to work out fine. Just wait and see."

Isn't it funny how sometimes we know everything and yet nothing at all?

So, was the wicked witch and her flying monkey the most exciting thing that happened all day? Yep. Afraid so.

Wednesday passed uneventfully, and all too soon, it was time for the toothpick class again – I mean, the sock class on Thursday night.

Knitters love a little drama. Did you know that? Very casually and as if it was the most normal thing in the world, Laurie knitted on her sock and very innocently mentioned that her house was broken into on Tuesday. Her house had been completely turned upside down.

Needles fell to the table. Mouths fell open. High drama indeed.

Laurie didn't miss a beat. "Nothing was taken," she said calmly. "The police say that they've never seen anything like it."

Apparently, it took all day Wednesday to put things back together, but luckily no one had been home when it happened except for Captain, their Jack Russell. He was fine too. Although, judging from the fact that this treat jar was almost empty, he had clearly been well paid for his silence and cooperation.

Still processing this news, Sarah decided to rock the group further with the news shared that her knitting bag had been tampered with the other day as well. She, too, said that nothing had been taken, but the contents had clearly been rummaged through. She very kindly did not mention the fact that it might have happened at Carolyn's store.

"I've seen your knitting bag, Sarah," Laurie said, somewhat put out that Sarah was stealing her limelight, "how

232

on earth you could possibly tell that someone had gone through it is beyond me."

Sarah scowled as the other ladies around the table giggled. Then a wicked grin lit up her face. "I've seen your house, too, Laurie," she said, "how on earth—" She would have finished her sentence if Laurie hadn't thrown a skein of sock yarn that landed right in Sarah's face.

"Ladies, ladies," I cried out, "please, please settle down." For heaven's sake, if they started throwing sock yarn around, I would have to rebuild the display from the ground up. Again.

Sarah threw the sock yarn back to Laurie before looking to Carolyn. "Do you have any idea what is going on with all of this Knitting Fairy nonsense, Carolyn?" she asked.

It was the question they were all dying to ask.

Looking beautiful in a lilac sweater with lace patterns running up and down the side, Carolyn shook her head regretfully. "No, my dear," she said, "I have absolutely no idea what is going on."

"But Carolyn," Helen protested, "surely you must have some idea of who the Knitting Fairy could be."

"I really don't," Carolyn protested, "I know as much as you do."

Sarah took a deep breath, as if she were gathering her courage, "Some people are saying that they think you're—"

She didn't get a chance to finish because Rachel slammed her knitting down onto the table. We all jumped – even Carolyn. "I just can't take this anymore," she said, "I just can't." Kicking her chair back, she stood up with both hands planted firmly on the table. "I think it's time for the Knitting Fairy to come forward."

Everyone stared at her, then glanced covertly around the table at their neighbors. I don't know what she was expecting to happen. Did she really think that the Knitting Fairy was amongst us this very minute?

"You think that someone here is the Knitting Fairy?" Helen asked. I could tell by her expression that she was

233

skeptical. After all, we had already tested that theory. But, we could hardly tell Rachel that now, could we?

"Someone is knitting for other people," Rachel said firmly. "That is a fact. Not a question. It may have started out innocently, but now it's harming more people than it's helping. Carolyn's good name is being tarnished, and if someone sitting around this table has some information that they would like to share, now would be a good time to do so. No one is going to think badly of you. Just tell us. Tell us now."

My goodness. And I had always thought that I had a nice, intimidating librarian's stare. Rachel's left me in the dust. Her stare was deep and penetrating. The Knitting Fairy would stand no chance against the Stare of Death that Rachel was now currently directing around the table. She paused at each person. When she felt that the person had squirmed enough and was not confessing, she moved on to the next person. When she got to me, I almost jumped to my feet and confessed. Just to get her to stop. And we all know that I am NOT the Knitting Fairy.

Well, no one confessed, but Rachel's little outburst sure put a damper on the rest of the evening. Snack time came and went, and I think everyone was a little bit glad to leave once 8:00 rolled around. No one lingered. No one would quite meet Rachel's eye anymore either.

As Carolyn and I went around performing our end of day chores, something on the counter caught my eye. It was a little slip of paper tucked under the tray of cookies. It was typed. It said, "I'm really sorry about what I took. I will bring it back soon. The patterns are so fascinating that I can't put it down. Please forgive me. I just have to know if I can do it."

"Carolyn!" I called, "You have got to come and see this!"

She studied it carefully. I wondered if she was as excited as I was. Here it was. Actual proof of the Knitting Fairy's existence.

"My goodness," Carolyn said softly, "this is very interesting."

I turned to her, "Carolyn," I said as firmly as I could, "you must have some idea of who is behind this."

Taking my arm, she guided me to the sofa and we sat down together side by side. She folded her hands primly in her lap. "Molly, dear," she said, "I am so sorry. I haven't been completely honest with you since you started here. But, please believe me when I say that I really do not know anything for certain." My expression must have betrayed me, because she reached over and gave my hand a quick pat, "I'm not saying I don't have my suspicions," she said, "but I do not know who the Knitting Fairy is."

I sighed. "I don't either," I said, "I'm completely stumped. Helen and I can't decide if it's one of your customers or someone from Happy Knits."

She twisted her mouth. "It is a mystery," she said, "and it's really getting out of hand."

Taking a deep breath, I decided to test our newly opened waters of mutual trust. "Do you think it has anything to do with the threats you've been receiving," I asked cautiously.

She paused to consider my question. "I don't know," she answered, "it might and it might not. The threats were always very non-specific. Somehow, I didn't get the impression that the person sending them was a knitter. And the Knitting Fairy is clearly a knitter."

It was no use discussing it any further. There were too many questions, and not enough answers. One thing was for certain. Word was getting around about the Knitting Fairy. And it did not reflect well on Crabapple Yarns.

THE KNITTING FAIRY

Chapter 33
Worse Than A Leaky Sink

I tried talking to Ryan about it on our ride to the store Friday morning. He was absolutely no help. For a man who worked so close to a yarn store, he really had no clue about knitters. Shaking his head, he kept saying, "It just doesn't make any sense." Like I said, absolutely no help.

Today, I had a phone call that was almost as disturbing as a crank phone call. It certainly made my heart sink and my throat close up with dread. The lady was friendly. Completely understandable. Very polite. She asked if I could please remind Carolyn that her account was a bit past due. She would very much appreciate payment as soon as possible.

Money must be tight. Of course. I knew that it had to be. I just hadn't realized that it was that tight already. Carolyn only smiled and patted me on the arm. "Oops," she had admitted, "I thought I had paid that one already. I'll take care of it tonight." My expression must have conveyed my worry. "Don't worry so much because we're slow, my dear. Things are always a bit slower at this time of year." But her smile didn't reach her eyes, and as she took the number that I had written down, her fingers weren't exactly steady.

It cheered me up a little bit when a few customers trickled in throughout the morning. It really cheered me up that they didn't all come in at the same time, and so Carolyn could handle most of the customers by herself. Don't worry – I did my fair share. I checked them all out on the cash register. And I worked on my sweater. I now had the back done and the front started. I felt a little panicky every time I thought about putting it together someday. The edges curled horribly. The back itself looked like it would need the arms of an octopus to hold it all down straight. Ryan's scarf, you ask? Well, one can't always knit on a scarf, now can they?

237

It was getting to be our little habit that if we should have no customers, Carolyn and I would sit down in the seating area, put our feet up and knit together. Unfortunately, we seemed to be doing it a lot lately. I absolutely loved sitting and knitting with Carolyn. She had a way of making you feel very at ease. Even in the midst of chaos.

I think she knitted three stitches to my one. Her fingers flew over the needles gracefully and with the experience of one who is comfortable with themselves.

Usually we talked about everything. But, today, we were quiet. At the moment, I think I would have jumped up on the sofa and started screaming if anyone even mentioned a word about the Knitting Fairy. Or Carolyn's possible money troubles. Or, quite possibly, anything at all.

But, just because we didn't talk, didn't mean I wasn't thinking. My brain was going full steam ahead, tossing and turning, throwing the same ideas around and around.

It all boiled down to this. Someone was harassing Carolyn. The Knitting Fairy had obviously turned rogue. Carolyn was having financial difficulties. Were these three things related? Or was it all a huge coincidence? Her financial troubles could be attributed to Happy Knits, this was true. But, who was the Knitting Fairy? And who was behind the threats?

I went over the list again in my head of all of the knitters that I knew. Somehow, it was just too hard to believe. Maybe Helen's plan hadn't worked because it was too obvious. Maybe it was one of the regular knitters. Maybe it was...

My heart was heavy, and I was starting to get a headache. I peeked at Carolyn. She was still knitting calmly. I thought back to our conversation about God and His plan for our lives. She didn't just believe it. She lived it. And, me? I didn't know what to do with myself anymore. I was so sick and tired of the Knitting Fairy. I was sick of Happy Knits. I was sick of cringing every time someone pulled their knitting out of their bag. I was sick of wondering and dreading, what would happen next. I was sick of Louise and the way she had turned so many people against me – or, at least, tried to. I was just sick of everything. And, not only that, but there was a feeling building up in my stomach that I couldn't quite define. I was anxious and, for some reason, very nervous.

In one of the better decisions I had ever made in my whole life, I decided to offer up a little prayer of my own. And then, after that, I decided not to think about it anymore.

And so, I knitted.

And knitted.

I became submerged in it. Absorbed by it. I forgot Carolyn's flying fingers and concentrated, instead, on the rhythm of my own stitches. I watched my needles go in and out, the soft yarn making swoops across the tips in graceful arcs. I knitted and knitted. And then, something happened. The hard lump around my heart loosened, and for the first time in a long time, I felt something that could almost be called peace. It was wonderful. I didn't dare stop – even to admire my stitches although I could see that my knitting was growing faster than I had ever thought possible. I was in Knitting Neverland, and I never wanted to come back.

And then, the worst thing happened.

Carolyn's niece, Irene, came in and ruined our beautiful little piece of peace.

She looked neat and trim in her matching grey suit. As usual, not a hair was out of place. She looked happy. I had never seen her look happy before. Because I am a terrible person, this made me inexplicably upset. She smiled her beautiful fake smile at us, and had I been close to the sock yarn display, I would have gladly thrown each and every skein at her.

"Aunt Carolyn," she gushed, "it's so nice to see you."

Yeah, right.

"Why, Irene," Carolyn said with a faint smile, "this is a surprise. What brings you out here today?"

Irene allowed her brows to come down in what I assumed was her version of a frown. "Why," she said, "I heard that you were having some difficulties, and so naturally I came down to see if there was anything I could do."

"I can't imagine where you would have heard a thing like that," Carolyn said, "but it was very thoughtful of you to check up on us. We're fine."

Irene sat down gracefully on the tapestry chair, her legs bent together sideways at the knee. She did her best to look concerned, "Now, Aunt Carolyn," she chided, "you shouldn't try to hide things from me. We're family."

Yep, I really didn't like her. What? You can't see why? Really?

Irene leaned forward and lowered her voice. "Are you having financial troubles?" she asked, her face the perfect picture of dismay.

Drat. It looked like her little guilt trip was working. Carolyn was wavering. "It's true that the last couple of weeks have been a little...difficult," Carolyn admitted, "but it's really nothing to worry about. Although, it's very sweet of you to be concerned."

Irene patted her hair – perhaps she felt a little hair slipping out of place. The horror. "Have you given any thought to closing?" she asked innocently.

The bad thing about knitting with bamboo needles as opposed to metal needles now became apparent. Mine snapped like a dry twig. I swallowed my cry of despair and valiantly tried to keep my stitches from slipping off the broken ends. I would let out my anxiety later. There was not a doubt in my mind that this wasn't something that Carolyn couldn't fix. I had seen her work miracles before. For now, I had a conversation to follow. Can you believe the nerve of this woman?

Carolyn looked a bit taken back, too. "Closing?" she said, surprise coloring her voice, "of course we're not even thinking about closing."

Irene sighed. "I know it must be hard to think about," she said sympathetically, "especially after so many years of being open. But, I heard that you have some competition now. Are you sure that there are enough people who knit in this town for the both of you?"

Was she even listening to Carolyn? We were not thinking about closing. Period.

"A little competition never hurt anyone," Carolyn said cheerfully.

Well, Irene stayed for about 45 minutes longer than I would have liked. Well, okay, if we're going to be honest, she stayed for 45 minutes. Annoyingly, for the length of her visit, she kept coming back to the subject that it might be time for Carolyn to close her store. In a very sweet and kind voice, she pointed out that Carolyn wasn't getting any younger. With a worried frown, she wondered aloud how Carolyn would be able to pay her bills if the other store took away too many customers. The comments kept coming. Carolyn was very polite, but firm. We were not closing.

She left in a little cloud of her own perfume.

Carolyn waited until she heard the door close, before she waved her hand as if she were clearing the air. "Now," she said, "let me see your knitting before you completely lose all circulation in your knuckles."

It was true. I had been gripping my needles so tightly, that my knuckles were currently white. "I can't let go," I said desperately, "the stitches will fall off."

Carolyn eased the needles out of my hands, and grabbing a spare needle from her knitting bag soon had my stitches neatly rescued.

"I apologize for my niece," Carolyn said, handing my knitting back to me, "she was a little out of line."

I frowned. "She sounded pretty certain that she thought you should close," I said. "You're not going to take her advice, are you?"

She leaned back and grinned. "If I listened to Irene, I would be sitting in a nursing home right now," she said.

"Well," I said, somewhat shocked, "let's not ever listen to her, then."

She shook her head solemnly "Never."

"She was right, though," I said, "you could lose a lot of money to Happy Knits." I paused and made a face. "That is, until the customers realize that Happy Knits is a total drag and come back here."

Carolyn took a deep breath, sat up straight, and slapped her hands against her legs. "I almost forgot," she said, "there's more than one way to make money." And with that, she stood up and headed towards the back room.

O-kay. That statement could have multiple meanings. My beautiful knitting-induced sense of peace was slowly ebbing away.

"Where are you going?" I asked, bewildered.

"You'll see," she said mysteriously. But, she turned to look at me, and my heart soared when I saw the mischievous twinkle in her eye. It was the same Carolyn that I had seen in the park. What in the world did Mother Goose have up her sleeve now?

When she came back downstairs, she looked extremely flustered. I stood up eagerly, anxious to see what she had. But, she walked right past me. She grabbed her purse from behind the counter and headed towards the front door.

"Molly dear," she said, "would you do me a favor?"

"Of course, Carolyn," I said, confused. "What is it?"

"Would you lock up for me?" she asked. "I don't know when I'll be back. Don't wait for me. I'll see you tomorrow."

And, with that. She was gone. I ran to the window, and yes, sure enough, she was walking briskly down the street, skirt flapping with her long strides.

We only had a half of an hour before I was supposed to close. I paced the floor impatiently. There was no peace left now. Curiosity consumed me. What on earth had Carolyn been up to in my apartment? My apartment. My heart rate sped up a little. I couldn't wait until I could really say that and mean it. In less than three weeks, I would be moving in. Was she looking for something up there? She definitely had walked upstairs with purpose.

The clocked chimed. Finally. The store was closed. I locked the door and ran upstairs.

Everything looked the same. Wasn't that strange? What had Carolyn been up to?

I opened cabinets at random, checking their contents. The last place I checked was the bathroom. I opened the cabinet under the sink. It was a very deep cabinet. I had to put my shoulders through the doors to reach the back. So, naturally, I lost my balance. My head knocked painfully against the pipes. Ouch. Oh, great. There was a terrible rushing in my ears. Something wet was running down my face. Was that...... blood?

I jumped backwards out of the cabinet and put a hand to my head. Nope. It was water. Thank goodness.

I'm embarrassed to tell you that it took me a few moments to realize that water was almost as bad as blood. The rushing had not been in my ears. The pipe was leaking. I should turn off the water. I stood up and looked at the sink. Rats. The sink wasn't on. So turning the water off at this level was probably not going to help a whole lot. Rats. Rats. Rats. Clearly there was somewhere else that one should turn the water off. Where that could be was anyone's guess. Maybe it would just stop by itself. Stranger things have happened. I stared at it expectantly.

It was a beautiful dream.

A jet of water was now emerging with a little more force than before. I ran to the kitchen and grabbed all of the towels I could find, placing them where the leak would hit. Rats. It didn't look like it was going to stop by itself at all.

Mr. Morrie. Surely he would know what to do. I ran down the stairs, out the front door and next door to Mr. Morrie's. He was already closed too, but I pounded on the door anyways.

"Mr. Morrie," I yelled, "I need your help." I pounded again and then took a step back to look through the dirty windows. Where was that man? Didn't he know that my sink was leaking?

"Molly?" a voice called, "is there something wrong?" Ryan was peeking his head out of the bakery.

I spun around, "Ryan," I said, frantically, "I was just...I need—"

The door creaked open to the hardware store.

243

"What?" Mr. Morrie was not the most loquacious man in the world.

I spun back and forth between the two men. "It's a leak—" I said, "It just keeps squirting and—"

Mr. Morrie turned back around and went back into his store, the door creaking shut behind him. I stared at it with my mouth open. Well, I certainly hadn't expected that. I mean, it's not like he was obligated to help me, but you would have thought that he would have at least...

The door creaked back open and Mr. Morrie emerged with toolbox in hand.

Oh.

Ryan was already heading our way as well. We walked quickly back to Crabapple Yarns, and I led the way up the stairs.

"It's in the bathroom," I said, "through here." But Mr. Morrie was already heading in the right direction. Obviously he had been here before.

Ryan stood behind me and we peered into the bathroom anxiously where Mr. Morrie was kneeling in a growing puddle of water. I felt a twinge of sympathy for him. It was cold water. Believe me, I know.

Mr. Morrie handed me a flashlight and grunted something. I guess he wanted me to hold it. So, bending my knees, I shone the light as best I could under the sink as Mr. Morrie got out a huge wrench.

Water spritzing in his face, he put the wrench up to the bolt thingie on the pipe and turned. Interesting. We had gone from a trickle to a stream.

"Lefty loosie, righty tightie," I said helpfully.

From behind me, Ryan sounded like he was choking.

Sitting back and wiping the water from his face, Mr. Morrie gave me a look that spoke volumes. Well, if he didn't want my advice, I wouldn't give it to him. I was only trying to help.

He turned his attention back to the pipe and gave the wrench a solid turn. The pipe creaked and groaned under the pressure. I glanced warily at Ryan. He raised his shaggy eyebrows and shrugged. I looked back at the pipe. Was it actually bending? Should a pipe do that? I didn't really want a river in my new apartment.

I was paralyzed with a horrifying thought. If there was a river upstairs there would be a waterfall downstairs. My breath caught in my throat, all of Carolyn's yarn would be ruined. And it would be all my fault.

"Uhhh...Mr. Morrie?" I said hesitantly "Would you be more comfortable if I called a plumber?"

I might be.

He did not reply. Perhaps I should run downstairs and start throwing yarn into plastic bags. How many plastic bags did I have?

But, with a final groan, the pipe shuddered and, miracle of miracles, the water stopped gushing.

"It's amazing," I said, almost reverently, "it stopped."

Mr. Morrie turned to stare at me. "Didn't you think it would?" he asked.

"Oh, um—"

"I think she means that she is amazed that you got it to stop so quickly," Ryan said.

Wow. He was good.

"Oh." Mr. Morrie said obviously appeased, "well, that should hold for now. I'll come back tomorrow and fix it properly."

"Thank you so much," I said sincerely. "You have no idea how grateful I am."

"I'll just mop this up for you," Mr. Morrie said.

"No, I'll do that," I objected.

"I'll help her," Ryan added.

"Well, don't forget the drawer under the cabinet," Mr. Morrie said, "if you've got anything in there it's probably ruined by now."

I stared at him. "What drawer?"

What was he talking about? There was no drawer under the cabinet. After all, I had cleaned the entire bathroom.

245

With a long-suffering sigh, Mr. Morrie leaned into the cabinet again. He scooped the water out that was lying still on the shelf. I shined the light into the cabinet, fascinated. He pushed down in the back right corner, and we could hear a little click. He then proceeded to lift out what I had always thought was the bottom of the cabinet.

Huh. Who would have thought? There was a little compartment, clearly some kind of safe, about the size of a sheet of paper and about an inch deep.

"Is there anything in there?" I leaned in to see better.

Mr. Morrie reached in and pulled out one sheet of paper. It was definitely wet. Carolyn really didn't pick a very smart place to put a safe. Not to mention, she should have picked a waterproof safe. In her defense, however, it did look very old. The safe, I mean.

The paper was covered with drawings. The details were all smudged out by the water stains, and the pictures ran together. But, it looked to be drawings of some type of garments. I smiled. This must have been Carolyn's secret pattern stash.

I paused. Could this have been what Carolyn had come up here to find? And, if so, why did she leave them here?

I turned the paper over and over in my hands, trying to find some clue. There was nothing on the paper but the little drawings. They were very colorful, but they didn't mean much to me. Anxiety squeezed my stomach again with its big hands.

I had an overwhelming urge to speak to Carolyn.

"I think I'm going to go call Carolyn," I said, "I'll be right back."

I went quickly back downstairs to find the phone. I dialed her number and waited anxiously for her to pick up. There was no answer. Her machine eventually picked up, but I didn't leave a message.

I bit my lip. All day I had been feeling out of sorts, and now that feeling was growing to a new emotion. I realized suddenly that I was scared. But why? Nothing had happened. Today had been just like any other day. Maybe it was because of the way that Carolyn had run out of the store so suddenly. She had looked flustered...and...something was fluttering at the back of my mind, but I couldn't focus on it.

Mr. Morrie and Ryan were coming back down the stairs. "Water's cleaned up," Mr. Morrie said. "I'll be back tomorrow." He continued his trek to the front of the store.

"Thanks again," I called out behind him. The front door slammed shut behind him.

Ryan looked at me. "He doesn't say a whole lot, does he?" he asked.

I shook my head, and my attention returned to the phone I still held in my hand. I hit the redial button and waited until I heard the answering machine again.

"What's the matter?" Ryan asked.

"I can't reach Carolyn," I said, frowning. "There's no answer."

"Is that unusual?" he asked. "Do you expect her to be home right now?"

I shook my head. "Not really," I said, "but, she just left so strangely. And, now, for some reason, I'm worried."

"Worried?" he repeated, looking concerned, "why are you worried? What happened?"

When the phone rang in my hand, it startled me so badly that I dropped it on the ground. We both stared at it as it rang again.

I scrambled to pick it up. Maybe it was Carolyn.

"Hello," I said breathlessly, "Carolyn?"

"It's not Carolyn," the caller said mockingly. I recognized the voice instantly. My heart started pounding. It was Carolyn's prank caller.

"I need the Knitting Fairy," the voice growled, "bring her to the store in two hours."

What? My mind reeled. "What?" I said shakily, "what are you talking about?"

"The Knitting Fairy," the voice repeated, "has taken something I need back. Bring it to the store."

"Why would I do that?"

"Because if you don't," he said, "you won't know where Carolyn is, will you?"

"What? Where's Carolyn? Who are you?"

But the phone was dead.

Shaking, I dropped the phone. Ryan picked it up from where it crashed to the floor.

"What's going on?" he demanded. "Who was that?"

I put a hand to my head, trying to gather my thoughts.

"You're as white as a sheet!" Ryan exclaimed. "Here, sit down," and he pulled a chair out for me to sit on.

As quickly as I could, I filled him in. The words tumbled out faster than my leaky sink. Then, he sank into a chair, looking a little peaked himself.

We were silent for a few minutes.

"Maybe we should call the police now," he said finally.

I stared at him. "Do you think we should include the part where we need to procure the Knitting Fairy in exchange for Carolyn's life?" I asked.

He twisted his lips and frowned. "I guess they might find it a little hard to take us seriously," he admitted, "but, we should at least try."

"By the time we convince them of what is going on, the two hours are going to be up."

He took a deep breath and pulled himself together. "Well then," he said, "I guess the only thing left to do is figure out who the Knitting Fairy is."

Chapter 34
Just Like Agatha Christie

"It's not as easy as that," I objected. "We've already laid one trap for the Knitting Fairy, and it didn't work. I have absolutely no idea who it could be."

Panic clawed at my heart. It was true. I really didn't know who the knitting fairy was. I had no idea, no idea at all. But if I didn't find out in less than two hours, Carolyn might be...It was too horrible to think about. I covered my face with my hands.

All of a sudden Ryan was kneeling in front of me. He took my hands in both of his. His hands were nice and warm.

"It's okay, Molly," he was saying, "just take a deep breath. We'll figure this out."

I took his advice, and felt a lot better after a couple of deep breaths. Funny. I didn't even realize how shallow I was breathing until he said something.

I opened my eyes and found myself staring at him. Lines I had never seen before were now framing his eyes, and his red hair was sticking up at odd intervals like he had run his hands through it recently. Obviously, he was not exactly calm, either. This made me feel better.

"But, Ryan," I said feebly, "I have absolutely no idea—"

He gave my hands a final squeeze and sat back to sit on his heels. "Let's look at this logically," he said. "Come on, I have an idea."

He grabbed a piece of paper and a pencil from behind the counter and we sat down at the table. "Now," he said, "let's put this down on paper. What do you know?"

"Well," I said, "I don't know all of the knitters that come here, of course, but I figured that it has to be a regular. There's Sarah and Abby and—"

249

"No, no," Ryan said patiently, "I meant tell me what you know about the Knitting Fairy. What exactly do you know? Not just think."

I thought hard for a minute. "Well," I said slowly, "I know that the first project, that we know of, that the Knitting Fairy 'helped' with was Carolyn's mohair scarf."

"Good," he muttered, "that's a start." He wrote that down. "What else?"

"Well, let's see. Then, she picked up a dropped stitch on Lacey's scarf. She did a Mobeius cast on, and she kitchenered Old Mrs. Harrison's toes together."

Ryan dropped his pencil to stare at me. "She did WHAT?" He looked appalled.

I snickered. Non-knitters. They were so funny. "Don't worry," I said, "it's not painful."

He shook his head. "Knitters are weird." Picking up his pencil, he paused again. "I wouldn't even know how to begin spelling a word like that." He stared at me suspiciously. "Are you making this up?"

I held up one hand. "No. Honestly I'm not. Allow me to rephrase. She kitchenered the toes on Mrs. Harrison's socks together."

"Let's just put down 'fixed socks'," he muttered. "It sounds a lot better than what you said. Plus, it doesn't sound like something a crazy person would do. What next?"

"Well, after that, she felted Helen's purse."

"Wow," he said, "that sure wasn't nice."

I snickered again, conveniently forgetting that several weeks ago I knew even less than he did about the world of knitters. "No," I said, trying to keep a straight face despite the circumstances, "felting is a good thing in this case." I struggled to remember more details. "And then she cracked the beads out of Abbey's shawl and then sewed Jean's sleeves shut."

It was his turn to try and not grin. "Sewed the sleeves shut?" he said. "That's kinda funny."

See? I'm not the only person who thought it was funny.

"Wait," I said, "first she sewed the sleeves shut and then she cracked the beads. No. Wait a minute. Well, actually, I don't know which order those two happened in."

"Doesn't matter," he said, writing them down. "Anything else?"

"I'm pretty sure she did the decreases in a hat pattern, too," I admitted. "Oh... and she bound off a scarf for someone with a fancy stitch. And there may have been other things. I just can't think of them all right now."

"Okay," he said, putting the list between us. "Let's look at this logically. Just look at the list and try not to think of one person. Look at the details. Is there anything on this list that strikes you as odd at all? Or maybe think about when they happened. Or—"

"Slow down," I protested, "let me think."

I stared hard at the list. Somehow, I had thought the Knitting Fairy had been busier than this. It didn't seem quite so bad when it was written down like this.

"Lace shawl, moebius, kitchener," I muttered to myself. "How would I know if there's a connection?" I grumbled. "They're all things that I can't do."

Ryan studied the list with grim determination. "That's too bad," he said, "I was hoping something would jump out if we just looked at it objectively."

I started to feel fidgety again. Maybe we should just get a printout of Carolyn's customers and go door to door, begging the Knitting Fairy to come forward. I let out a ragged sigh. There just wasn't enough time. Who could the Knitting Fairy be? And why would the crank caller need the Knitting Fairy? A knitting emergency? A dropped stitch, perhaps?

We were wasting time with this list. Ryan was still staring at it. "Sure is a lot of variety," he commented. "Are you sure you can't see some kind of connection?"

I shook my head desperately. "I'm sorry, Ryan," I said, "I just don't. Like I said, I haven't done almost any of these things." Proof again that Carolyn should have hired a real knitter and not me. I held up my head with my hands, trying to think. Was it only last week that I had sat, giggling with Helen under this very table? It was hard to believe.

This was all becoming a little too unreal for me. I could feel myself disconnecting from the situation. It was like I was out of my body, watching pretend-Molly and Ryan sit by the table staring at the list dastardly deeds of the Knitting Fairy.

"Life was so much easier when I worked at the library," I said, almost to myself.

"What do you mean?" Ryan asked, half-heartedly. His hand was itching towards the pencil again.

I sighed. "No one went around knitting on other people's knitting. No one got kidnapped at the library. I only had to worry about other people when they were in a book." I sighed again. "It's too bad this isn't just a book. I would just flip ahead to the ending and read that first. And then we would know who the Knitting Fairy is."

He tilted his head and looked at me quizzically. He probably thought I was losing my mind and it would be best to humor me. "I suppose that if this were a book," he said slowly, "it would be one of those mysteries where at the end you're like, 'Of course, I knew it all along.'"

My mind was slowly returning to my body. I stared at him so hard that I think he felt uncomfortable. "You mean like an Agatha Christie?" I asked, just as slowly as he had spoken. Something was coming together. I could feel it. But the pieces were still fragile, and if I moved too fast, they would be gone.

He nodded, and I stared at the list again. "What did you say again?" I asked.

"I suppose that if this were a book—"

"No," I cut him off, "about this list? You said something a minute ago."

"Oh. Right." he paused, "I think I said that there was a lot of variety in this list."

My heart was starting to pound again. This was it. We had to go carefully, but I knew we were on the right track.

"You're right about that," I said, "this list is very diversified."

"But what does that mean?" I think he was holding his breath as he turned to me. Maybe he could feel it too.

"I don't know," I murmured, "but it means something."

We stared at the list like we were waiting for it to speak further to us.

"I don't know a lot about knitting," Ryan said, "but does it seem like the Knitting Fairy is doing repair work for people or does she just want to knit?"

"That's just it," I said, "she's doing a little of both. Not to mention the fact that she's ruined people's knitting too. I just don't get it," I admitted, "why on earth would someone want to knit on someone else's knitting? Why would they do that? Why not just stick to your own knitting?"

"Knitters are crazy?" Ryan suggested. He had my vote with that one.

"It's got to be more than just craziness," I muttered desperately. "As Shakespeare would say, there has to be a method to this madness". I felt a brief stab of panic. My inspiration was sliding away. The beautiful bloom of hope began to wither. I felt like crying.

"Unless," Ryan said slowly, "it's a knitter who doesn't want you to know she can knit." He looked at me skeptically and shrugged. "But that's ridiculous. Isn't it? And a little hard to believe." He picked up the list again. "Look at this list. The variety could mean that she is building her skills—"

I can't believe that I didn't see it before.

I grabbed Ryan's arm in my excitement. "You did it, Ryan!" I said. "You've figured it out!" I jumped off my chair. "I know who the Knitting Fairy is!" I said excitedly. "I have to go."

"Whoa, whoa." It was Ryan's turn to grab me by the arm. "Where do you think you're going?"

I tried to get away from him, but he held tight, so I settled for pulling him along with me as I headed to the door in determination. "We don't have a minute to lose," I said, "I have to go. I think I know what's going on."

"Then you're not going by yourself," he said, "I'm coming too."

253

"Great," I pulled him through the door. "You can drive."

We hopped into his car, and I gave him the address. "Do I get to know now or do I have to wait until later to find out what's going on?" he demanded irritably, speeding through the night.

I barely heard him. The pieces were still slightly wobbly around the edges, not quite together and still dancing a little bit out of my reach. I was afraid my big idea had holes the size of boulders in it, and my fear now was that I was completely wrong. If this was true, we were wasting precious time that we didn't have. I begged him for his indulgence so that I could think things through, and, to his credit, he didn't say a word until we arrived at our destination.

There was a light in the window. Relief washed through me. Good. They were home. I didn't bother with the doorbell, instead, I pounded on the door until my fist hurt. Ryan calmly reached around me and rang the bell several times.

The door eventually opened. Helen looked shocked to see us. "Molly," she gasped, "what on earth is going on?"

I pushed past her. "Can we come in?" I asked as I walked right into her living room.

Patrick stood up from the sofa as I barged in. "Molly!" he said, "what on earth is going on?"

Was that all these people could say?

Ryan had trailed Helen into the living room, looking a little bit embarrassed to be there.

"I've figured it out, Helen," I said, "I'm sorry."

Helen's mouth couldn't have fallen any lower. Patrick sank back down onto the sofa.

"What on earth—"

If she said that one more time I was going to scream.

"I know who the Knitting Fairy is!" I blurted out.

Helen and Patrick continued to gape at me. After several seconds, Helen closed her mouth, swallowed, and said, "That's great, Molly," clearly still puzzled, "but who is it?" She sank onto the sofa next to Patrick. He put his arm around her.

I started to pace the living room. "Something happened tonight and we realized that we needed to know who the Knitting Fairy was," I said. "So, Ryan," and here I gestured towards Ryan who quickly looked down at his feet sheepishly, "had the wonderful idea of making a list of everything that the Knitting Fairy has done. Setting it all down on paper like that made me realize that the Knitting Fairy is not just knitting on other people's knitting. It is doing things that are difficult and challenging. It's doing things that I have no idea how to even begin doing." I paused to look at my audience. They were rapt with attention. And still completely clueless. I sighed. They were going to make this hard, weren't they?

"I also wondered why someone would be knitting on other people's knitting instead of their own. Besides the dropped stitch, the Knitting Fairy only did things that other people could have done for themselves. It wasn't rescuing them from knitting disasters or really even helping...it was just... knitting...trying new things."

I stared hard at Helen, willing her to figure this out. "It must be someone who doesn't want anyone else to know that they can knit."

Helen was staring back at me just as intently as I was staring at her. "But who could that be?" she asked, clearly bewildered.

"I think you know, Helen," I said, "don't you?"

Helen looked shocked and then indignant. "It's not me!" she protested. "Everyone knows I knit."

I sighed. "I know it's not you, Helen." This really was going to be difficult.

And with everyone still staring at me, I walked over to the sofa, got down on my hands and knees, and reaching under as far as I could, pulled out a stack of patterns.

Ryan's freckles were standing out again. Patrick looked slightly ill. Helen looked alarmed.

And then, I pulled out piece after piece of knitting.

"Where on earth did that come from?" Helen exclaimed. "Who put that knitting under my sofa?"

255

Patrick let his head fall forward into his hands and groaned. "I knew that under the sofa was the last place you would ever go," he said. "You only move it once a year."

Ryan's face lit up with awareness, and he looked between us with a dumbstruck expression. Evidently, he was catching on.

Poor Helen was still flabbergasted. "What on earth are you talking about, Patrick? Why did you put that stuff under the sofa? Whose knitting are you hiding? And why on earth are you hiding knitting for someone?" She narrowed her eyes. "Are you seeing another woman?"

Poor Helen really didn't get it.

Still kneeling in front of Patrick and Helen, I put a gentle hand on Helen's arm, "Helen," I said softly, "Patrick is the Knitting Fairy."

Patrick groaned again. Helen remained frozen in place for exactly three seconds. I was counting. Then, she turned slowly to Patrick. "You're the Knitting Fairy?" she asked. "You're the Knitting Fairy?" Her voice was rapidly rising in volume. "You're the Knitting Fairy? That means that all this time you knew how to knit and you didn't tell me? What were you thinking?"

Patrick looked broken. "I-I," he stuttered. "I was too embarrassed to tell you. It just didn't seem like something a guy should be doing."

"What are you talking about?" she all but shouted. "Lots of guys knit!" She paused, putting a hand to her head, suddenly suspicious. "Who taught you how to knit, anyways?"

Cheeks flaming, Patrick admitted to teaching himself out of one of Helen's books. He had become addicted and could not stop. Being too embarrassed to buy his own yarn, yet endlessly fascinated by all of the knitting techniques, he had stooped to knitting whenever and wherever he could – not caring whose knitting he knitted on. Without even trying, he had become a knitting junkie. He literally couldn't stop. He wouldn't stop. He just wanted to learn one more thing and then one more thing and then...He pointed out that we were just as sexist as he was

– we had never even considered the possibility that the Knitting Fairy wasn't female. And even though I hated to admit it – he was right. But, I was still a new knitter. And so was Helen. We had a lot to learn.

Helen stopped his rant and grabbed him by the arms. "Think of all the fun we've missed by not knitting together," she said with a cry of exasperation. "I can't believe you knitted all of this stuff by yourself. Without me!"

Patrick was speechless. Clearly this was not the reaction Patrick had feared. Ryan was trying very hard not to laugh. I was still sitting on the floor between them.

"I'm so sorry honey," Patrick said, "I just—"

I could see where this was going. They were going to spend the next few hours arguing and making up, and I didn't have time for it. I hit Patrick on the knee. Hard.

He stared at me, stunned. "Patrick," I said, "this is very, very important. Where did you get these patterns? I have to know. Please, please tell me," I begged. Because I knew that, for some reason, these patterns were what the prank caller wanted back. Badly.

He took a deep breath. "I left a note," he said, looking guilty. "I was going to bring them back."

"I don't care about any of that," I said, gathering the patterns together. Ryan joined me in stacking up the knitting. "I just need a name. Please."

He hesitated, looking back and forth between us and then back at Helen again.

"Please." I asked again, not quite stopping the break in my voice.

"Rachel," he said quietly, "I stole the patterns from Rachel. But," he said, his face brightening, "I didn't steal the yarn. I bought that at the grocery store. I hid it in the new tackle box that I bought at the same time until I got up to the register. "

Rachel! I cracked myself on the head and looked at Ryan, No wonder she didn't have her knitting bag with her this week. Patrick had stolen it. Why? I had no idea. But, at least, this was a start. "It is like Agatha Christie!" I exclaimed. "I should have known. It all makes sense now."

"Maybe to you," Ryan muttered.

"Oh, honey," Helen was really shocked now, "don't tell me you've been knitting with acrylic yarn all this time!"

We really didn't have time for this. We stood up, our arms full of knitting and patterns. "I know you won't understand," I said, "but we have to take these with us."

I doubted that they even realized we were gone. They had a lot to talk about.

Chapter 35

In Which I Don't Make A Good Sherlock

As we raced back to Crabapple Yarns, Ryan wasted no time in demanding an explanation.

"Well, when we said 'Agatha Christie' earlier, it made me remember a conversation I had just had the other day with Patrick and Helen. I had said almost the same thing. I remembered the strange look on Patrick's face at the time. I thought he was trying to accuse me of being the Knitting Fairy, but I think he was trying to communicate something. He must have been feeling a little guilty about the trouble he was causing. But, he didn't know how to stop, and I don't think he wanted to stop knitting either. And then, when he came to pick Helen up the other day, he picked up Laurie's shawl that had dropped on the floor. He hid it well, but when he picked it up, he picked it up like a knitter, the yarn wrapped around his finger and everything." I hit myself on the head again, "I'm so stupid. I saw it all. And yet, I saw nothing."

"Well," Ryan said, "if it makes you feel any better, I would never have guessed that Patrick was the Knitting Fairy. How did you know that stuff was under the couch?"

"I didn't," I confessed, "it was just a guess. But when I was at their house for lunch, there was a pattern peeking out from under the sofa. Patrick said Helen was hiding her patterns down there. It didn't make sense at the time, but when you said that maybe the Knitting Fairy was someone who didn't want anyone else to know that they knitted, it all started to click into place. And then I remembered the note."

"What note?"

"Oh," I said, "I guess I forgot to tell you about the note that the Knitting Fairy left."

"Well," he said, somewhat sarcastically, "I'm so glad you forgot to tell me half the clues, Sherlock."

I huffed. "Sorry," I said. "The Knitting Fairy left a note. And, the last part said something about needing to know if he could do it. And, I once heard Patrick say, 'you never know what you can't do until you know you can't do it.'"

"Oh," Ryan said, "well, had I known that, I would have figured it out too."

"I really don't know how I put it all together," I said honestly. "It was like there were all of these pieces floating around in the air and I knew that they fit together somehow, but I had no idea how. Or why."

"Sometimes your subconscious is working even when you don't realize it," Ryan said.

"Maybe it was God," I suggested timidly. "I think maybe He helped me." I held my breath, wondering what Ryan would say about that.

He just nodded. "Could be," he said, "if we ever needed help, it was tonight." Ryan didn't sound shocked at all about including God in everyday conversation. He paused thoughtfully, "I guess, as a plumber, Patrick had access to a lot of knitters."

"That's right," I said, "I didn't even think about how he had done it. I bet if we took our list and cross-referenced it, we would find that Patrick had been in these people's homes at some point to fix a plumbing issue."

"And everyone was so sure that it was a woman, no one even considered that the plumber was knitting for them." In the light from the dashboard, I could see Ryan's brow furrow in thought. "But why did he sew people's sleeves together...and—"

"He didn't," I said grimly, "Rachel did. I don't know why, but I know it was her."

He was quiet for a long moment. "I can't believe it. I just can't believe it."

But, we didn't have any more time for discussion. We were back at Crabapple Yarns.

Chapter 36
Fear

Ryan leaned over me in the car. "So, you're sure that this guy wants these patterns?" he asked, looking at the patterns in my hand as best he could in the dim light. The knitting sat on my lap in a pitiful little pile of acrylic.

"It has to be," I said desperately. "I don't know why, but it's the only thing that makes sense."

I looked at the darkened store. We still had half an hour before the deadline. My heart was beginning to pound hard again.

"Give them here," Ryan said quietly.

"What?"

"Give me the patterns. I'll bring them in. You wait out here."

"Yeah, right," I said, "that's not going to happen."

His eyebrows pulled together in a scowl. "There is a man coming to the store who threatened Carolyn's life if we didn't bring the Knitting Fairy. This is not a joke."

"He didn't really want the Knitting Fairy," I objected. "He wants these. The Knitting Fairy stole them from Rachel. "

"I understand that," Ryan said patiently, "and that's what I'm going to give to him."

"No, you're not," I said, just as patiently, "I am. I'm the one who talked to him. If he sees you and not me, he could leave and then C-Carolyn..." my voice wavered.

Ryan's hand closed over mine as he gently tried to pry the papers away from me. "Carolyn's going to be fine," he said. "Give me the patterns."

"I'm bringing them in," I said stubbornly. "We can't risk Carolyn like this."

"I can't let you do that," he said. "Somebody could get hurt tonight. Have you forgotten the van? Or the bookcase? Stay out here. Call the police if—"

But, I was already jumping out of the car, patterns and knitting firmly clutched in hand. Ryan's misplaced sense of chivalry was very sweet, but completely out of line. Playing games with Carolyn's life wasn't an option.

Ryan said a bad word, and I heard him scrambling to get out of the car after me. He was quick. But I was faster. My hand was already on the door handle when he grabbed my arm. And, just so you know, grabbing that handle was not an easy thing to do with my arms full of knitting and papers.

"Molly," he hissed, "I really think—"

The handle turned in my hand. I looked at him. "Did we forget to lock the door?" I whispered.

With the sigh of a man who knows he will not win, he pushed himself ahead of me and opened the door. He stretched out a long arm to brush the light switches, but the room remained shrouded in darkness. He made the mistake of moving aside to try the switches again at closer range, and I zipped past him.

I had seen Carolyn. "Carolyn!" I cried, running towards her.

Ryan called out a warning, but I didn't listen. I never listen. Maybe someday I'll learn.

She was sitting behind the counter. I could only see her dimly in the shadows. Why wasn't she moving? Why wasn't she talking? My heart pounding heavily in my throat, I was only a few steps away from her when a shadow disentangled itself from one of the shelves. He was wearing a ski mask and baggy sweat pants. I've never seen anything quite so terrifying in my life.

"That's far enough," he said. It was him. The voice. "Put the patterns on the table."

And now I could see why Carolyn wasn't moving. She had been tied to a chair. Her mouth firmly gagged.

Cold fear pounding in my veins, I walked slowly back to the table and dropped the patterns and knitting on it, slowly backing away. In case you ever want to know – extreme fear tastes like metal in your mouth. It's awful. You feel like being sick and shaking and crying and hiding all at the same time. He had a gun. I could see it gleaming in what light that there was.

Was that all there was? Would he take the patterns now and go? His gun swiveled back and forth between me and Ryan. My knees were shaking. "There they are," I said in a voice that sounded much braver than I felt. "Take them and go."

He approached the table slowly, his feet moving oddly – rather like a robot. "Oh, I'll take them," he said, facing me, "but I'm not quite ready to leave yet."

My heart twisted inside of me when I saw the gas can sitting on the floor. A fresh wave of horror washed over me. No. This was all going wrong. This couldn't be happening.

There was a sudden blur of motion to my right. Ryan had taken advantage of the man's momentary distraction and rushed at him. The man was quick. Faster than I have ever seen anything happen, he had his arm raised, gun pointed towards the shape of Ryan.

"No!" I yelled. I, too, rushed at the man, trying to knock aside the hand that held the gun. He grabbed me, twisting my arm with one hand to pull me closer. I tried to throw him off-balance, but he was too solid.

The sound of the gunshot was deafening. It was an awful sound. A life-changing sound. A sound you will never forget. I could hear it ringing in my ears, over and over again.

Never, ever in my life do I ever want to relive those five seconds. They were the worst five seconds. I didn't know that one could live an eternity in that amount of time. In the vast expanse of time present and past, how could five seconds even mean that much? But, I can still see them so clearly in my mind. The gun went off with a puff of smoke and, even as he pulled me towards him, I saw Ryan fall. I don't remember screaming, but my throat hurt, so I guess I did. The smell from the gunpowder burned my nose. In one motion, he had turned his gun towards me, holding me with one arm and the gun pointed at me with the other.

Ryan! Where was he? I couldn't see where he had fallen behind the table. I struggled to get away, but his grip only tightened. I couldn't help the sob that escaped me.

"I am so sick of all of you knitters," he snarled. "This ends now."

But, the fun was not over yet. A small form burst through the door, and the man covered my mouth with his grimy hand to prevent me from screaming. He also covered half my nose. I could hardly breathe. I struggled, trying to re-adjust his grip, as he dragged me backwards into the store – back into the darkness. I knew the gun was pointed at me. Ryan still had not moved.

"That's enough, Pete," a familiar voice said. "It's too late."

"Shut up," the man spat. "Get out of here."

My struggles succeeded in loosening his grip a little, and I took advantage of the freedom to breathe and then twisted my leg and stepped backwards on his foot. Ow. I wasn't expecting that. I think I might have broken my foot. He had some kind of hard covering over his foot and leg. Through my fear, reasoning began to kick in.

I knew who this man was. Rachel's brother. The one with the broken leg. The pieces were coming together.

From the direction of the table, I heard a groan. My heart leaped. Ryan!

"No, Pete," Rachel said firmly, "this has got to stop."

"It's too late for that," he said, and I heard the note of desperation in his voice. Not good. Not good at all. "I don't have a choice. You know that."

Rachel came slowly through the store. "It doesn't matter anymore, Pete," she said. "We're in way over our heads. We can't go on like this." She sidestepped Ryan's body, still lying on the floor. Her face was drawn and white and anxious. "I'm not going to keep quiet anymore. I'll tell everyone. You're going to have to face up to your mistakes just like I'm going to have to face up to mine. And I was wrong to let it get this far."

"That's not going to happen, Rach," he said, "it's too late."

"It's not too late, Pete," she pleaded, "it's never too late. We were wrong. Please, just stop. Let Molly go."

His grip did not loosen, but I could feel the hesitation in his body. I held my breath. I think Rachel was holding hers, too. Tears were streaming down her face.

"No," Pete said finally, "No, Rachel. Go home. Before you get hurt too."

TOO? Oh dear.

Ryan was struggling to get to his feet. Pete grabbed me tighter, and I cried out as he twisted my arm further. He had my right arm stretched over my left arm. I couldn't move either. For the first time in my life I was physically helpless. I hated that feeling. Rachel winced. "Let her go, Pete," she said, "there's no way out of this."

Ryan's legs were wobbly as he clung to a chair, trying to stand. "She's right, Pete," he said weakly, "there's no way out."

Pete swung the gun at Ryan. "You stay back!" he shouted. "Just stay back!"

Rachel took a step forward, as did Ryan. Pete swung the gun back to me. I could feel the cold metal on my temple and I closed my eyes. I'm ashamed to tell you that I couldn't stop the tears that rolled down my cheeks. I had never been so scared in my life.

"Stay back," Pete said again. "I'm warning you. Come any closer, and I'll...I'll—"

"You'll what?" Rachel challenged. "Kill her?"

Oh great, I thought hysterically, encourage him. I could feel Pete starting to shake behind me. Could it be that he was scared, too? And, then, strangely enough, I felt a sudden surge of pity for him. Isn't that odd? I was feeling sorry for the man holding a gun to my head. I must be a true knitter now because I was clearly crazy.

Ryan stopped mid-stride and held up both hands. "Easy," he said softly, "let's just take it easy. You don't want to hurt anybody." He took a small step forward.

Pete swung the gun back to Ryan. "Don't tell me what to do!" he yelled. I decided to forget that I felt sorry for him and renewed my struggle to escape. I knew he couldn't hold on to me and hold his gun up and steady at the same time. He would never be able to shoot and hit Ryan or Carolyn, or even Rachel for that matter if I squirmed enough. Swearing, he swung me away from his body, holding me tight at his right side, the gun pointed back at me once more.

Oh. Yeah. There was a flaw in my wiggling plan.

Ryan stopped, his face white, and a trickle of blood running down from his forehead.

"Please, Pete," Rachel begged. "Please."

Ryan took a couple of steps forward again. Pete was enraged. "I told you to stay back," he snarled. He pointed his gun at Ryan once more, and I could tell by the look on his face that this time, he just might shoot.

Rachel saw the same thing, too. "No, Pete!" she yelled. "No!"

I looked around desperately. Pete's hand was like a vise around my arm. Rachel dove towards Ryan, trying to push him out of the way. With a start, I realized that we were standing next to the needle display. Being the little marketer that she was, there was a little can on the display with samples of the needles that we sell. By some miracle or stroke of luck, the can was at just the right height.

I felt Pete gather his breath, and I knew something was going to happen. Something that could turn out badly. I would have to act fast. I kicked him with all the strength that I had on his broken leg. I know. It wasn't very nice. But, it was effective. He howled with pain, and loosened his grip on my arms just enough for me to wiggle my hand and grab the closest thing out of the can that I could reach. I'm pretty sure it was a metal double-pointed needle. Size 2, I should think. Small. Very pointy. And painful.

I stabbed him in the leg as hard as I could, and he howled in pain as he pulled the trigger. I think the bullet ended up somewhere in Mr. Morrie's newly rebuilt shelves. I remember thinking that Mr. Morrie would not be pleased. The gun clattered to the floor, and Pete let go of me.

Ryan was already halfway across the room when the shot rang out. He ducked, but kept coming, tackling Pete to the ground. Pete did not put up a fight.

Rachel collapsed by the table, shaking and crying. With hands that were shaking quite hard myself, I picked up the gun very, very, very carefully and tucked it high up on the shelf with the cashmere yarn.

Then, I raced to untie Carolyn. She, too, was shaking like a leaf, and as I untied her hands and pulled the gag from her mouth, the first thing she did was wrap me in a bone-crushing hug, "Oh, thank God, you're safe, Molly!" she breathed. "I was so scared."

I hugged her back just as hard as I could.

Ryan had one of Pete's arms behind his back, and he walked Pete back to the table, pushing on his shoulder to make him sit down. He had taken Pete's ski mask off. Funny how Pete didn't look quite so scary any more. He didn't even look that old.

"Do you have anything to tie him up with?" Ryan asked, "Just in case he decides to cause more trouble?"

I doubted that Pete would be causing any more trouble for quite some time. His shoulders were slumped in defeat, and despair was written over every line in his face. He didn't make eye contact.

Ryan had to repeat his question before it sank in. "Do we have anything to tie him up with?" I asked, looking at him dumbfounded. "What kind of question is that? This is a yarn store."

"The wool/hemp blend right behind you would do very nicely, Molly, dear," Carolyn said, her throat still a little scratchy sounding. "It's especially sturdy."

Have you ever noticed that after a crisis, people act strangely and say the oddest things? This may have been one of those times. Because, instead of tying our bad guy up as fast as we could, we ended up debating on which type of yarn we should use.

"Are you serious, Carolyn?" I said, "that would be a complete waste of wool. Let's use the kid's acrylic blend."

"Oh no," Carolyn said, "I really don't think that would hold up."

"But it wears well," I countered. "I'm sure it would be strong enough. We could use the super bulky."

With a sigh and a roll of his eyes, Ryan ignored us and grabbed the closest skein to him, tying Pete's arms securely behind his back. It was pink. Mostly acrylic. It had intervals of pink sparkly eyelash sticking out at random intervals. Certainly not the choice of hardened criminals. He didn't bother tying his legs. One had a cast. And the other was bleeding just a bit from the stab wound. A size 2 doesn't make that much of a hole.

I really wasn't too happy about that. I think that for the rest of my life I will remember the sucking sound the needle made as it came back out of Pete's leg. It's a good thing it was just a short needle. He would probably need a tetanus shot, though.

After that, we all sat rather weakly down around the table. It was over. But, there were still some questions that needed answering. Ryan was holding a wet dishcloth to his head. He had not been shot. Instead, as he was diving for the ground, he had hit his head on the table. He was shaking, too. So, we just sat there, not quite looking at either Pete or Rachel. Carolyn sat between Ryan and Rachel. I think we were all in a bit of a daze. No one seemed in a real hurry to call the police.

Strangely enough, it was Pete who broke the silence. "I didn't mean for all of this to happen," he said rather pitifully. "One thing just led to another, and then I couldn't stop."

"Would you really have hurt someone tonight?" Carolyn asked. Her gaze was sharp and piercing.

Pete hung his head. "I don't know," he said honestly. "I didn't want to hurt anyone, but I just felt so desperate."

"Violence is never the answer to anything," Carolyn said crisply. "But, the fact that you're being honest about it counts for a lot." Her eyes went over to the gas can on the floor. "And I assume you were going to burn my store down?" she asked.

Pete looked shocked. "No ma'am," he said, "that was gas for my motorcycle. I was just being prepared. Can you imagine running out of gas on your getaway?"

I think he was serious. To my astonishment, I felt the corners of my mouth tugging up in an unwilling smile. I hid it quickly behind my hand.

Carolyn then turned her piercing gaze to Rachel. "And you, young lady," she said, "what have you got to say for yourself?"

"Nothing," Rachel whispered, her tear-stained gaze never leaving the top of the table. "I'm so sorry."

Ryan set his washcloth down on the table. "Well," he said, "I, for one, am absolutely dying of curiosity of why you, Rachel, of all people, would sew people's sleeves shut and crack beads and...what was that other word, Molly...kitchen?...oh, yeah, kitchener some poor old lady's toes together? It just doesn't seem like you at all."

"I never kitchenered anyone's toes," Rachel said, almost indignantly, finally raising her eyes. "That was the Knitting Fairy."

"We know," I said gently. "You were the naughty half of the Knitting Fairy, weren't you?"

She nodded miserably. Fresh tears streamed down her face. She looked like a mess. Carolyn put a motherly arm around her, "Why don't you just tell us everything," she suggested. "You'll feel a lot better. I knew something was troubling you lately, but I had no idea it was this serious. Why didn't you say something?"

Rachel let out a small sob and put her head in her hands, "B-Because—" she sobbed, "I stole your knitting patterns."

"Ah," Carolyn said, "I know. I figured that out this afternoon. I was on my way over to talk to you when your brother decided to detain me."

Rachel sent him a frustrated look. Tears welled up in his eyes, too. "I'm so sorry," she said again, "I don't know when this got so out of hand." She took a deep breath. A couple of months ago, Pete got into some trouble. Gambling. He owes...quite a lot of money. We just didn't have it. I tried talking them into payments or something, but they wanted the whole amount. Or else. Pete's my brother. I tried getting a loan, but my credit hasn't been too good since my parent's died. The funeral expenses last year just about wiped us out. And then, you had a doctor's appointment, and I was helping Louise watch the store. There was a customer in the bathroom, and I had to...well...it was the oddest thing. I dropped my earring, and, somehow, it got under the sink. When I saw your drawings, I knew they would be successful. It was almost like it was meant to be. I took them home and worked on them and wrote the patterns up." She shrugged her shoulders, helplessly, unable to continue.

We were all surprised when Pete spoke up. "The phone calls were my idea, Carolyn," he said suddenly. "Rachel was angry at me for doing that, but I thought if we kept you busy wondering who was harassing you, you wouldn't start working on your patterns." He sighed. "And then you hired Molly, and we were scared that since you had more help, you would have more time to get back to them. Rachel already had a distributor who was interested in the patterns."

"So it was you who tried to scare Molly with the van," Ryan said darkly. "And you knocked over the bookcase." He leaned across the table. "Don't you realize that you could really have hurt someone?"

Pete hung his head again. "It was me with the van," he admitted. "I never thought that she wouldn't tell Carolyn about it. I just wanted to scare Carolyn. Rachel didn't know I was going to do that."

"But it was me with the bookcase," Rachel admitted quietly. "I never dreamed that Molly would be in the store when it happened. I thought everyone would stay in the back room. I loosened the shelf with a crowbar the Sunday before. I've just been sick ever since then thinking about what could have happened. I was miserable because I was hurting you, and you didn't even know it. I tried to call it off then. I was going to stop.

Really, I was. I couldn't do it anymore. Just the thought of scaring you is more than I can think of. But, then Pete was attacked. And he broke his leg."

"You mean they actually broke his kneecaps?" I goggled at her.

"Oh no," she said, "they threw a few punches, and he broke his leg trying to run away and fell down the stairs. But they were going to come back and hurt him for real if we didn't have the money soon." She was crying harder now. "I just didn't know what to do. I felt so alone. I couldn't go to anyone. It was like I had dug this deep hole, and there was no way out, so I just had to keep digging. I had heard Helen talking about the Knitting Fairy, and with Happy Knits opening, I knew Carolyn would start losing money. She would go back to working on her patterns. I just couldn't risk her finishing them before me. I thought it would give Carolyn and Molly something else to think about if the Knitting Fairy started behaving badly." She covered her face with her hands and sobbed harder. "I can't believe all of the terrible things I've done," she cried, "things that make me sick."

Tears were rolling down Pete's cheeks too. "Don't cry, Rachel," he said desperately. "It's my fault, not yours." He turned to Carolyn. "I-I—"

Rachel turned to Carolyn. "I know you won't believe me," she said, "but I was going to pay you back for the pattern ideas. I really was. I just needed the money right away and—" She didn't get the chance to finish because the door flew open and about a hundred men jumped inside.

I didn't think I had the energy to be scared again, but strangely enough, I did.

It was the police and Mr. Morrie. I sagged against the table.

I might have exaggerated just a tad about the number of men. There were three (including Mr. Morrie).

"Mr. Morrie," Carolyn gasped, "what on earth—"

Let's stop for a moment, shall we? Does it strike anyone else here as odd that people tend to use the phrase, "What on earth—" a whole lot when they're confused? Just checking. I find it extremely odd. And just a little bit boring. I really expected better from Carolyn.

Anyways, back on planet earth...

"I thought you might need some help," Mr. Morrie said, scratching his head, his voice trailing off. "But it looks like everything is under control."

Ryan had jumped to his feet when they burst through the door. Now, he gestured to the empty chair between me and Pete, "Have a seat," he said to Mr. Morrie, sitting back down himself.

"Good evening officers," Carolyn said sweetly.

The officers were quick to notice that something strange was going on. Perhaps the pink yarn tying Pete's wrist together was their first clue.

"Did you have a little trouble here tonight?" one of the men asked.

Rachel cleared her throat. "Yes, sir," she said, valiantly fighting back tears. "You should know that...owwww—"

"That this troubled young man broke into my store, obviously looking for money," Carolyn finished. Rachel leaned an arm under the table. It looked like she was rubbing her foot.

Rachel looked bewildered. Pete's head shot up. He looked bewildered too.

"Someone called in a complaint that they thought there might have been a kidnapping—" the other officer said slowly. "Any of you know anything about that?"

"Well, sir," Ryan began. He didn't finish, though. His face contorted slightly in pain and he stared indignantly at Carolyn.

"Kidnapping?" Carolyn echoed. "No, officer. Nothing like that happened here. Are you sure you're at the right address?"

"How about you, miss?" the first man said to me, "you look a mite frazzled. Do you know anything about a kidnapping?"

I doubted she could reach this far, but just in case, I replied quickly, "No sir."

Well, look at that. Mother Goose had turned us all into liars.

I really feel like I need to say that normally, I don't tell falsehoods to police officers, and it's not something I would advocate, either. However, the police aren't really equipped to deal with bad knitting fairies, so I felt it was justified. Evidently, Ryan agreed too. Either that or he just didn't want to get kicked again.

Thirty minutes later, Carolyn had very calmly and with great efficiency bundled Pete and the policeman out the door. She had insisted that it had been a case of breaking and entering – that we had caught the perpetrator, no one had been harmed, and to please let her know if she needed to appear in court to testify. Pete did not object.

Rachel hadn't stopped crying. Not noisy, gushing sobs or anything like that. Just tears that wouldn't stop running down her face. She watched Carolyn with an expression I had never seen before. Like she could not believe what she was seeing.

I sympathized with her completely. It was the first time I had ever seen grace used as a verb too.

The police came and went, and we were still sitting around the table. I'm afraid I was having another out-of-body experience. I guess I just don't handle stress very well. It was like I was watching the events unfold from somewhere outside of myself. Ryan, at least, made himself useful and made a pot of coffee. He set a cup in front of everyone. I drank mine even though I still hated coffee. No one said much. Not that Mr. Morrie ever said much.

"Why?" Rachel finally asked. "Why?" She tried wiping tears away, but they kept flowing.

Carolyn knew what she meant. She patted Rachel's hand. "What's in your heart isn't always what's in your head," she said. "When you're desperate, you do things that you never thought you would be capable of.

"But I did terrible things," Rachel sobbed. "You should be angry with me—"

"Well," Carolyn said with a sigh, "I'm not exactly happy with you. But, in many ways, I do understand. Love is the fiercest emotion there is, even when it's misguided. Pete needed to face up to his mistakes not try to cover them up with another one. Stealing my drawings wasn't your best idea, either," she chided gently. "But I think you've punished yourself enough just by living through each day with the knowledge that you were going against everything you believed in as a knitter."

Rachel sobbed again. Misery was etched into her face. "I don't know what to say," she said. "You should have told the police the truth. I want to take responsibility for what I did."

"Nonsense," Carolyn said briskly. "The best way to take responsibility is to help me get these patterns ready to be sold. They might have been my ideas, but you did all the work. From what I can see, even from here, they're adorable. We'll split the profits. I'll even advance you what Pete owes. You can pay me back once we start making money."

"I don't know," Rachel said doubtfully, shaking her head, but I could almost see the faintest glimmering of hope in her eyes.

"Well," Carolyn said, "I do know. And, of course, you'll have to promise me that your days as the bad Knitting Fairy are over. It also goes without saying that you won't knock over any more bookcases." She was teasing, and Rachel couldn't help but give her a small smile.

"But you can't afford that," Rachel protested, quickly sobering. "Not with Happy Knits opening and everything."

Carolyn waved her hand loftily. "Do you really think that this store is my only source of income?" she asked. "Don't be silly."

It must have been kind of funny to watch Ryan, Mr. Morrie, and myself throughout this exchange. We said nothing, our heads swinging back and forth between each woman as she spoke. I was literally speechless. A strange occurrence for me.

Carolyn stood up and, standing behind Rachel, patted her shoulder affectionately, "One mistake shouldn't dictate the rest of your life," she said softly. "I'm afraid Pete is going to have to spend a little time in a correctional facility unless he gets community service. Judge Hopper is usually pretty lenient towards first-time offenders. But, this is a one-time deal. If he gambles again, I won't help him."

She sent Rachel home, but not before offering her one more piece of advice. "Love may be one of the fiercest emotions," she said, "but regret is one of the most debilitating. Take my advice. Don't look back. Just look forward. On Tuesday I told you that everything would be fine. Of course, I didn't quite expect all of this to happen, but I was right. Pete's debt will be paid off, and you and I will have a new line of patterns to sell. What's done is done. Don't look back at it and wish you had done things differently. It won't change anything but your attitude – and that for the worse."

Rachel hugged Carolyn. "Thank you," she whispered, and then she was gone into the night. I hoped she would be alright. Carolyn had certainly given her a lot to think about, and a reason to hope again. There was finally a light at the end of Rachel's tunnel.

Mr. Morrie got up walked around the table. He kissed Carolyn on the cheek and walked slowly out the door.

Ryan rescued the gun from the cashmere, removed the bullets, and promised us that he would take care of it discretely and anonymously. I was glad for that. I never wanted to see a gun again in my life.

Chapter 37
In Which The End Is A Beginning

I spent the night at Carolyn's house. I told myself that she shouldn't be alone after such a terrifying ordeal. But the truth was, I didn't want to be alone. Because, despite the fact that things had turned out happily ever after, it had been a terrifying ordeal. Carolyn had been kidnapped and tied to a chair. That wasn't something you just forget right away. I didn't exactly forget the fact that someone had held a gun to my head, either. We invited Ryan to spend the night, too. Carolyn had a couch that would have fit him just about right, but he declined. He was clearly braver than I was. Either that or he was just plain tired of dealing with crazy knitters. Who could blame him?

After we had breakfast, I headed to my apartment to change my clothes and shower. Carolyn went to the store. She said she wanted to get another look at those patterns.

To my surprise, after I showered and was getting ready to leave, Ryan rang my doorbell. "But Ryan," I said in surprise, "you don't have to pick me up anymore, remember? There's no more bad guy."

He just smiled a crooked smile and said that with all the trouble I was capable of getting into, a ride to work in the morning couldn't hurt.

He walked with me down to Crabapple Yarns. I think he wanted to see for himself that everything was fine. Things do tend to look differently in the cheery sunshine of morning, and as we walked through the door, the bright rays of sunshine illuminated the store beautifully. There was no darkness here anymore. Rachel was sitting by the table with Carolyn.

"I was thinking we could call the line of patterns 'Pipsqueaks'," Rachel said.

"I love it!" Carolyn exclaimed, "it's perfect. I just can't believe that you wrote all of these patterns based on my silly little drawings. What a lot of work. And in all the different sizes!"

They had Patrick's knitting laid out on the table. For the first time, I studied the patterns and the prototypes closely. They were absolutely adorable. It was a whole line of children's patterns. But, not just ordinary patterns. Everything buttoned together. The vest had optional sleeves that you could button in. The sleeves were short with longer pieces available to button on for added length. Each panel of the vest was also interchangeable. Patrick had knitted each panel in different colors. The left front was pink. The right front was yellow. The back was orange. The orange back was also able to be buttoned to a purple front to make a pullover. There was even an optional, knitted, ruffled border that could be buttoned onto the bottom of any piece. It was just too cute. Pipsqueaks were going to be very, very popular.

I was examining my new tentacle hat when Patrick and Helen walked in, hand in hand. The hat was from Louise. There had been no grand apology. No wasted words. No words at all, actually, she had just given me the hat and left. It was the ugliest hat I had ever seen. I cuddled it to my chest like a treasure and watched Patrick apologize profusely to Carolyn. And then he apologized profusely to Rachel. And then they both apologized for calling the police. Apparently, after Ryan and I left, it had occurred to them that we had entered and exited rather strangely. So they called Mr. Morrie and the police.

Carolyn just smiled. She hugged Patrick and told him that you should never, ever deny your inner knitter.

And then she swore everyone in the store to secrecy. There was no need, she said, for upsetting the other knitters. A little mystery now and then was good for the soul.

When they left, Helen was chattering happily. She was already planning their first knitting project together. Matching Aran sweaters. "You mean with cables?" Patrick asked excitedly, "that's one thing that I didn't try."

"Oh, honey," Helen answered, "let's go home and cable."

Later, sitting on my favorite tapestry chair, listening to Rachel and Carolyn plan and dream, I realized that some of my most life-changing moments had happened here in this chair. Sitting here, I had taken a job to work at a yarn store, my heart pounding in my chest and wondering if indeed, a yarn store could possibly have customers. Sitting here, I had knitted and found friends. Sitting here, I had realized that Carolyn trusted me. Sitting here, now, holding my tentacle hat, I was filled with contentment and peace.

And that, my friends, is what Crabapple Yarns was really all about. There is a big difference between a store that sells yarn and a yarn store. Anyone can throw yarn onto a shelf and sell it. What made Crabapple Yarns a great yarn store was the great woman that owned it. Someone who knew that you needed more than yarn and needles to make beautiful things. You also needed love.

And, then I knew... I knew what I had been missing all along. It was so simple... It was so simple that I never saw it. It was so simple that I think I've known it all along. Life isn't a secret that you suddenly know the answer to, and there is no possible way to plan your whole life. As trite as it sounds, you really do just have to take one step at a time and see where you are... and then take another and then another. The truth was clear now, and I can see that The Plan would never have worked. And that's a good thing. If it had, I would have been miserable. It did look cute on the refrigerator, though.

Carolyn was right. You can't look back. Everyone should learn from their mistakes and move forward. Move forward because otherwise you're not moving at all. And knitters hate to sit still. One mistake doesn't mean you rip everything out and give up knitting. You look for someone with experience to help you fix things. And once you've learned from your errors, it's your job to help the next person learn from theirs. It's a beautiful, never-ending circle of love and friendship.

You know, when I first started knitting, I looked up the definition of knitting in the Merriam-Webster dictionary (I doubt I'll ever outgrow my librarian tendencies). This is what it said:

- To form by interlacing yarn or thread in a series of connected loops with needles
- To tie together

I usually have great respect for Mr. Merriam-Webster; however, I know that, in this case at least, he is totally, completely and hopelessly wrong.

This is the knitting definition that <u>should be</u> in the dictionary:

- The mystifying and magical process whereby linear fiber is twisted and reshaped by needles of varying sizes not only knitting fabric together, but hearts and minds as well, resulting in lifetime friendships, a sense of self-satisfaction, and personal identity.

There. Doesn't that sound better? If it doesn't, that can only mean one thing. You must still be denying your inner knitter. Oh, yes. That reminds me. I almost forgot. I learned one more very important thing from Crabapple Yarns – knitters come in all shapes and sizes. Never judge... never assume...and never, ever deny your inner knitter. It's much too dangerous.

The End

(and...the beginning)

By the way, Ryan loved his scarf.

ABOUT THE AUTHOR

Since the age of three, Jaime Marsman has long been fascinated with the simple shifting of letters to create different words, thoughts, and sentences. As a knitwear designer for Live.Knit.Love, she has found the same thing to also be true of yarn. Perhaps that would explain the joy she feels every time she picks up her pen or her needles. Inspiring others with her work is one of Jaime's fondest goals and dreams. She wants people to realize the joy of creating and following their dreams in their own special ways. Jaime is so grateful to God for His love and guiding hand in her life. She prays that everyone comes to have the joy and peace of knowing Him.

- **Jaime's FaceBook:**
  http://www.facebook.com/JaimeMarsman2
- **Jaime's Web-site:**
  http://jaime.liveknitlove.com

ACKNOWLEDGEMENTS

Thank you, God, for all of Your blessings.
I love You.

Thank you to my dear and wonderful family,
especially my mom and dad, for believing in me
even when I didn't believe in myself.
'Thank you' seems a very inadequate phrase to say
how much I love you and how much I appreciate
all of your love and support, but I'm going to say it anyways
Thank you!
I love you.

And thank you to my friends, You are a gift from God.
I am so grateful and so thankful for your friendship.
More than you will ever know.
I love you.